Praise for

OBLIVION

"Readers will feel unmoored until the last few pages of this novel, and that's all right—so does the story's narrator, Callie."
—starred, *Booklist*

"Thoroughly compelling."
—*Kirkus Reviews*

"An exciting page-turner."
—*School Library Journal*

"[A] gripping, psychologically intense mystery . . ."
—*VOYA*

"I could see the tension rippling through every scene. A fabulous book that readers are going to inhale."
—Jessica Warman, author of
The Last Good Day of the Year and *Between*

A New York Public Library Best Book for Teens 2014

A 2016 Illinois Reads selection

SPLINTER

SASHA DAWN

carolrhoda LAB

MINNEAPOLIS

Carolrhoda Lab™ is a trademark of Lerner Publishing Group, Inc.

Carolrhoda Lab™
An imprint of Carolrhoda Books
A division of Lerner Publishing Group, Inc.
241 First Avenue North
Minneapolis, MN 55401 USA

For reading levels and more information, look up this title at www.lernerbooks.com.

Cover and interior images: © imagenavi/Getty Images (fragments); iStockphoto.com/
raywoo (tally marks).

Main body text set in Janson Text LT Std 10.5/15.
Typeface provided by Linotype AG.

Library of Congress Cataloging-in-Publication Data

Names: Dawn, Sasha, author.
Title: Splinter / by Sasha Dawn.
Description: Minneapolis : Carolrhoda Lab, [2017] | Summary: "Sami's mother
    disappeared ten years ago, and the police have always suspected that Sami's father
    killed her. But they've never had any convincing evidence . . . until now. Sami's
    sure her father's innocent. Or is she?" —Provided by publisher.
Identifiers: LCCN 2016008994 (print) | LCCN 2016036377 (ebook) |
    ISBN 9781512411515 (th : alk. paper) | ISBN 9781512426953 (eb pdf)
Subjects: | CYAC: Mothers and daughters—Fiction. | Missing persons—Fiction. |
    Identity—Fiction. | Mystery and detective stories.
Classification: LCC PZ7.D32178 Sp 2017 (print) | LCC PZ7.D32178 (ebook) | DDC
    [Fic]—dc23

LC record available at https://lccn.loc.gov/2016008994

Manufactured in the United States of America
1-39668-21289-8/23/2016

FOR MY HICKORY AND SUNFLOWERS:
JMD, SMK, AND MJM.

"People disappeared, reappeared, made plans to go somewhere, and then lost each other, searched for each other, found each other a few feet away."

—*F. Scott Fitzgerald, The Great Gatsby*

1

My feet hit the pavement in even cadence, keeping time with a song that's been repeating in my head: "Photograph" by Def Leppard. I haven't heard the song in a long time, maybe even since before my mother left. Glam bands of the late eighties were definitely her thing, not Dad's.

I can't shake free from the song. It came to me the moment I pulled the mail from the box and saw the postcard. This one came from Charleston, South Carolina, and it's adorned with a picture of an old mansion, situated among thick-trunked, moss-draped trees, the kind of place where ladies might eat scones and sip English tea.

Like all the other postcards I've received over the years, this one is vague. She didn't sign it, or even address it by hand. My name and address are typed on a label pasted to the right side of the card. Directly opposite is the same message she sends me time and again—a handwritten *11/7*, usually scrawled in Sharpie. Sometimes, she writes *117*. Sometimes *XI* and *VII*.

November seventh. The date my mother, Delilah Jennifer Lang, was supposed to return home. The date she never came home.

Eleven and seven are also Mom's favorite numbers—used to be, anyway, which is why they're my favorite numbers too. Both prime. Indivisible by anything but themselves.

Plus, they rhyme, which I got a kick out of when I was a kid.

And if I wanted to rationalize it, maybe I'd say Mom writes numerical poems on these postcards, and poetry means something. But I'm well past rationalization, well past trying to understand her.

In accompaniment with the music in my head, the early autumn wind rustles through the gold and burgundy leaves overhead. The trees reach from both sides of the road and create the illusion of an arbor above me. This is a common sight in neighborhoods like mine, neighborhoods planned and constructed on a predictable grid in the Victorian era, when everything was straight and proper, thank you very much, with shade trees planted at intervals in the parkways.

These trees have been here a long time.

Likely, they watched as my mother walked out the front door.

And they, like me, couldn't do a thing to stop her.

I see her in the archives of my mind, crouching in front of me, the very last time I saw her: caramel waves of hair streaked with pale blonde, bright blue eyes like mine, freckles sprayed over her cheeks like stars in the sky. *See you Wednesday, Samantha-girl.* The sunflower locket strung around her neck bouncing against a yellow tank top. The pink caterpillar keychain spinning as she jingled the keys in her hand. My fingers feathering over holes in her denim capris. Cork-heeled wedges on her feet, carrying her far away from me.

For a while, I kept waiting for the next Wednesday and the next. But over five hundred Wednesdays, and ten November sevenths, have passed since she uttered those words, and honestly, I think I lost faith in Wednesday somewhere around my twelfth birthday.

Mom obviously hasn't, if she keeps writing *11/*7 on these cards. But I mean, would it kill her to actually *say* something to me, if she's going to write anything at all?

I left a message for Lieutenant Eschermann just before my run, letting him know that another of Mom's postcards had shown up. Not that it's likely to change his mind about anything. Eschermann has had the same theory about my mom for years. That she's dead. But if she's sending postcards, it means she's alive, right? And if she's alive, the good lieutenant's hypotheses are wrong.

Eschermann is a veteran from the first conflict in the Gulf, and for the past ten years he's been the police detective in charge of finding my mom. But he's found people before—soldiers who'd disappeared in the dunes of the Middle East—and if he can do that, my believing he'll find my mom can't be that unrealistic.

It's a lose-lose scenario, though. Either she can't come back, which means she's in a bad situation, or she chooses not to, which means she isn't thinking of me at all and I shouldn't think of her.

And frankly, this postcard today did more to piss me off than give me hope anyway. If she's out there, I need more than a random *11/*7 on the backs of postcards of places I've never been. Blank postcards are no substitute for having a mom at home with you, playing rummy with you, praising your school projects, baking cookies for you.

Technically, I *do* have a mom in Heather, even though she and Dad separated a few months ago. She's been around a long time—almost as long as Mom's been gone. The gist is that she and Dad were childhood friends and high school sweethearts, and that fate brought them back together. Fate did more than that, actually. It brought me a sister. In a way, Cassidy and I melded long before our parents made the official jump to husband and wife.

It took them a while to get married, but I can't blame Heather for that. After Mom left, Dad starting drinking way too much. Heather insisted that Dad get permanently sober before they tied the knot. And in the meantime, she picked up the slack. If I needed a ride to Little League—this was before I realized I was too uncoordinated to play baseball—Heather served as taxi. If I needed a costume for a class play, Heather stepped up. And when I was in tears over the disaster of my *Bridge to Terabithia* diorama in fifth grade, it was Heather who helped me pull it together. She never tried to replace Mom in my life, though, for the eight years she lived with us. She knew nobody could do that.

I'm rounding the corner at Schmidt's place, which bears the honor of being the oldest and largest house in the neighborhood. It's kitty-corner from the rear of my house. Prime real estate. A red-bricked path—which winds through an arbor of vines, clinging to their last breaths of life for the season—leads to the front door. The house itself is white with navy blue trim and a door the color of black cherries. A bronze plaque is affixed to the siding next to the door, declaring it a landmark. An identical one adorns our carriage house, which was originally part of the same property.

The sweeping lawn holds more trees than I can count. There used to be sunflowers, too, when I was little. The scent of a backyard bonfire fills the air. Schmidt's always burning lawn refuse, and although it's against city code, no one seems to bother him about it.

I breathe in the smell of it, which always makes me think of Mom, who often stood at an open window to relish the scents and sounds of autumn. "Listen, Samantha," she'd say. "Do you hear the crackle of the leaves?"

I listen for it now and smile when the sizzle and pop of Schmidt's fire reaches my ears. Yes, Mom. I hear it. Angry as I am about this postcard, I wonder if she's standing at a bonfire in South Carolina right now, saying the same thing to some other kid—a kid she deemed worthy of sticking around for.

When my mother first disappeared, I thought she was hiding at Schmidt's place. It would be an easy house to hide in. According to town records, there's an underground tunnel connecting his place with our carriage house. Rumor has it, it was a means to carry contraband liquor from the street to the house during Prohibition, which makes it sort of mysterious. And there is a door in the floor of the carriage house that makes the rumors actually seem possible.

Dad put a lock on the door in the carriage house floor when I was little. It both intrigued and terrified me to think of people descending into a dank cellar and worming through a narrow tunnel to emerge hundreds of feet away, in the basement of Schmidt's grand house. Maybe that's why I used to imagine that Mom had escaped down through the carriage house floor to Schmidt's house. Intriguing and terrifying.

The familiar feeling of loss creeps in again, along with a sense of inadequacy. If she'd loved me the way moms are supposed to love their kids, wouldn't she have come back by now?

My feet fall a bit faster on the pavement.

My breath comes in sharp intakes. I close my eyes for a second or two.

Look for the map in my mind. Watch the pushpins pop up from the tiny towns that Mom has sent postcards from, and see them connect to one another with veins of a road system. Breathe.

I know it's weird, but it works. Some people envision serene landscapes or oceans to calm down. I see maps when I close my eyes. It helps me remember that even if Mom is far away, all towns are connected somehow.

I open my eyes and breathe deeply, inhaling the scent of burning leaves. Inhale for eleven seconds, exhale for seven. Inhale for eleven, exhale for seven. Okay. Better now.

Schmidt's nephew, Ryan, is in the front yard, trimming branches off the sadder-looking hickories. He's visiting for the week, probably helping with the enormous task of tending to the plants and trees on the property. He waves, and I raise a hand in return before I round the corner.

Ryan used to come here often when I was younger, and I have vague recollections of playing with him when we were little. I haven't seen him in about five years. Can't imagine hanging out with him now. He's grown into one of those unapproachably good-looking guys, and since he arrived last Sunday, I've kept my distance, if only to avoid looking like an idiot in front of him.

Besides, it's not as if my dad and I are on especially friendly terms with Ryan's uncle. Schmidt's an older guy, single, not very sociable. Our households have an unspoken agreement to mutually keep our distance.

I run through the neighborhood, all the way to the lake, and down the shoreline to the strip of shops where Cassidy, my once-step-but-always-sister, is closing up at the Funky Nun.

Streetlamps begin to buzz, washing the bricked path with

their amber light, and the sun is dipping in the sky, painting the horizon apricot. I don't usually go running this late. Because where there's light, there's shadow. I pick up my pace. The shop is all the way at the end of the Lakefront Walk.

When I enter the shop, some low-volume, drum-heavy soundtrack greets me. Cassidy is at the register, probably adding up the day's receipts. She glances up at me. "Whatcha doing, chickie?"

"Knitting a scarf." I flip Heather's homemade sign from open *(COME IN AND LOSE YOURSELF)* to closed *(GET LOST AND FIND YOURSELF)* and turn the lock. "What's it look like I've been doing?"

"Well, duh. But at this hour?" She knows I hate running at dusk.

"Got a late start thanks to Charleston, South Carolina."

"Huh?"

"I got another postcard today."

"Oh, Sam." She tilts her head a little to the left, and her brows slant downward. She never knows what to say when this happens.

"It's okay. I'm fine."

She takes my words at face value and quickly changes the subject. "Is Dad home?"

"Wasn't when I left."

My dad's not her real father, but she still calls him Dad. Her biological father was never interested in filling the job, and ever since Heather married Dad, the four of us seemed to fit together naturally.

We were meant to be. At least that's what we thought up until their abrupt end this past spring.

They filed for divorce on vague grounds. Irreconcilable

differences. Which is Lawyer Speak for Sami-and-Cassidy-don't-have-to-know-exactly-what-happened. But Dad and Heather are eternally entwined, connected by the sisterly bond Cass and I share, and by the bond Cass has with my dad, whether they like it or not.

"You should try running in the morning instead of the afternoon," Cassidy says in her best imitation of my father. "Invigorating!"

I roll my eyes. She knows better than anyone that I'm not quite myself until noon, and I'd probably fall flat on my face if I laced up my Nikes at six in the morning. "While you finish, I'm going upstairs to see Kismet"—yellow lab extraordinaire—"and maybe grab a shower."

"No time." Cassidy clips the receipts together and flips her long black hair over her shoulder. "We'll be late."

On Thursdays, Heather teaches an evening textiles class at the community college, so Cassidy has dinner with us and often spends the night. But if she's worried about being late, I must've run for longer than I thought. I mentally retrace my winding route. "What time is it?"

"Five thirty-six."

So very like Cassidy to be so exact. It's probably why she and Dad get along so well.

"Well, then. We're already late, by Dad's timetable." We're still twenty-four minutes early, as he dictates six as dinnertime. Yet if I know my father, he'll be checking his watch at the window, waiting.

"By the time you shower, we'll be at least ten minutes late," Cassidy says. "And the food will be getting cold—it's Chinese tonight, remember—and he puts a lot of effort into our Thursdays. We should be on time."

8

"Okay."

We walk through the shop to the back door. I punch off the sound system, silencing the clanks and clatter of the tribal drums, while Cassidy hits the lights and turns on the security system. Good night, Funky Nun.

Cassidy's Jeep Wrangler smells faintly of vanilla, thanks to the satchel Heather made to mask the stench of wet dog after Cassidy and I took Kismet to the dog beach last summer. Dad originally bought the Jeep for us to share, but now I only see it when Cass is chauffeuring me.

Def Leppard serenades me in my head once more as we buckle up.

"Zack texted me during government today," says Cassidy.

I offer a fist for a bump.

"I mean"—her fist meets mine—"I didn't actually get the text during class—"

"Of course not." That would require her taking her eyes off the Smart Board, and Cassidy just doesn't do that.

"—but once class was over, I got the text he sent *during* class. And . . . apparently Brooke's been putting in a good word, so . . . he wants to hang out."

"Awesome. So what's the plan?"

"Friday night. Party at their place."

"Brooke's grounded."

"She doesn't seem to care. Their parents are in Door County."

"Is this a *party* party? Or, you know, just the four of us?"

"She didn't say. Knowing Brooke, she'll invite Alex at least"

Not that it matters, really. I'll go, either way. I just prefer smaller gatherings to big bashes, and I prefer not to be a fifth wheel.

"Zack's a senior," Cassidy continues. "It's now or never. He's going to Virginia next year."

Yeah. Full-ride scholarship. Brooke's older brother is amazing with a soccer ball.

"Shit," Cassidy says under her breath as we near my house.

An Echo Lake Police cruiser is parked at the curb.

I figured Eschermann might show up when I left him a message about the postcard, but I wish he would've called instead. This display leads our neighbors in the wrong direction, makes them think things that aren't true. When people don't have all the information, they tend to fill in the blanks.

I've heard the story a thousand times: Mom was planning to go away for the weekend, so on Friday night Dad got me a sitter while he and Heather were out. When they came back from dinner, the sitter was gone, I wasn't home, and neither was Mom. They assumed Mom had left for her trip and taken me with her. A couple of hours later, Schmidt found me in his basement and walked me home. No one ever saw or heard from Mom again.

There's a lot I don't remember, but there's plenty I know for sure.

I don't know why it's so hard for Eschermann to grasp.

Mom's gone because she didn't want to be here anymore.

Dad didn't kill her.

||

The Jeep bumps over the curb when Cassidy pulls into the driveway.

"You okay?" she asks me.

"Yeah." But my mouth is dry. Beads of sweat roll down my back, and they're not just from my run.

And I'm acutely aware of the fact that curtains are parted and noses are pressed to windows in every house on this street.

I open the car door; my feet hit the red-bricked driveway.

"Good evening, Miss Lang."

"Evening." I count four officers in front of me. The only tolerable one is Neilla Cooper, who babysat me a lifetime ago. Nothing differentiates the other three—closely shaved heads, broad shoulders—except for the slight paunch on the one who just spoke, Lieutenant Ken Eschermann. I've known him since I was six, since before he moved up the ranks.

His hands are hooked on his belt, near his weapon. He nods to Cassidy, who's getting out of the driver's seat. "Miss Solomon."

"Hi." She's quieter than usual in their company. Always has been.

"Do you know where your father is?"

Wait. He isn't home yet?

"What time is it?" I ask Cassidy.

"Five forty-eight," she answers, in unison with another officer.

"He's usually home by now."

"He didn't come to the door when I rang the bell. And given your call this afternoon, he should've known we'd be by." Eschermann and my father are somewhat friendly, which is weird when you consider their relationship is based upon certain suspicions.

"I didn't tell him about the postcard," I admit. "I was going to tell him about it tonight."

"So where's this one from?" The lieutenant squints down at me, the day's last rays of sun in his eyes.

I figured Eschermann would want to see it, that he'd have questions about it. This isn't unusual. I've been questioned nearly a dozen times about the day my mother left. But it still irks me that he's chosen to show up like this, drawing the whole block's attention.

"We have to do this here?" I ask. "Why can't you call me back like a normal person? Why can't I just give you the postcard—you can dust it for prints, the whole rigmarole—and conclude, like always, that it's been handled too many times, and—"

"Samantha." His sigh is long and drawn-out.

"No, you know what this looks like," I tell him. "And you know how hard this is. Tomorrow at school, everyone will be talking about a parade of cops on my lawn."

"Samantha," he says again. "Someday you'll see this is as much for your benefit as ours. It isn't a punishment."

It is, sort of. Sit a girl down year after year after year, and remind her that her mother isn't here. While you're at it, fill her head with all your horrible theories about what might have happened to her. I don't know why they don't get it. Sometimes, mothers just don't stick around. Their families aren't enough to make them stay.

"We're trying to get to the truth, regardless of what that truth is," he tells me.

If I had a dollar for every time I've heard that line from him, I could've bought the Jeep from Cassidy.

"Talk to our father when he gets home," Cassidy says. Her hand is at my elbow, gently guiding me toward the brick path to the back door.

"There's been a development," Eschermann says.

Cassidy's fingers tighten at my elbow. We stop.

"Could be nothing, but I wouldn't be doing my job if I didn't ask you about it. And your father."

Cassidy reaches for me, even as I step back toward the cops.

"What kind of development?" I ask quickly.

"Does the name Trina Jordan mean anything to you?"

"Trina Jordan?" I shake my head.

"Girls."

I turn toward my father's voice. He's standing in the now-open doorway, his lips thinned into a crooked, angry line. "Dinner's getting cold."

"Chris." Eschermann nods.

"Ken."

"I'd like to talk to you and Sam. We've come across—"

"It's not a good time." If I know Dad, and I do, this is the end of the conversation.

Cassidy's already inside. I'm taking my time walking up the steps.

"We'll arrange a better time for an interview, then."

I look over my shoulder at the lieutenant. He was about to tell me something about my mother. He was going to tell me about Trina Jordan.

"Tomorrow," Eschermann says. "It's important."

"Maybe," Dad says. "Sam. Inside." We step inside and the door closes behind us.

"Hi, Cass." Dad wraps her in a big hug. "What've you been up to?"

"Oh, you know. Making the world a better place."

"You must be exhausted."

"Yeah, well, someone's got to do it."

If I weren't so preoccupied, I might have laughed, like Dad does.

Dad's different with Cassidy than he is with me—more affectionate, which I think says more about the way she feels about him than the way he feels about me. It's easier for Cass. Heather didn't bring her around during the dark days; Cass's relationship with Dad began to grow a few years ago, when he was already sober.

Cass disappears into the kitchen and Dad turns to me. "What did Eschermann have to say?" He rests a hand on my shoulder.

I shrug away. Too sweaty to be touched right now. "If you were really that curious, you could've answered the door when they rang the bell."

"Your tone." It's his way of telling me I'm being disrespectful, but I call it like it is.

"I didn't hear the bell," he says after he's sure his message is received. "Must be broken again."

Of course. It's the charm of living in an old house. Everything in it is in some state of disrepair. I choose to ignore the fact that Eschermann probably also knocked.

I hear Cassidy bustling in the kitchen. The clangs of plates and utensils against the granite countertops echo through the hallway. I guess this is as good a time as any to tell him: "I got another postcard."

"And you called Ken before you called me."

"What can *you* do about it?" I push my hair back from my forehead. Besides—and I won't say this out loud, not after I've already been warned about my *tone*—these little bits of news from my mother tend to shut my father down. I know what would've happened, had I told him: he'd close up, withdraw. And I'd be stuck here, being a shadow around the one parent I still have. "There's nothing on it. Just like the other ones. The same pointless *eleven-seven*. I wonder why she bothers at all."

Dad opens his mouth, as if he's about to say something, maybe comforting words, but the words don't come.

"At least when she left *you*, you got some semblance of closure when you signed the divorce papers." I shove my running shoes into the cabinet designated as my locker.

Still silent, he leans against the doorframe, blocking the path to the kitchen. "Samantha, I know this is hard. And I don't understand it either. She loved you, and I can't explain why she would do this to you. But if she's chosen to walk away from you because she walked away from me, it's her loss."

This is more than he's usually willing to say about Mom, and under other circumstances, it would mean a lot. But I'm not putting up with this dodgeball routine.

"Who's Trina Jordan?" I cross my arms.

For a split second, his mouth hangs agape, but he quickly regains his composure. "I don't . . ." He shakes his head with a minute jerk. "*What?*"

"Eschermann asked about someone named Trina Jordan. Who is she?"

"I don't know."

"She has something to do with Mom."

"I *don't know*, Sam."

For a good few seconds, we stand there, staring at each other.

"You coming?" Cassidy calls. "I might eat all the egg rolls before you get here."

"Come on." Dad pats me awkwardly on the shoulder, moving out of the doorway. "She really might eat all those egg rolls."

I don't budge.

"I ordered the veggie ones," he offers. "Just for you."

I take a few steps toward the kitchen.

Dad follows.

But I hear him let out a tense, weary sigh—the sigh of someone who's won a temporary reprieve from whatever's weighing on him.

He knows.

He knows who Trina Jordan is.

And he just lied to me about it.

III

I don't remember the day I realized my mother wasn't coming home again. One day, it just became a reality.

Despite rumors of my mother's infidelities—which I've heard only from Cassidy, who swears she overheard Dad and Heather talking about it—the divorce had been amicable. So much so, in fact, that I got to stay in the house all the time. It was my parents who visited me, not the other way around. Dad would come in the front door, while Mom slipped out the back. They shared the space for what seemed like forever but was probably only a couple of months.

And one day, she just stopped coming. Wednesday, November seventh, came and went without a sign of her.

At first, the fact that she'd gone didn't alarm my father. She'd been planning to take a weekend trip to Georgia. When she didn't return that Wednesday, he figured she'd prolonged her stay—or just decided not to come back. She'd started packing her things. Since those boxes—like her car—never turned up, I assume she took everything with her.

She'd neglected to pack the framed portraits of the two of us, which speaks volumes, if you ask me.

I mean, it's possible that she took along another picture of me. I have no idea how many pictures of us existed in the first place, let alone which specific ones are left. But recently, I've come to realize that in all likelihood, Mom just wanted out. Something about me, about being a mother, didn't jibe with her plans.

Then, when Dad married Heather, pictures of Mom joined the ranks of old stuff in the attic. Nearly every trace of my mother was wiped out with one pass of Heather's eraser, and by that time, I couldn't even resent my stepmother for insisting on it. My mother was gone. Images of her had haunted us from the edges of end tables, from the arched niche in the foyer. And why did we keep them there? To remind us that she'd left?

A few things remain: Her classic novels, of course, still line the highest shelf in our family room. Found in any library, they're generic-enough possessions that they could belong to anyone. They don't scream *Delilah* any more than our cheese grater does.

But I still have a few distinctly-Mom things too: her favorite recipes for butter cookies and snickerdoodles, a locket, a snapshot of the two of us, taken shortly before the divorce. I keep these things in the drawer of my bedside table. I don't look at the picture much anymore, but I've memorized every detail: Mom in a black sundress, me on her lap in a pale yellow romper. Our matching golden-brown tresses flowing together like a confluence of two rivers. Identical lockets—silver hearts embossed with sunflowers—strung around our necks on silver chains. We wore them every day.

Dad bought mine for my third or fourth birthday; Mom bought one for herself so we'd match.

Thinking about it now, my fingers ache to hold my locket, which I hardly wear anymore, just to feel close to her again.

"You okay?" Cassidy asks.

"What?" I shake free from the photograph in my mind.

Cassidy's sitting on the bench in the mudroom and shoving her feet into her boots. We've just left the kitchen, where Dad is loading up the dishwasher after a nearly silent dinner.

"You gonna be okay?" Cassidy asks. Before I have a chance to answer, she follows up with, "Who's Trina Jordan, anyway?"

I shrug a shoulder. "Who knows?"

"Do you think Dad knows?"

I do, but I don't want Cassidy to think that too. Not unless there's a concrete reason. "He said he didn't."

"Here's the great thing about my mom and me moving out," she says.

"You mean aside from the fact that you got custody of the dog?"

"I have somewhere else to go when he gets all mopey," Cassidy says. "And you know . . . you can come too."

I do know. Heather has told me countless times I'm welcome, but I belong here with Dad.

"I don't know how you do it." Cassidy gives her head a slight shake. "He gets so quiet."

"I know."

"*Uncomfortably* quiet. Doesn't it ever irk you? Stopping your life every few months when he zaps into depression mode? I mean, no offense, but he just can't stand to be happy. Not even when he was with my mom."

Maybe she's right. For almost a year after my mom left, not knowing what happened to her practically debilitated him. And even now, whenever something happens to remind him of her, he'll get like this. It's one reason that I know he had nothing to do with Mom's leaving.

But still, we adjust. He does whatever it is he does—incessant P90X, regular AA meetings, teaching his economics classes at Northwestern University, scheduling his days to death—and I get used to bumming rides off people.

While his moodiness is sometimes tough to take, we manage to make do. The day Heather and Cassidy moved out, we'd played rummy late into the night. We both were emotionally drained, and it should have been one of the worst nights in my memory. I'd lost another mother, who'd taken with her my best friend. Yet whenever I think of it, I feel a sense of warmth and protection. Dad rose above his own despair because he knew I was hurting too. I needed him that night, and he needs me now.

"Pick you up tomorrow morning." Cassidy is dawdling at the door now. "You sure you're okay?"

"I'm fine. And hey . . . awesome news about Zack."

She grins. "I know, right?"

////

I have a bad headache, brought on by tension, and there's plenty of that hanging between Dad and me. Why won't he just tell me what he knows? Has there ever been a time that he hasn't answered one of my questions?

No.

But maybe that's because I've never asked a particularly difficult one.

My head pounds, and the walls of the room seem to be closing in on me. I reach for my Imitrex and down a pill without water to ward off what seems to be a migraine-in-the-making.

My trigonometry textbook is open, but instead of working on the assigned functions, I'm staring at my laptop screen, at dozens of profile pictures of Trina Jordans. Any one of them could be the woman Eschermann referenced.

I try another search—Trina's name in connection with my mother's—but nothing substantial comes up with that, either.

One more: Trina Jordan Missing.

The screen fills with links and thumbnail photos, and I hear her, my mother, in the back of my mind, winding through gray matter:

Sami-girl?

"Sami?"

I startle. Whip around.

Dad.

I close my laptop fast.

"How's homework?"

Silver halos encircle the triangles on the page before me, and the beat of ancient rock 'n' roll rattles my brain. "Just one last problem."

Dad clears his throat. "Going bowling tomorrow night?"

"Yeah, with Brooke and Cassidy. Maybe Zack." If Dad ever actually saw my bowling score, he'd realize I can't possibly bowl as often as I say I do. But I never tell Dad when we're having a party, even if it's a smallish one.

He's staring past me, as if the wall behind me is the most interesting thing in the world. "Stressful day."

"Stressful evening, anyway." I tap the eraser of my pencil against my notebook and wait. *Please tell me about Trina Jordan.* I know that if I ask again, he'll only withdraw deeper into his abyss.

"So." He rubs his hands together. "Charleston, South Carolina."

"Yeah."

"Call me at work next time? Before you call Eschermann?"

"What difference does it make? It's not like I was going to hide it from you." I pause. "*I* don't hide things from *you*."

He chooses to ignore that. "But you're distant tonight."

I answer with a guttural sound, but what I really mean is *so are you*.

"We've already lost so much." Dad's voice is low and not quite steady. "Heather and Cassidy, your mother . . . I can't imagine how I'd survive without you."

I don't say so, but I don't know what I'd do without him, either. Once, when I was little and we were shopping for school clothes, I lost track of him at the mall. Those three minutes without him felt like an eternity. And to calm me down after the ordeal, we split one of those huge, soft pretzels. *See the twist in the middle?* he'd asked. *That's you and me, laced together.*

These days, I wonder if we aren't unraveling a bit, and if we'll end up two separate halves of what used to be a whole family unit.

"We can't shut each other out," Dad says.

"Take your own advice." *Tell me about Trina Jordan. Tell me what you know.*

"Sam." Regret seeps into his voice. "I know this gets frustrating for you. You and I—we deal with things differently. Sometimes I don't communicate with you as well as I should. That's on me, I know that. Maybe if this thing with your mom hadn't been hanging over us for so long—" He cuts himself off. "Anyway, I just don't want us to be at odds."

I say nothing. We wouldn't be at odds if he'd just be straight with me, instead of backhandedly apologizing for *not* being straight with me.

"Do you think she's out there?" he says suddenly.

I flinch. We never talk about her, so this is unexpected.

"Don't *you*?" I ask.

"I don't know anymore. I just don't know."

There's a tickle in my nose suddenly, and an itchiness in my eyes, like I'm about to cry. "I feel her sometimes."

He pauses. "Me too."

I should say something about her, something to prove I remember her, something to show him he's not alone in wondering where she is.

"Certain things you do . . . you remind me of her," he says. "Some of the things she used to say . . . the way you look at me when you're angry . . . And you don't eat meat. You used to, you know. When you were little, hot dogs were your favorite."

A memory, or maybe a flash of a dream, wafts into my mind: I'm roasting a hot dog on a stick over a fire. Mom's laughter fills my ears for a split second—she's laughing at something someone said, something Schmidt said—*Schmidt?*—and then, just as I'm about to grasp the moment, the whole thing is gone.

I try to get it back.

What had Schmidt said?

Why was Mom laughing?

Why were we there? Roasting hot dogs?

Was Dad there too?

But the memory's gone.

I think back to what Dad just said. "Mom didn't eat meat?" Maybe I knew that once, but she isn't the reason I stopped eating animal carcass. I stopped because I don't like leaving little skeletons or pools of blood on my plate.

"No." A hint of a smile appears on his lips. "She loved animals too much to eat them, she used to say. That's why I learned to cook. Didn't want to give up bacon. And you love animals too. Watching you with Kismet . . . you should've always had a dog. Your mother wanted one."

"She did?" What else have I forgotten about her?

"Maybe we should get another."

"You mean . . . replace Kismet? Like you tried to replace Mom with Heather?" I didn't know I was going to say that; I'm still angry about Trina Jordan, I guess.

"I didn't *replace* your mother. *No one* can replace her."

"Really?" I beg to differ. My father wasted no time in dating Heather after their divorce. I never questioned it, because I quickly came to love Heather, and it seemed clear that she and Dad were meant to be. But Dad's quick resurgence into the dating world is one reason Eschermann suspects that Dad knows what happened to Mom. Even if they were divorced, even if her disappearance sent him down a long, dark road with a bottle in his hand . . . "You and Heather packed away all the pictures of her. It's like she was never here, like you don't want to acknowledge her existence. We don't talk about her. Ever."

"Because it used to upset you to talk about her."

"When I was little."

"You'd cry with just the mention of her."

"But that was ages ago. And now I'm forgetting. She's slipping away. And if we *never* talk about her . . ."

Maybe that's why her music has been haunting me lately. Maybe it's a subconscious urge to remember.

He slips his hands into his pockets and trails his glance from the window to the items on my bulletin board—pictures of me with Brooke, with Cassidy. But the one picture I have of Mom, I keep hidden in a drawer. So, if I'm playing devil's advocate, who's willing to forget?

"Your mother's favorite color was light yellow."

"Sugar-cookie yellow," I say with him.

He offers a brief smile. "And that's why the foyer is still painted a pale yellow. The family room throw pillows are pale yellow. The kitchen cabinets . . . that same pale yellow."

I close my eyes and savor the memory of her staining the porch swing. It's weathered and gray now, but it, too, had an opaque yellow cast to it when I was a little girl. *The color of sugar cookies right out of the oven.*

"She may be gone, Sam, but she's still here. In this house. And even though we got divorced, she's still here." He pats his knuckles against his heart. "She's here because you're here. Nothing and no one is going to squeeze her out."

We're staring at each other now. His eyes are misty with so many things unsaid.

This might be one of those times when storybook daughters hug their fathers-of-the-year, but I'm not a hugger. Dad and I have never had that type of relationship. He isn't touchy-feely, either. I know he loves me. I assume he knows I love him. We don't have to put on spectacular shows of affection to prove it.

After a few moments of silence, he says, "We'll talk more in the morning, okay?" Without waiting for an answer, he pulls out his cell phone and turns around. "Good night, Sami."

And just like that, the moment's gone.

At least for him.

"'Night, Dad." I close my text book and cradle my aching head in my arms.

I hear Dad as he heads down the hall.

"To do tomorrow." He talks through his plans for the next day on the voice recorder on his cell phone. "Finish workout by seven and protein shake by seven fifteen. Shower by seven thirty."

So regimented. I think I must be more like Mom. Breaking a day into fifteen-minute increments doesn't make any sense to me. Dad says that's how he gets the most out of every day. But what if something unexpected comes up and you can't enjoy it because it doesn't fit into your schedule?

I think he used to be more fun . . . before. But maybe he was more fun because of the alcohol. And the alcohol, I know firsthand, was *not* fun after a certain number of swallows. He'd drink until he was numb. He'd stare quietly at the television, out the window, or at the wall, even. If he'd look at me, he'd look right through me. At first it scared me. But eventually I got used to it. I'd cover him with a blanket after he passed out on the couch or at the table. I'd put myself to bed and cry myself to sleep, praying that he'd be Dad again when I woke up in the morning. And usually, he was. He'd mutter something about losing track of time last night, and we'd get on with our day. Now, I suspect the regimen, the schedule, is part of what helps him stay sober. If that's the case, maybe it makes sense after all.

After he kills the hall light, I hear the soft murmuring sounds of his fan down the hall—Dad can't sleep without white noise—as a background to his mapping out of the day. I open the drawer of my bedside table and find my locket. I pick it up by its silver chain and carry it to the window seat. Along with my laptop.

Staring down at links to articles and webpages containing the words *Trina Jordan Missing*, I loop the chain twice around my ankle and fasten it. I sink into the hypnotic rhythm of the white noise down the hall and imagine a map of the United States. Mentally, I stick pushpins in all the places Mom's been, and try to get her laughter back in my head.

Pins pop up on the map in my mind: Providence, Dover, Richmond, Tallahassee . . .

The lines between cities create triangles. *Cosine "A" equals adjacent over hypotenuse.*

Originally, my parents met in Atlanta, but they moved out here, to the Chicago 'burbs where Dad grew up, when he got a tenure-track position at NU. I was a baby at the time; I don't remember living anywhere else. It makes sense that she'd go back to the southeast once she and Dad called it quits, even though she doesn't have any family left there and none of her old friends in Atlanta have heard from her in the past ten years.

What doesn't make sense is the fact that she never bothered to contact anyone—*anyone*—to confirm that she was alive. To tell the police that there was no need to mount a manhunt for her.

What doesn't make sense is that she left me behind.

And even now, she's just a car ride away. It's not like she moved to Zimbabwe. I wonder how she can't want to see me. I'm her daughter. Shouldn't she feel my absence the way I feel hers?

I travel through the hourglass in my mind, rewinding time. The mother I remember—just snippets, a caricature, really—was affectionate, loving. Not the type of woman who'd take off and not say good-bye. She'd blare her music—*Photograph*—and twirl me around while we were supposed to be cleaning the kitchen.

Sometimes I hate her for leaving me to deal with this mess.

But one thing I know for certain: she *did* leave.

Dad isn't capable of doing what the cops think he did. He couldn't have hurt her. It's a ridiculous thought, and most of the time, I think the police know that. But then they find a connection in something like Trina Jordan, whoever she is, and they have to investigate. Like Eschermann says, he's just doing his job.

I click on a link. *Remember Trina Jordan* spans the top of the screen. A beautiful brunette with black-as-night eyes stares at me from immediately below the headline. I scan the words on the welcome page:

Trina Jordan lived in a suburb of Atlanta.

Atlanta!

Took the dog for a walk ten years ago.

Never came home, and neither did the dog.

Family and police assumed she'd run away—she'd run away before.

Her sister questioned Trina's significant other at the time, but only in regards to whether he'd seen her, or if he knew where she'd gone.

Significant other's name? Christopher Joseph Lang.

My father.

He told me he didn't know her.

She disappeared ten years ago, a few months before my mom left. And he was dating her at the time? How could he have been dating a woman in Georgia before his divorce was even final?

A lump forms in my throat, and my mouth is suddenly so dry that I can't swallow.

Trina's been missing a long time, but people assumed it was her choice to be gone.

Just like Mom.

A recent "development"—one the police haven't disclosed to the general public— has changed all that, so the case is being reopened. Now there are webpages devoted to her remembrance. Which is what you do for people who are not just missing, but dead.

And she used to be my father's girlfriend.

The thought fills me with a tingling sensation in my fingers, my toes. I'm dizzied, numb, hot. Too hot, as if I'm surrounded with flames.

Get it together, Sami.

I'm safe.

I've lived with Dad my whole life. He's never hurt me, not even when he was drinking.

I know I'm safe.

But we're only safe until we're not. Aren't we? And *he lied to me* about Trina Jordan.

My phone drones a humming alert; I have a text from Brooke, but I can't read it now. Can't worry about Friday, and Brooke and Alex, and Zack and Cassidy.

My room spins around me, or maybe I'm walking in circles.

I crank open the window. The scent of burning leaves wafts through the air. I look over at Schmidt's place. The place I was forbidden to go, once Mom was gone.

If Dad figures out I'm second-guessing his innocence . . .

Is that what I'm actually doing?

If I doubt him, what will he do? How might he react?

Can I make it out this window and across the lawn to Schmidt's place? If I have to?

I leap toward my door, close it, and lock it with the slender skeleton key that's always shoved into the keyhole.

The locket bounces against my ankle when I sink into the comfort of my bed. I pull the duvet up to my chin, as if hiding makes everything better. My aching head sinks into the pillow.

Trina Jordan is a coincidence. Maybe my dad has just always been drawn to flighty women who are prone to taking off without warning. The article said Trina Jordan had run away before. Maybe that's his type. After all, my mother had left her *daughter* behind. And her postcards prove she's out there somewhere. Of course, Heather is as steady as a rock, even if she is free-spirited, so maybe I'm wrong.

The dog was gone too, though. Trina took the dog. If she'd left the dog behind, that'd be another story.

But Mom couldn't be bothered to take her own daughter.

Come home, Mom.

It would be easy enough to do, especially considering how much ground she's covered in the past ten years.

I see the triangles in my mind, angles connecting to cities all over the country. All she has to do is find the right in-between and follow the hypotenuse. I'm waiting here at the end of it.

I close my eyes and concentrate until I hear the peal of Mom's laughter. It's a gem, something I can't lose. I may never hear it again in real life.

Shortly after Mom left, I had a dream.

It was vivid, vibrant. She'd come back, out of the secret passageway, to play with me in the sunflowers one more time.

She came back, if only while I was asleep.

I have to believe she'll come back again, if only to prove Trina Jordan's disappearance is a coincidence.

And it has to be, or everything I know, everything I've always believed about my father, could be a gargantuan lie.

||||

I see Trina Jordan's face in my mind.

It's there when I traipse to my shower, there as I dress and pack my backpack.

Even the too-loud club music accompanying Dad's morning workout in his basement gym doesn't help to distract me.

I slip two pieces of wheat bread into our ancient chrome toaster and find the cinnamon shaker on its designated shelf.

She took the dog for a walk, and she never returned. Neither did the dog.

I grab a clementine from the bowl of fresh fruit on the island and peel it over the trash.

I pour myself a glass of almond milk.

Business as usual, right?

The music from the basement comes to a dead stop. A creeping dread crawls through me, chewing at the back of my neck.

Who's coming up the stairs? The father who'll reminisce about sugar-cookie yellow? Or the man whose exes seem to disappear without a trace?

"Morning, Sami."

I flinch a little, even though I knew he was coming, but hope he doesn't notice. "Hi, Dad."

He opens a cabinet, selects a stainless steel shaker from the third shelf up, and proceeds to mix a protein shake. Although he's toweled off, sweat bleeds through his T-shirt in a V down his back. "You're up early."

"Couldn't sleep." My toast pops up.

"Me neither." Two scoops of protein. Chocolate flavored. Ice cold water from the filtered tap. Shake, shake, shake. "I have an early conference call with that guy about the grant and there's a meeting after my classes about the December conference."

The shake gurgles as he pours it into a glass, and the shaker clangs as he places it into the copper farmhouse sink. Sip. Silence. Sip.

I eat the last section of my clementine and then clear my throat. "I did some research last night. Online."

He avoids my stare, simply takes another sip and pulls up the weather forecast on his tablet.

"I looked up Trina Jordan."

His gaze snaps up. "Why did you do that, Sam? I told you—"

"You knew her, Dad. Why didn't you just tell me you—"

His body tenses. "Because I'm the father, and you're the kid, and sometimes I know what's best, okay? I don't think involving you in Eschermann's half-baked theories is going to help anything. When I say I don't want to talk about it—"

"But you didn't say that, Dad. You said you didn't know who she was. You *lied* to me about it." Tears gather in my eyes, but I blink and inhale, trying to make them go away.

"Samantha . . ."

"Were you cheating on Mom with her?"

"No, Sam. Trina and I hadn't been involved for some time before I met your mom. And I haven't heard from Trina in a decade."

"Did you know she's been reported missing?"

He closes his eyes briefly and nods. "I did know that, yes. I looked it up online last night, too. But it's got nothing to do with me, Sam. Trina's been off the radar for ages. Her sister did get in touch with me years ago to see if I'd heard from her, and I wasn't able to help her."

"Why did this thing with Trina come up now, if it's such old news?"

"I don't know. You saw the website, I take it. Apparently there's been a *development.*" He says the word as if it's nothing more than theoretical bullshit. But maybe it isn't.

"Why wouldn't you just tell me about it—about her—when I asked? She was your girlfriend, and she disappeared."

"She wasn't my girlfriend when she disappeared, Sam, and that's an important distinction to make. I knew her before I met your mom."

"The website I saw said you were her significant other."

"Anyone can write anything on a website. You know it doesn't make it true. My guess is her family published that site, and frankly, they never knew much about Trina. They sure didn't know when we began or ended our relationship."

"Okay, but *tell* me about her. What happened? Dad . . . look, you were mad that I called Eschermann before I told you about the postcard, right?"

"I wasn't mad, I was—"

"This is the same thing, here, isn't it? I'm going to find out. Someone's going to tell me. It should've been you."

He doesn't reply right away.

He nods. He pats the countertop, a few inches from a barstool. "Sit down. We can talk if you want."

I take a seat, bringing my plate with me.

"First, whatever I tell you," he says, "stays here. You can't tell Cass."

"We're sisters. Isn't that what you and Heather said? Sisters, divorce aside. Sisters rely on each other. Sisters—"

"You're sisters, yes. But this information . . . look, I love Cassidy, and I love Heather—"

This floors me for a second. They're getting divorced. But he loves Heather? I mean, sure, exes can care about each other. But Dad's never said that he still loves Mom—not in those words, not even last night.

"—but I don't want to talk to them about Trina. At least not yet. They're not levelheaded like you and me. They have a tendency to blow things out of proportion sometimes, and this is one instance when a level head is *absolutely necessary*. Why do you think I didn't invite Ken Eschermann in last night?"

I look him in the eye for what feels like the first time this morning.

"Because I didn't want to get into it in front of Cass. And then later, I tried to talk to you about Trina, but you were so defensive, and so worked up, and convinced I'd lied to you—"

"You *did* lie to me."

"I prefer to think of it as delaying the conversation until a more appropriate time."

And I prefer to think of *that* as rationalization.

"And then we started talking about your mom. Sam, I didn't want to ruin that."

That makes sense, I guess.

"I should've known you'd look her up. I should've thought it through and talked with you last night. Is this why you didn't sleep?"

"It's part of it. I mean, not knowing about Mom? Okay, I'm

34

sort of used to it, but it still eats at me sometimes. And then last night, to feel like you know things you're not telling me . . . Dad, come on. Don't do that to me."

"I'll tell you the same thing I told her family a decade ago," he says. "The same thing I'll tell the police again today if they want to talk with me about it. Trina went through a hard time with her family. Whether or not I wanted to see her, she showed up from time to time. She dropped in a few months before Delilah left. But after that I never saw her again. And Sam, we were never—romantically involved during those visits. I was married by then to your mom."

"Happily?"

He pauses on this one and meets my gaze. "Not as happily as I would've liked. Obviously."

"Cass said Mom cheated on you."

"She said that, huh?"

"Yeah. She said you and Heather used to talk about it."

"Maybe we speculated once or twice, but that doesn't mean it's true." He shakes his head. "That's exactly why I don't want you discussing this Trina business with your sister."

I think of the memories resurfacing lately. The bonfires, Mom's laugh. I almost can't believe I'm about to ask this. For years, our neighbor has been a quiet, slightly standoffish fixture across the lawn, watering his hydrangeas. I'll get an occasional smile or wave from him, but he and Dad aren't on speaking terms, and honestly he doesn't seem to be on speaking terms with most of the world. He may as well be a garden fountain these days.

But lately, I'm remembering he wasn't always that way. Maybe something happened that turned him inward.

Most of my sunflowers have thirty-four petals. Some of the bigger ones'll have fifty-five, but . . .

"Was it Schmidt? With Mom?"

Dad looks startled. "What makes you say that?"

"I don't know. Mom used to love sunflowers."

He nods and even smiles a little, then slurps up a gulp of shake. "She did."

"Schmidt grew them when I was little," I go on. "He doesn't grow them anymore. I thought maybe he grew them for Mom."

"So this theory that your mother had an affair is based on sunflowers."

"Well, yeah. I guess."

And in the early days after Mom left, Lieutenant Eschermann asked me where I thought she'd gone. I figured she'd moved into Schmidt's enormous place, and that she'd come back when she stopped being mad at Dad. The house is big enough that she could've sneaked in through the underground tunnel, I'd fantasized, and Schmidt wouldn't have even noticed. I never considered, until now, he might've offered her refuge in his arms.

"Henry Schmidt wasn't your mom's style."

I want to ask how he can be so sure.

Schmidt made my mother laugh. At least once.

For a few seconds, the only sounds in the house are comprised of chewing and sipping.

"Anyway, about Trina. I promise you, when all the dust clears, she's going to turn up somewhere, with a new life of her choosing. Safe and far away from her family."

Maybe he's right. And for a second or two, I feel better.

But if Trina took off ten years ago, Dad wasn't exactly married anymore, either. He and my mom weren't together. He was with Heather. It's another lie.

And the pieces of a puzzle I didn't know I was working on

are beginning to spread out in front of me. Suddenly, I'm struggling to understand the mystery that is my father—the one constant in my life. Predictable ever since he worked through the twelve steps of AA, regimented, *boring* in some respects. But he's an enormous question mark now.

He brings his protein shake to his lips for another sip.

I have more questions, but what's the point in asking, if he's only going to fill my head with half-truths?

Maybe he's trying to protect me from something.

Whatever he's protecting me from, it's bad.

"Sami, it'll be okay." He chucks me under the chin. "I promise."

"Okay."

He presses a kiss to the part in my hair.

Instinctively, I wrap a hand around whatever I can grasp onto—his arm, as it turns out—as if holding him here will keep us both safe from the past and the future.

I feel the warmth of him near me, feel loved and close and safe.

Guilt floods my heart.

Just last night I made a mental escape plan out of this house in case I thought my father might harm me.

Maybe he's lying to me, but he loves me. He could never . . .

What kind of a daughter thinks things like that?

"I gotta hit the shower, Sam. We'll talk more tonight?"

I sniffle through an affirmation. Unless he actually put it in his plan for the day—*7:35, reassure Sami for five to seven minutes*—he's taken time out of his meticulously scheduled routine to have this talk.

"I assume you'll already be bowling by the time I get home. Long agenda today."

"Probably, then."

"In that case, I'll see you when you get home."

When he leaves the room, I dab at my tears with my napkin.

Amidst the silence of the house, I hear Dad's shower running.

The sound of the Jeep horn signifies Cassidy is here.

I check my reflection in the toaster. It's plain I've been crying, but at least my mascara hasn't smudged. I don't have time to touch up my makeup.

"You turned your phone off," Cassidy says before I even pull the seat belt around me. "And it was such a crazy night that I cannot *believe* I couldn't get a hold of you."

I glance at my phone. I'd turned the ringer off last night, and I'd been so preoccupied that I hadn't turned it back on. "Did you talk to Zack?"

"Dad lied to you."

My hackles rise in defense, even though it's true.

"I looked her up," she continues. "Trina Jordan. And you wanna know what?"

"She was his girlfriend."

Cassidy looks almost disappointed. "Yeah."

"He told me this morning. But they haven't been in touch in a long time."

"Did he tell you she's missing?"

"I—"

"I swear, when you weren't answering last night . . . God, I don't even want to *tell* you the things that were going through my mind."

"Sorry. I just couldn't—"

"My mom was *freaking out*. I half-thought I'd pull up today to an empty house."

"What? Like you thought we'd leave? In the middle of the night? Don't be dramatic, Cass."

"The woman's *missing*."

"It doesn't have anything to do with Dad."

"Well, if either of you had answered your phones last night—"

"Cass, you should know better than to think like that. And your mom? She's known him her whole life. Why would she start thinking those things now?" I ignore the fact that I was thinking some of those same things not so long ago.

She sighs and glances in the rearview mirror before backing out of the driveway. "To be honest—and don't get mad, okay? But Mom's starting to say stuff that makes me think . . . I mean, it seems like—she's not so sure Dad's in the clear."

I shake my head. Cassidy is clearly taking Heather's comments out of context, blowing them out of proportion—*something*. Heather would never actually accuse Dad of something like this. "She's mad at him. They're getting divorced. Of course she isn't going to say nice things about him right now. But that doesn't mean she thinks he's capable of . . . you know."

"I know. But, God, what *else* can happen, right?"

"You know what Dad said today?" I help myself to Cassidy's compact. "He said he loves your mom."

She raises a brow. "He *loves* her. That's what he said?"

"He said, *I love Cass, and I love Heather.*"

"Huh."

"Does your mom ever say things like that, or say anything about why they split?"

"You mean, besides the standard we're-too-different discussion? No. But they *are* different. Divorce doesn't have to mean you don't love someone anymore. Just that you can't live together."

"You think that's what happened?" I wonder, in that case, if Dad could live with anyone.

"Maybe. If you think about it, they'd been at each other a lot over the past year. Maybe Dad saw the writing on the wall. Mom wasn't going to live with his bouts of silence forever, and lately, he's been—"

"Hey!" I snap. "I'd like to see how Heather would cope if your sperm-donor father suddenly took off—"

"He did!" Cassidy says. "Dad didn't miss a single soccer game last year. You want to know how many games the sperm donor has been to in my whole life? Try zero. But Mom doesn't let his absence rule her days."

"Maybe because it's obvious he's still breathing, even if he doesn't keep in touch." An emptiness floods my heart, stirring memories of Mom clacking away at an ancient typewriter—she preferred it to the computer—and tears prick at me. I press a few fingers to my lips, as if I can take back what I just said.

"Sam." Cassidy pats my knee. It's obvious she realized it too.

For the first time ever, I've admitted what so many other people—the police, the press, the whole town—have always assumed.

That my mom might really be dead.

"What do you mean, you don't know if you can come?" Brooke's leaning on a sink in the girls' room, unnecessarily touching up her dark red lipstick.

"Aren't you grounded, anyway?" She's always grounded.

"Yeah, but the Ps are going out of town this weekend. They said I couldn't leave the house, except for school or work. So I'm not leaving the house. And you'd better be there."

"My dad," I say, rubbing a temple. There's still a dull ache in my head. Probably due to lack of sleep. "Something's going on."

"You have to come." She glances at me in the mirror and offers, "I'll buy stuff for s'mores. Your favorite."

She blots her lipstick on a tissue, then tends to her eyelashes, which probably don't need curling—or another coat of mascara—any more than her lips needed more color. But we have trig next hour, and Alex Perry's locker is on our way to class. He and Brooke have a sort of love/hate relationship. They've been dancing around an inevitable hookup for years. "You can't leave me alone with Cassidy and my brother. They'll probably start making out within five minutes. I need you there tonight."

"Is Alex going?"

"Don't know yet. I mean, do I want him there? Do I not?"

"If he's there, and you ditch me to hot tub with him—"

"Wouldn't dream of it." She flips her dark blonde hair over her shoulder and pivots toward me for approval. "Do I look okay?"

"Stunning." She may have lipstick on her teeth for how closely I looked at her, but it doesn't matter. She knows she looks great. "I'm going to class."

"Wait, wait." Brooke digs in her bag and produces a tablet. After a few touches on the screen, she presents me with a Bible app. "Solemnly swear you'll be there tonight."

"You're cracked." I'm already halfway out the door.

"That's why we're friends!" she calls after me.

One step into the hallway, I feel a shift in the atmosphere, like everyone's looking at me. The pressure in my head intensifies.

A few feet down the hallway, I see the subtle turn of a few heads as we pass, and I wonder if maybe I have toilet paper stuck to the sole of my shoe or something. I glance down, and when I don't see anything that would put a target on my back, a funny sensation—like a sliver of ice injected into my blood—pumps through me.

"Omigod, here he comes," Brooke whispers.

"Ladies." Alex sidles up next to us, which isn't altogether unusual. He shakes his too-long blond hair out of his eyes. "Going out tonight?"

"Actually, no." Brooke hugs her books more tightly to her chest. "Staying in."

"Slumber party?"

"If I said yes, would you be interested?"

"Depends on the sleeping accommodations."

The chilly feeling now settles in my fingertips, my toes. I feel as if I'm all alone, even though I'm obviously among hundreds of people.

A moment before I duck into our trig classroom, I catch the gape and subsequent smirk of a girl across the hall. By the time I turn toward her, she's already turned away, but I still feel the remnants of her stare.

And I know something's different the moment I enter the classroom too. Everyone sort of shuts up for a split second when I drop my books atop my desk. When I glance around, no one's looking at me, but I feel like they all turned away only a moment ago.

My brain rattles. Oh, no. I slide into my seat, yank my shoulder bag off my arm, and rifle through it in search of my Imitrex. Have to stop this headache in its tracks.

A whisper behind me: "I wonder if she's looking for her mother in that bag."

I whip around, but see no one's lips moving.

Behind me again: "Maybe she should look in her basement."

"Or buried under the patio in her backyard."

I close my fingers around my vial of pills, which I'm not supposed to have at my disposal at school. No one understands that when the migraines hit, I don't have time for a teacher to maybe give me a pass to the office and wait for the nurse to look up my medication release and maybe find it in time. So I sneak it.

Behind me: "Probably an antianxiety, considering . . ."

"Samantha Lang."

Busted. I look up to see Mr. Peters entering the room.

"Is that prescription?" my teacher says.

"Yes."

Mr. Peters' brows slant downward. "You know you're supposed to report to the nurse for medication."

"Sorry. I just—"

"I have to send you."

I scoop up my books amidst what I'm certain is a snicker at my expense. Uncertainty hollows in my chest. And I head back out, past Brooke and Alex, who are making plans for tonight.

Maybe I'm imagining the whispers as I pass through the horde of students who ought to be scrambling to get to class. Maybe I'm paranoid.

Maybe.

"Sam!" Brooke calls after me.

I keep moving.

Along the way, I count eleven steps, then seven, eleven steps, then seven, but the white noise in my head is only getting louder.

"Sami!"

I keep walking and pass the commons, where the face of the local news anchor fills the television screen. The transcription of her words flashes up on the screen, and certain phrases catch my attention—*new development, local professor*—but I just quicken my pace.

The bell rings as I hook a right to the nurse's office.

I'm unbelievably exhausted, as if someone drilled a hole in the bottom of my foot and drained every ounce of energy out of me. This *new development* in the case of a random woman my father *used to date* might bring on the worst migraine of my life.

"Can I help you?"

"Migraine." I take a seat and cradle my head.

Somewhere in this room, one of the bars of a fluorescent light is flickering, and I can't concentrate. Its steady hum, coupled with the inconsistent brightening and waning of light, is making me nauseous.

Or maybe it's the whole situation that's wreaking havoc on my system. How selfish could my mother be to let the world think she's dead? To abandon her only child? And let my father face the fallout?

On the other hand . . . if what they're saying about Dad is true . . .

And the fact that I'm even considering *the other hand is* evidence enough that I'm losing my grip on reality. I know better than to buy into all this hype. Dad explained it all, and pretty soon, the whole world will know these suspicions are bogus.

"Your name?" I hear the nurse in the periphery and have to struggle to formulate my response.

"Samantha Lang."

"Samantha?"

I look up when the nurse says my name, but she's only a watery image before me.

Nothing is static. It's all a silvery crescent-shaped aura. I shift so I can lay my head against the back of the chair.

"Should I call home?" Her voice sounds as if it's in a tunnel.

I shake my head. Dad has a big day. The conference. The grant. He can't come get me, even if I wanted to go home, which I don't. And whether or not he deserves it, he's the last person I want to see right now. I can't help it. I have to blame someone, and there's no one else here to throw darts at. I mean, how much more am I supposed to take?

Maybe I could ask her to call Heather. No, I just need to let the medication work its magic. Just need to wait it out. Twenty minutes or so, and I should be fine. I swallow over too much saliva pooling in my mouth. Heather's not my stepmother anymore, anyway. I don't even know if her name is on my emergency release papers this year.

It's better that I deal with this alone. No one else understands my splintered existence. They don't get that I can still long for my mother, even though she's the reason my life is in pieces. They don't see that my father, for all his faults, is not only my cross to bear, but also the pillar that holds me up.

I need my father more than ever before, especially now that Dad and Heather have split.

Cassidy's commentary during our trip to school this morning revisits me. Heather actually thought we'd skip town! What else does she think?

If the public has just learned about the coincidence that is Trina Jordan, I can't afford to listen to anything anyone has to say—not even Heather. Not if I still want to believe in my father.

ⅢⅢ Ⅰ

Cassidy is waiting by my locker by the time I emerge from the maze of administrative offices in which I've spent my day. Her backpack is secure on one shoulder, and the Jeep keys dangle from her hand. "Zack Snapchatted me about ten times today. We have a streak going."

Okay. I guess that's as important as everything else that happened today.

"And there he is again." Her phone alerts, and a silly smile takes over her face. While responding to her new message, she says, "Where were you all day?"

"I went to the nurse."

"You were there *all day?*"

"For about an hour." I spin the dial on the combination lock around, and glance up at my stepsister when I say, "Then I had to go to the counselor." Lot of help that did. The woman's questions about my feelings were completely pointless. How did she *think* it made me feel to know the news was on in the commons? *Actually, I feel great. I'm glad everyone knows another half-truth about my father's past.*

"Yeah," Cassidy says. "Lots of talk today."

A sense of exasperation weighs on me, and I feel the

pressure building. I open the compartment in my mind where I keep the map. No need to unfold it just yet, but I keep it at the ready. "For a while, there, I was wondering if maybe you lived on another planet where Zack MacElroy is the center of the universe."

"Sami, come on. Of course I heard. Everyone was whispering incessantly about it after fourth hour."

I make no effort to disguise my groan of disgust. "You set them straight, right?"

"Well, no. I mean, it's been my experience that if you just ignore them—"

My locker opens with a clang and rattle. "Really, Cass? Some of those jerks think silence is confirmation. You *know* what they're saying now, right? They're saying *Cassidy Solomon was right there, and she didn't deny it.*"

"Well . . . I didn't think of it that way. It's not like there's a rule book for this sort of thing." She cups a hand over the top of my locker door and leans in a little closer. "And besides. I was talking to Mom about this last night. It's a little weird that Dad never said anything about this girl before."

"Why would he?" I feel my defenses starting to bubble and boil over, despite the fact that I've been wondering the same thing since I learned of Trina's existence. "I mean, how many of your ex-boyfriends do you still talk to? And not on Instagram."

Cassidy shrugs, but before she can utter whatever logical argument is dancing on the tip of her tongue, I press on. "Dad and this girl went their separate ways, and that's that. What happened to her later has nothing to do with Dad."

"Right. I'll say that next time."

I slam my locker door. An uncontrollable sense of irritation with my sister needles at me. She agrees with me. Or does she?

There's nothing to fight about, but I can't let it go. I'm angry, and I can't seem to talk myself out of staying that way.

She said it herself last night: she has somewhere else to go. This isn't her life anymore. Worrying about Dad, worrying about how other people see Dad. She can walk away from it without leaving a piece of herself behind.

"What?" she asks. "I'm sorry I didn't defend Dad, okay? I will next time."

She got the Jeep.

She got Kismet.

I got a perpetual headache and a cloud hanging over me.

"Okay." I pull my phone from a pocket in my bag. "Listen, you go ahead. I'm going to go home with Brooke"—I'm already texting her so she doesn't leave without me—"so she can catch me up in trig."

"Brooke's working at the Nun this afternoon. And I thought you're coming by anyway. For those new leggings."

"Oh yeah, sure. But first I have to . . . I'll ride there with Brooke, okay? And if I don't make it today—"

"You're still going tonight, though, aren't you?"

"Yeah. If I don't make it to the Nun, pick me up at seven, all right?"

Her brow crinkles a little, but she backs off. "All right."

"See you then." I practically throw myself down the hallway in the opposite direction.

A few strides later, I nearly bump into Brooke.

I don't even give her time to say hello. "I swear, it must be great to be Cassidy. She gets all the easy parts of being Dad's daughter. Today was hard, okay? And what's she focused on?"

"Let me guess. My idiot of a brother." Brooke hooks an arm through mine, and we pivot down a hallway. "You okay?"

"I guess." I fill her in on the migraine, the long hours I spent crashed on the counselor's sofa. "Meanwhile, Cass apparently acted like it was any other day."

"Maybe it's just easier for her to ignore it all."

"Sure, it's *easier*. I just don't see how it's *possible*."

"Want me to talk to her?"

Could anything good come from Brooke intervening? "I'll get over it. It just irked me, that's all. I mean, I know that since the separation, she has a reason to distance herself from the mess, but Dad's the only real father she's had." And she should know better than anyone that my father isn't the reason Trina Jordan's gone.

"Maybe this is the only way she can deal, Sam."

"Okay, but she's actually suggesting that maybe my dad's hiding something."

"She said that?"

"Not in those exact words, but—"

"So you just want to come with me, then? Alex and I were going to stop at the Madelaine before my shift at the Nun. You want a bubble tea or something?"

"No, thanks." What I really want is answers. Explanations. "Can you drop me off at the police station?"

"Sure, but . . . why?"

Because I know there's more to the story, details of Trina Jordan's case that the police can't share with the media. And if Lieutenant Eschermann wanted to talk to me yesterday, maybe he'll disclose more today.

ⲏⲏ II

I close my eyes, and instantly the map appears and towns push up out of the parchment.

"I'm glad you came in." I open my eyes, and Eschermann's gaze doesn't break as he joins me at the table where I've been instructed to sit. "I wish we could've handled this last night. Before the media got hold of the story."

I try to nod. The truth is I do understand, and even appreciate, his wanting to talk to me. But that doesn't change the fact that the cops are putting me in a tough position every time they convene on our lawn.

Neilla Cooper sits at the far end of the table and flips open a notebook. She gives me a wink, as if I'm still six. *Relax*, she says with just a look. *It's just me. Just the girl who used to babysit you, just the girl who used to catch rides to the NU campus with your parents.* Her familiar, sympathetic face does make this a little easier to endure.

The lieutenant takes a seat across from me, in front of a file folder I've seen countless times. It's about half an inch thick—the sign of a cold case without much to go on—and I don't have to look at its worn edges to know its tab bears my mother's name.

"Can you do me a favor?" I take a sip of the water Neilla offered me upon my arrival. "Before you show up at my house again, can you call? Can we deal with some of these things over the phone, maybe? I mean, I get that it's your job to find my mom, but—"

"Good," he says. "It *is* my job, and you're a witness to her disappearance. Even if she simply decided to walk away."

"That's what happened," I assure him for the hundredth time. I glance at Neilla, who probably remembers more about that time than I do. I gauge her reaction. Does she agree with me? She tilts her head and gives me a little shrug.

"Okay, why?" Eschermann asks. "Why would she just up and leave? No good-bye to you, no note—"

"I never told you she didn't say good-bye," I interject. "She said 'see you Wednesday,' which is sort of like good-bye."

"But you never saw her Wednesday, did you? And she's made no contact since."

"That's not true, either. She sends the postcards." That reminds me. I open my backpack and pull out the postcard from Charleston. "I put it in a plastic bag this time. You know, just in case."

"Did your father handle it before you put it in the bag?"

"I don't think so."

"So we shouldn't find his prints on it."

I catch on to what he's insinuating.

"He may have taken it out *after* I put it in the bag, but . . . I don't think so." I slide Charleston across the table. "Here."

"Thank you." He pushes the postcard to the edge of the table, where Neilla is sitting.

In the momentary silence, the scuttle of the police force at work beyond the wall fills the dead air. Proof of life going

52

on as scheduled, even though I feel as if mine will never be the same . . . and not only because my mother took off ten years ago, but because of whatever development has come to light in Trina Jordan's case. "It's been a long time, Sami."

I nod. I didn't come here to get into this again, but Eschermann seizes any opportunity to work me over. I decide to let it play out. Maybe if I listen patiently and don't get too mouthy, he'll feel like sharing some new information with me.

"Why . . . *How* does a mother like Delilah Lang stay away from her child for ten years without a word? How do we have a mother telling her ex-husband she's going to Georgia for the weekend, then never returning? And how is it that the ex-husband never calls the police when, weeks later, Delilah still hasn't returned home to retrieve her daughter, and won't answer her phone? We don't have a missing persons report filed until six weeks after she's gone. And even *then*, the call came from one of your mother's friends. Not your father."

"I know." They've been asking Dad to explain this scenario for as long as I can remember. "They were divorced. Doesn't that mean it isn't—wasn't—Dad's job to keep track of her anymore?"

"Does that also mean it wasn't your mother's job to tell anyone in her life that she was alive? Even after her absence sparked widespread publicity? Wouldn't she want to set the record straight, let us know that there was no need to search for her?"

I set my cup of water on the table as carefully as I can. If I keep holding it in my shaking hand, I might spill it. "I think my mother is selfish. I think all the things that seem suspicious to you are just evidence of her selfishness, her inability to care about the consequences of her leaving."

He ignores me, presses on. "Furthermore, we have the

issue with the neighbor. Have you remembered why you were in his basement?"

I shrug. We've been over this before too. The day Mom left, I turned up in Schmidt's basement and he walked me home. "I don't remember. I know I used to play with his nephew, but . . . I don't even know if Ryan was there that day."

"You were supposed to have had a sitter, yet no one in the neighborhood remembers sitting for you that day," Neilla reminds me. "I sat with you all the time. I was always your parents' first choice. I was free that day, but your parents didn't call me. And you don't remember who was supposed to have been there, either."

"Well, I also don't remember Heather being around back then, but obviously, if she was my father's alibi . . ." The police know Dad and Heather were childhood friends, reunited after my parents' divorce. The situation with my mother had kept Heather at a distance for a while, but eventually they'd found their way back to each other.

Kismet, they'd said.

Which is how we'd named our dog.

"You know what's always bothered me about the alibi?" Eschermann says. "The officer who talked with your dad interviewed Heather at the same time. They were afforded a chance to sync their stories. Heather could've simply followed your dad's lead, agreed with whatever he said. I've always wondered if Heather would've cooperated, had we interviewed them separately."

Cooperated? You don't *cooperate* with the truth. You simply tell it. "You think Heather lied for Dad."

"Your memories of Heather in your life come *after* your mother's disappearance. You father's explanation was that he and Heather didn't involve you and Cass in the early days."

I read between the lines: Eschermann thinks Heather covered for Dad, and they didn't actually get back together until *after* she lied for him, which isn't impossible, considering it took them a couple of years to get married.

Of course, Heather's always said that before she could commit to Dad, she wanted him to prove he could live without alcohol. He worked a program, but he slipped up a few times in the earlier years. So that always made sense as the rationale for Heather taking their relationship slowly. But Eschermann's idea makes sense too.

"Sami. Do you believe your mother is out there?"

"I believe she was in South Carolina recently. And Rhode Island last year."

He leans back in his chair, super casual, and laces his fingers together. "I'm going to share something with you, something that won't be made public. Can I trust you not to talk about it? You understand how important that is, right?"

I do.

"A passport renewal application in your mother's name was submitted some weeks ago."

"What?" I tighten my grip on the straps of my backpack. "That means . . ." *It's more proof she's alive.* I can't even say it. I don't want to jinx it.

"The authorities alerted us," Eschermann says, "and they opted to process it to see if it established a lead."

"It was delivered to a box in one of those delivery suites," Neilla tells me. "A passport can't be renewed through the mail unless the address is the same as on the original application. This means someone applied in person with your mother's credentials."

In person. The thought of seeing my mom . . . in the flesh . . . "In person *where*?"

"In Georgia," Neilla says, "in a suburb of Atlanta."

Atlanta!

"Trouble is," Eschermann says before I have a chance to crescendo, "the box isn't registered to Delilah. It's registered to a C. J. Lang."

"My father? Why would he have a mailbox—"

"We don't think it's likely that he rented it. Besides, he couldn't apply in person for your mother's passport, and how would he accept delivery of it in Georgia? But in any case, by the time we were alerted it was out for delivery, we were too late to intercept delivery at the box, and whoever is renting in C. J. Lang's name had already collected the passport."

"So all you have to do is find C. J. Lang." There's too much excitement in my words, but I can't contain it. This is a real lead! An honest-to-goodness lead! And if Dad had let me talk to Eschermann last night I would've known about it yesterday!

"We've checked the information on the application at the delivery suite. It's untraceable. Whoever rented it paid with a pay-as-you-go credit card. The card defaulted the week after the passport delivery. C. J. Lang doesn't exist."

I feel myself deflate like a balloon with the helium escaping. Dead end.

"But the passport *does*," Neilla says. "We know that for certain. So the question is . . . was it your mother or someone else who ordered the passport? If it was your mother, why would someone wanting to remain hidden apply for a passport renewal in her own name?"

"Maybe she wants to head to Europe."

"Maybe." Eschermann nods. "Or maybe someone wants us to *think* she's going abroad. Someone wants us to *think* she's still alive."

My stomach clenches. I know what he's not saying: that he believes *someone* killed my mother, and that this *someone* is throwing red herrings at us to cover up the crime.

"In any case, we'll be alerted to any travel plans, and we'll secure DNA from anyone traveling under your mother's name."

"And you already have my DNA on file to compare." I wish there was more I could do. Knocking on doors in an Atlanta suburb sounds like something Brooke might spearhead with me, even if I know my father would never allow it.

"Sami . . . there's more."

If there's *more*, which I take to be good news, I wonder why he looks as if he just accidentally ran over someone's golden retriever.

Eschermann moves aside my mother's file and opens one hiding beneath it. "This is Trina Jordan." He slides toward me an eight-by-ten glossy photograph.

I peruse the photograph I saw online last night. In person, it looks dated—at least ten, maybe twenty, years old. But still recognizable as the pretty woman whose image has been stuck in my head all day. Shoulder-length dark hair in haphazard waves, parted off-center on the right side. "I looked her up online yesterday."

He drums his fingertips on the table. "Your father married Trina Jordan before he married your mother."

I look up. My father was married before my mom? Married to this woman, whom he initially told me he'd never even heard of?

Something tumbles in my gut, like I'm going to be sick. I force a swallow. Try not to show that I'm shocked, that I didn't know. But in my head, triangles are forming, and I'm trying to put the pieces together but none of them fit.

"They weren't married long. Less than a year. This is Trina Jordan's college graduation photo, taken a few months before she married your dad. Less than a year later, their marriage was annulled. Some time after that, he married your mom and moved up here. Meanwhile, Trina Jordan took her dog for a walk one day and never returned home. She and her family weren't on good terms, and they assumed she'd left of her own volition. A few months ago, she was reported missing by a younger sister, who'd finally figured Trina would have come back . . . if she *could* have. Turns out the remains of a woman were found about ten years ago in rural Georgia, classified as a Jane Doe. We were just alerted of a possible correlation to your mother's case."

"You think the Jane Doe in Georgia is my mother?"

"Authorities there think it's more likely she's Trina Jordan."

Dad's words replay in my head: *when the dust clears, Trina Jordan will be living a new life of her choosing . . .*

Or maybe she's dead. Better her than Mom, but either way, it's bad news. Either way, if the Jane Doe turns out to be Mom or Trina, they're looking at my father. Lose-lose. "How did she die?"

"I can't disclose that."

With a slight tremor in my hands, I shove the photograph of the maybe-dead girl back across the table.

"All those years ago, before Trina was classified as a missing person, after you turned up in your neighbor's basement and were so insistent that your mother was hiding in your neighbor's house, I brought a team of dogs out. Do you remember that?"

"Vaguely."

"The dogs alerted behind the barn."

"They . . . what?" My hands are full-out shaking now, and splintered fragments of memories come back to me. The digging. The dogs. "What does that mean? Alerted?"

"It means there was a body there at one time."

"But you didn't find anything. I'd remember if you found something."

He presses his lips together and shakes his head. "We didn't find anything."

He never told me that the dogs alerted, though. Maybe because, at first, I was too little to understand. And then, as I got older, I refused to listen to anything he said, shut him down with blanket denials and dismissals of my father's possible guilt.

"*At one time*, you said."

"The dogs aren't always right. Could be they responded to something else, old remains, maybe."

"But you didn't find old remains. So that means . . . you think my mom was there, at some point?"

He pauses longer than usual. "It's a possibility, Sami, considering what's happening in Georgia."

A slideshow plays in my mind. Memories of Mom placing a plate of cookies on the table. A hand reaching for one. A male voice: *I might gain ten pounds if you keep making these cookies.* Mom, laughing: *You might try not eating the whole batch.*

"This Jane Doe has spurred a theory," Eschermann says.

I blink back to the present.

"Could be, if there was a body behind the barn, it was

moved, maybe to Atlanta. Your father, at the time, drove a Chevy Express 1500."

Big enough to hide a woman's body in the back.

And Eschermann thinks my father may have transported one.

"But . . . Dad never went to Atlanta. You'd know if he had."

"Actually, like I said, the missing persons report in your mother's case wasn't filed until six weeks after the disappearance. And in Trina's case, no one reported her missing for nearly ten years. The police did talk with Heather and your father about their whereabouts during that six-week period, but as I said, the interviews occurred at the same time."

"And they said they didn't take a trip."

"I'm hoping *you* can help me with that. Do *you* remember your father taking a trip?"

"No." I can't look at him. "I've told you everything I know."

"I believe you think that's true. Someday, though, a mundane detail may surface, and it may not even seem significant. But trust me when I say that those mundane details crack cases."

I just shake my head. It's such a long time ago now. And how can he expect me to remember something I didn't even know at the time?

"I've mentioned it before," he says. "Hypnosis. Your father will never consent to it—"

"Because he doesn't want me to relive the worst day of my life."

"—but if we're still in this position a year or two from now, when you're of legal age to consent, I hope you'll consider it. The longer we wait, the more ineffective it will be."

"So it's probably a moot point already. It's been *ten years*. And this girl . . . this Trina . . . she was hardly even married to my dad, you said so yourself. And you don't even know that the body in Georgia used to be behind the barn—is there any way to tell?—and she's been gone a long time—"

"The more sophisticated our networks become, the more easily information is shared across the country. Not uncommon these days for a Jane Doe to be identified a decade after remains are recovered."

"It's a coincidence," I say.

"If she'd died in a car accident, I'd 100 percent agree with you, but—"

"I'm sorry this happened to Trina Jordan, but my dad doesn't know anything about it. And I'm sorry my mom didn't want to be a mom, but she isn't dead. She just renewed her passport. And if she renewed her passport, she obviously wants to go somewhere even farther away. It's all a coincidence."

Eschermann's nodding. "Could be." Thumbs still twiddling, head bobbing in a nod. "One theory in Trina's case names your mother as a person of interest. Ex-wife Number Two goes missing around the time ex-wife Number One's last seen. And now that Number One may be identified as this Jane Doe, there's suddenly a passport renewed—in the second wife's name."

I don't have a choice now. I have to meet his stare.

"It would explain why your mother's been gone as long as she has been, wouldn't it? And according to your father, your mother had planned to go back to Georgia."

I wipe tears from my eyes.

"All these years," he continues, "it's been an enigma I couldn't wrap my head around. Why would a mother leave her daughter, drop off the face of the earth and allow the world to think she could be dead? If she had something to do with Trina Jordan's disappearance, it might make more sense."

My heart pounds. "So you think she's been hiding because . . . because she murdered someone." That's just as bad as her being dead. Worse, maybe. "My mom wouldn't hurt a fly. She's a vegetarian, can't justify killing animals to eat. She . . . she used to put cocoons in jars so the birds wouldn't eat them, and she released the butterflies when they hatched! And you think she's capable of putting someone in a ditch?"

"Huh." A look of deep concentration crosses Eschermann's face.

"And my dad doesn't know anything about Trina Jordan." There's got to be a scenario that doesn't involve one of my parents being a murderer. But if there is, Eschermann apparently hasn't found it. I stand and hike my bag onto my shoulder. "And he sure as hell wouldn't have done anything to my mom. And you"—I look to Neilla—"you should know that. You knew them! You saw them together. You know he couldn't have done anything to—"

"Look, Sami," Neilla says soothingly. "I've known you since you were a little girl. Your mother's case is the reason I became a cop. Trust me. We just want to find her. The whole community. As much as you do."

She slides a box of tissues toward me, and I instinctively reach down to take one.

"Then actually *look* for her instead of obsessing about my dad!"

Eschermann leans forward, his hands clasped on the table. "I know you think I want to pin your mom's disappearance on your dad, but that's not my goal here, Sami. If you can give me information to prove something in your dad's favor, I'm looking for that too. My goal? Justice. Justice for whoever's responsible for Trina Jordan. Justice for your mom, if indeed she needs it."

I mechanically blot away my tears with the tissue I took. He's not lying. That's why I've never been able to hate him, as much as he infuriates me. "How long until you know? About the Jane Doe?"

"It takes about a month or so, depending on the backlog at the lab. It's already been a few weeks."

"Then pretty soon you'll know. You'll know this is all a coincidence."

"And if it isn't a coincidence," he says, "I guess we'll know that soon enough too. Your father has a third ex-wife now, doesn't he?"

Heather.

"Anything happens to her, and we won't be able to call it a coincidence, will we?"

I stare at him, appalled at what he's implying. "Nothing's happened to her." I can barely choke it out.

"Let's hope it stays that way."

||||| |||

Neilla drives me home. Just as she's about to turn her squad car onto my street, she veers back onto Charles Avenue. "Channel Five," she says.

I peer down the road as we pass through the intersection. Sure enough, there's a crew standing outside my house, filming.

"I can escort you to the door, but you'll still be on camera." She sighs and drums her fingertips against the steering wheel. "Your call: you want to go to the Nun?"

I probably should, if only to apologize for being nasty to Cassidy earlier today, but I want to change clothes and fix my makeup first. "Can you drop me at Schmidt's place? I'll cut through the backyard." It's going to be a trick to get in without being seen, even through the back door, but it's worth a shot.

Too bad the tunnel connecting our place and Schmidt's is out of commission, or I might use it now.

"Sam, are you and Mr. Schmidt . . ." Her head bobbles from side to side, like she's trying to find the right words. ". . . neighborly? Do you see him around? Talk to him?"

"Not much. Why?"

"Something I keep coming back to." She rounds the corner of Schmidt's block. "I remember it from back then, but I also

64

keep seeing it in the file. You said it more than once: right after your mother disappeared, you were sure she'd been at Schmidt's place."

"Mmm-hmm."

"Why?" She pulls up to the curb in front of Schmidt's enormous Victorian.

"I'm not sure." I study the place now. All its windows, like eyes, staring out at the world. All the nooks and secret niches it must hide within its walls.

"I used to think it was just because of the size of the place, or maybe because I couldn't imagine where else she'd go, but lately, I've been wondering . . ." I stop myself. Does what I'm about to say sound utterly ridiculous? "I wonder if my mom and Schmidt were . . . more than friends."

"Is that what you think?"

I shrug. "I have no proof. My father says it's not true. But I remember spending time there."

"Because of the nephew, maybe."

Maybe.

"Let me ask you something." Her brow furrows, as if she's concentrating. "Do you think there's any chance your mother arranged a playdate with the nephew that day? And then took off? It would explain why there's no record of a sitter."

"I don't remember ever being at Schmidt's without my mother. And the police checked him out back then, right? Schmidt?"

"They interviewed him."

"Because, you'd think, if I insisted my mother was at his house, and then, with the dogs alerting—"

"They ruled him out."

Of course they did. But I can't afford to simply trust that

65

the police would've thought to look into it—especially when all fingers are pointing to my dad. If they made a mistake with Dad and Heather's alibi, maybe they made a mistake with something else. "Could you check for me? Make sure?"

When she meets my gaze, the afternoon sun washes her hair an even lighter shade of blonde, and her eyes look as green-gold as leaves about to mellow in the fall. "Sure," she finally says. "I'll check on it."

"Thanks." I get out of the car.

I see our carriage house and our enclosed breezeway, which connects the carriage house to our home. Couple hundred feet, and I'm home free. I wave to Neilla one last time.

I'm off the driveway now and walking across the soft grass, alongside Schmidt's barn, which he now uses as a garage. When I was little, Schmidt grew his sunflowers against this barn. I remember weaving in and out of them, following them along the perimeter of the old wooden structure. Later, after my mother left, I'd wondered if the smiling faces of the flowers would ever grow tall enough to see into the hayloft. And if so, what would they see? Perhaps my mother was camping there, waiting for the right moment to come home to me.

How idiotic of me to think such things, considering a German shepherd sniffed out a cadaver here: either a body my mother put there, according to Lieutenant Eschermann, or my mother's own body.

Instinctively, I drop to my knees and press my hands against the cool, dry soil.

There are no sunflowers now. No fuzzy stems to tickle my fingers. No stray petals raining down on me when the wind blows. Just a mystery in the dirt, and the line of shagbark hickory trees that stood witness to it all.

I cup the dirt in my hands and imagine it filling in the caverns around my mother's lifeless body, filtering into her blue eyes, her nostrils, her ears, her mouth. If she had to be buried, she would've wanted to be buried under sunflowers, I think. But it's a gruesome image.

"You okay?"

I jump. Ryan, Schmidt's nephew, is suddenly standing before me in flannel and a work jacket, the epitome of strong farm boy.

"Yeah, I'm—" I wipe away tears with the sleeve of my shirt and scramble to my feet.

"Sami." He's about six-two. Broad-shouldered. A far cry from the boy whom I used to match, stride-for-stride, during games of tag. He smells of a combination of earth and Calvin Klein. Hazel-brown eyes look down at me. He's offering a hand clad in a garden glove. "Hi. I'm Ryan. We used to play together."

His voice carries a hint of the South. My heart warms. I'd forgotten that about him, the accent.

Like Mom's. Not an all-out twang, but a lilt, particularly evident in the *I*.

"Yeah, I know." I take his hand and feel the residue of dust or dirt from his glove on my fingertips once he pulls away. "I remember. You're the one who lives in . . ." I used to know this.

"Kentucky."

That's right. "Yeah. Hi." Brilliant, Sami. I catch another tear on one of my knuckles before I remember they're dirty. My eye burns as the soil mixes with my tears. "Holy *Jesus*."

"Whoa." His left hand cups my elbow. "Hold still." With his right thumb, now out of the glove, he wipes the corner of my eye.

"I should get this rinsed out."

"I agree. But . . . with what's going on over there . . . what *is* going on over there?"

"What?" I look at him with one eye pinched shut. "You mean a reporter standing on someone's front lawn, surrounded by a camera crew, isn't normal?"

"It is if you just won the sweepstakes."

"Yeah, you guessed it. My family's notoriously lucky at games of chance."

He chuckles and gestures toward Schmidt's back door. "Come on inside. I have something of yours anyway."

"Something of mine?"

"Well, sort of. I was going to drop it off later, but . . . come on."

A few minutes later, with enough grime and mascara staining one of Schmidt's dish towels that I feel I should replace it, I'm sitting at a counter stool at a freestanding worktable in the middle of my neighbor's kitchen.

The air smells like a mixture of lemon furniture polish and old library books no one's checked out in ages. But it's comforting in a way, and I wonder if that's because I used to spend time within these walls—which happen to be painted the same sugar-cookie yellow Dad referenced yesterday.

On the far end of the room, narrow cabinets, with what appears to be a recent bright white refinishing, reach from the floor to the ceiling. To my left, a sink perched on cast-iron table legs is skirted with a striped curtain. Dishes are stacked on bracketed, open shelves astride the window.

The floor practically dances with a tiny hexagonal ceramic pattern—black and white—and if I stare at it too long, it starts to screw with my vision. It *moves*. I do remember that. I remember staring at it, daring the floor to move beneath my feet.

And there's a serving pantry . . .

I meander to the far end of the kitchen, toward the small niche of mullioned-glass cabinetry fitted into a hallway between the kitchen and enormous dining room. I remember seeing dishes adorned with ivy and pink roses stored in this little pantry. I take a breath before I peek at the niche now.

I crane my neck to see around the corner, and sure enough. Ivy. Pink roses. And if I were to continue through the pantry, and out to the left instead of to the right, there'd be a hallway, and off the hallway, a bathroom big enough to house a sofa . . . and it did, once . . . with the same mosaic tile as the kitchen.

"Here we are."

I jump a little when I hear Ryan's voice.

But he doesn't seem to notice or care that I've ventured from my seat.

He's carrying a cardboard box—it's about fifteen inches cubed—that he places atop the worktable.

I slip back onto my counter stool.

"I was reading *The Great Gatsby* the other night. My uncle collects hardcover editions of the classics."

I do a double take. My mother did too. Well, not only *classics*. Mom had wide-ranging literary tastes. In addition to Hemingway and Hawthorne, we have Ray Bradbury's entire collection, as well as Mary Higgins Clark's. Still, I wonder if our neighbor talked about books with my mother.

"He used to read to us," Ryan says. "*Huck Finn*, as I recall. Anyway. I found this box in the barn, and this was in it." He slaps a book down in front of me. "Maybe I wouldn't have looked at it twice, if I didn't happen to be reading the same book in hardcover right now. But . . . here."

It's a paperback copy of *The Great Gatsby*.

"I was looking for the chainsaw," he says. "For trimming the trees. And I found this box, tucked behind the lathe."

"Like, in the wall?"

"Sort of. I mean, there's no plaster, but it was in a crevice over the wine cellar. Uncle Henry asked me to board it up, to stop critters from getting in there."

"And the box was hidden there?"

"Pushed in there pretty good. Anyway, I thought you should have it."

"Well . . . thanks." But I don't recall owning a copy of *Gatsby*, or ever reading it, for that matter.

"Open it," he says. I turn back the worn cover, which I now realize has been laminated at the edges. He reaches across the table and taps the inside cover with a blunt finger. "See?"

Once he moves his hand, I see it: a small rectangular sticker with my mother's typewritten name and address alongside an image of a sunflower—a return address label, proof that once, she lived at my house.

But Ryan takes the book and starts flipping the pages before I have a chance to study the label in its entirety, before I have a chance to memorize the way her name looks in print.

"And here . . ." He taps a finger at the bottom of page 117— eleven, seven—where my mother had doodled three sunflowers, which appear to have sprouted up from each digit. "My uncle says she used to love those flowers. He grew them against the barn, didn't he?" He looks up at me.

I meet his gaze. "Thank you. For getting this back to me."

"No problem." His eyes now hold a question. "Been a long time, Sam."

"Yeah."

"I'm glad you came through the yard today. I was wondering how long you'd keep your distance."

I feel my cheeks grow warm. "You could've come over to say hello when you got here."

"I've only been here a couple of days, and you've been in school."

"Why aren't *you* at school?"

"I'm homeschooled. Just finished my senior year, as a matter of fact, so now I have time to help my uncle."

"Why'd you stop visiting? You used to be here all the time."

"Was there anything to do here—once you stopped coming around, anyway?"

I guess it was no secret that my father didn't want me to speak to Schmidt, let alone spend time on his property, after Mom was gone. From the little that Dad's said, I gather Schmidt was pretty vocal about his belief that Dad was responsible for whatever happened to my mother.

"But really," he adds, "let's just say as I got bigger, I was needed at home. Lots of land to take care of."

"Yeah." I sort of remember he has horses. Or something. "You said . . . your uncle talks about my mom? About the sunflowers?"

He shrugs a shoulder. "Just when I asked about the book— why he had it, why it was shoved in a box with the rest of these things."

The rest of these things?

I peek into the box, which appears to be filled with old papers. Syllabi, applications for employment . . . with my mother's signature on them.

The moment my fingers meet the pages, a sense of coziness darts through me, as if the warmth of my mother's touch has remained embedded in the aging fibers of these papers.

Dad was right. Judging by the letters of reference addressed to deans at Clark Atlanta, Clayton State, and Coastal Georgia, Mom *was* planning to go home to Georgia—for good. But wouldn't she have needed these things to secure a job there? And why leave them here if she needed them?

I should call Eschermann. This is something else my mother left behind. And Ryan found it in the exact location I'd assumed my mother had gone!

"Why would Schmidt have been storing all this stuff in his barn?" I murmur.

"He said your mom asked him if she could keep a few things there. He was fine with it, and—I mean, she never came back for them."

I look up at Ryan, almost guiltily. "I—I feel like the police might want to see this."

"Yeah, maybe." He shrugs. "Uncle Henry said he turned everything of Delilah's over to the police . . . you know, when it happened. But they must've missed this box." I wonder how he's interpreting all this. From his point of view, has he stumbled over memories a former playmate's mom left behind? Or did he find clues suggesting foul play in her disappearance?

I can't decide. With most people, this would be easy. My family's history is like a horror movie people can't help but watch, peeking through their fingers as they cover their eyes.

But Ryan—so far, anyway—doesn't pass judgment. My mother is gone, but it's just a fact to him. There's no attempt to point his finger at anyone, or even try to explain the inexplicable. It just is.

"Your uncle and my mom . . . they were friends, right?"

A smile spreads in his lips. "Yeah. Neighbors, friends. Somewhere in between, maybe."

In between. Maybe less than friends. But not more.

Then why did my mother leave these things in his barn?

In ten years, surely Schmidt could've gotten rid of this stuff if he'd felt like it. Especially if he was convinced that my mom would never come back to reclaim her belongings. Yet he'd kept it. Why?

Out of the corner of my eye, I see movement on my property.

I practically jump when I see it: a motor home pulls up my driveway. It's an off-white contraption, yellowed with age, with a fine orange pin-striping along the base. "Damn," I whisper, walking to the kitchen window for a closer look.

"What's up?" Ryan's behind me now, looking out the window too.

I haven't seen this glorified van in years. I suspect Dad calls my grandmother when things are getting hot, whenever the dust settling around my mother's case gets stirred up again. Whatever the reason, her being here isn't a good sign.

"My grandmother's here."

"Huh."

I know he doesn't get why I sound less than excited to see her. Even as a little kid, I knew her being here meant things were about to get uncomfortable.

"You know those grandmothers who sort of annoy you because they insist on giving you kisses that leave lipstick marks on your cheeks?" I ask. "And you don't know how to talk to them, but you try because they keep asking questions, and the whole thing is really awkward? But in the end, they're your grandparents, so you love them anyway?"

He chuckles. "Yeah."

"Well, my grandmother isn't like that."

He leans against the countertop and crosses his arms over his chest. "What's she like?"

"In a word? Controlling. And usually drunk. When I was a little girl and she was watching me one night, she stared at me across the table for three hours while I took tiny sip of milk after tiny sip of milk, insisting I finish it all. Do you know how gross milk is at room temperature?"

"Yeah."

"And I don't even like it when it's cold. And I'm lactose intolerant, but she doesn't *believe* in lactose intolerance. I would've been there all night, if Dad and Heather hadn't come home and put a stop to it."

"Geez. She sounds delightful."

Of course, Gram's dietary tyranny is hardly the worst thing about her. But I'm not going to burden Ryan with my other memories. I imagine my too-thin grandmother, ever-present drink in hand. Sip after sip. Words slurring by dinnertime.

One memory in particular is hard to shake. She'd been visiting the summer after Mom left—the summer the air conditioning was on the fritz—and we'd been watching television in the basement because it was too hot upstairs.

Dad retreated after a few drinks, when he got that glazed look in his eyes. Gram went up after him. Just to check on Dad and get another drink, she'd said. She left me in the basement. A storm rolled in, and I was down there alone while thunder and lightning crashed and the house shook. She never came back. I know now that she probably just passed out on the sofa, but at the time I felt completely alone. I was too afraid to go upstairs, because I didn't want to see my father depressed and blank; his drunken episodes were still new enough to scare me.

So I'd huddled in the corner of Dad's office, by Dad's desk, and cried myself to sleep.

I glance at Ryan, who is sort of frowning but sort of looking sad, as if to say sorry-you-had-to-deal-with-that.

I summon a breezy tone. "Anyway, we just don't get along very well. At least I don't have to deal with her all that often." And I'm old enough now to come out of the basement. "Dad only calls her when he's desperate for someone to help fill the gaps while he's busy."

Busy, in this regard, means under suspicion.

"And sometimes, she comes just because she's breezing through town. But every time, she takes over like she belongs here."

"Sounds disruptive."

"To say the least." I pull my phone out of my pocket. I wonder if Dad invited her this time or if she's here of her own volition again. "I have to call my dad."

|||| ||||

My mom used to make cookies by the hundreds. But she made them in multiples of eleven instead of twelve.

I was in a hotel once that didn't have a thirteenth floor. The buttons on the elevator went from twelve to fourteen. There was still a thirteenth floor, of course, but calling it number fourteen must have made things more bearable for the superstitious people staying there. Still, how gullible could they have been to have simply accepted a different number?

Strange what people do to make themselves comfortable.

And I'm wondering what adjustments I've made over the years to remain comfortable. Comfortable with Dad. Comfortable with the fragments of truth I've gathered along the way and somehow pieced together as an explanation for what must've happened to my mother.

But based on what I know now—the Trina Jordan connection, the box of job-hunting materials left behind in Schmidt's barn—I can't afford to be ignorant anymore.

Ryan takes his eyes off the road long enough to glance at me. "So . . . bowling?"

"No, that's just what I told my dad." I left Dad a message, telling him that Gram had arrived and that Cassidy needed my help at the shop before our plans tonight. I didn't mention the hostile atmosphere at school, the box Ryan found in the loft, or even that I stopped by the police station to see Lieutenant Eschermann. I could have at least texted it to him, but truth be told, I just don't feel like he *deserves* to know right now. He was *married*. Trina Jordan wasn't just some girl he used to know. She was his ex-wife.

I wonder what else my dad is hiding. What else isn't he telling me?

I glance at Ryan, who offered to drop me off at the Funky Nun when I decided I didn't want to go home and see Gram. "We're really just hanging out at Brooke's," I explain to him. "Not doing anything special, but you're welcome to join. I mean, I'm sure you have your own plans, but . . ." My phone chimes. Dad's calling back. I can't take the call. Not now. Not in front of Ryan. I send it to voice mail.

"You okay?" Ryan asks.

"Yeah." I don't tell him the truth: that I'm confused. That I feel duped. That I'm angry and frustrated. With everyone. With my mom—obviously—for leaving us in this mess. With my dad for leaving so much to question, and with Eschermann for not figuring it out already. Even with Schmidt, who maybe through no fault of his own, or maybe through *every* fault, had been harboring a box of what might be evidence *for ten years*!

I'm even a little irked that Ryan found the damn box to begin with.

The windows in Ryan's truck are rolled all the way down. Despite the slight nip in the air, it's nearly sixty degrees. This is the time of year my mother used to call "second chance summer."

Let's roll the windows down, Sami-girl! Last chance to feel this free until spring!

Is there any chance someone like Mom could have something to do with Trina's disappearance? Not the mother I remember. But then again, the mother I remember also wouldn't have left me.

There's a little charm dangling from Ryan's rearview mirror: a white ghost with big, black eyes and a cheesy smile. And I can't help thinking that my mother, whether she's alive or not—my heart sinks with the thought of the latter possibility—is a lot like a ghost. Mysterious. Residual. *But not here.*

"This is it." I point toward the end of the Lakefront Walk.

Ryan expertly parallel parks. Across the street, in front of the Madelaine Café, Alex Perry is sitting outside in the alfresco dining section, reading, with an oversized mug in front of him. He looks up and waves when he sees me.

I wave back.

He goes back to his book.

Ryan kills the engine. "I'll walk you in."

"Oh, you don't . . ." I shut up. If I tell him he doesn't have to, he might think I don't want him to. It's not that I necessarily *want* him to, either, but it's not like I mind. "Thanks. You can meet my friends."

Together we approach the Funky Nun, which is bustling. Most of Heather's orders come through the website. I don't know that I've ever seen six shoppers in the quaint showroom at the same time before tonight.

Ryan's hand meets the door before I reach it, and he opens it for me. "After you," he says.

Tonight's soundtrack consists of heavy base and repetition. A new mix. Patrons leaf through racks, and some actually stand in wait with hangers hooked on their fingers, but Brooke hasn't moved from her position behind the counter, where she's flipping the pages of *New Dawn* magazine.

She looks up when she sees us, offers a bored wave.

"Hey." I drop my backpack behind the counter and do a quick introduction: "Ryan, this is Brooke."

She raises her chin. "Sup?"

"Excuse me." A woman in professional dress leans over Brooke's magazine. "I need a fitting room? If it's not too much of an inconvenience?"

I might guess this isn't the first time she'd asked for one.

"Sami," Brooke says. "Fitting room."

I raise a brow. "Really?" I'm not even on the clock.

"What?" Brooke grabs a scarf from a rack on the counter and drops it around her shoulders. She peers into a small mirror, which Heather hung on the wall behind the counter, to check her lipstick. "You know the drill. You want information on a voodoo doll? I'm your girl. Fitting room? Entirely out of my realm of expertise."

"Where's Cassidy?" I ask. "Filling online orders?"

"Nah, inventory." Brooke turns another page.

I turn to woman-in-pants-suit. "Right this way."

Three people with outfits hooked on their fingers follow me.

"Here." Brooke hands Ryan a Magic 8 Ball. "Keep yourself busy."

He shakes it. "Will I get accepted at Northwestern?"

I unlock three fitting rooms, admit the customers, and return for the verdict:

"You may rely on it."

"That thing's never wrong." Brooke moistens her finger and turns another page.

"I guess we know where I'll be next fall, then," Ryan says.

"The real question is"—Brooke finally closes her magazine—"where will you be tonight?"

"Brooke." Nothing like putting the guy on the spot, especially because he never answered when I invited him earlier. I turn to a customer approaching the register. "All set?"

"No, really," Brooke says, slouching out from behind the counter so I have room to work. "You should come to my place tonight. Just a smallish gathering. Sami, Cass, and me." She walks right up to Ryan, stands toe-to-toe, and cranes her neck to stare up at him. "And some dweebs you could step on, if you wanted to. How tall are you, anyway?"

"Six-two. But I should probably take a rain check. I got lots to do, so . . ."

"Like what?"

"Brooke!" I say. "Give the guy a break, all right?"

"Fine," she says, still staring up at him. "Be boring."

"Oh, no." Cassidy enters the showroom with a stack of embroidered jeans. She looks me over from top to toe and back again. "You're not wearing that tonight."

"What?" I look down at my standard outfit: leggings, tank top, and hoodie. Nothing fancy, but I'll take this outfit over a run-in with my grandmother any day of the week, so I'm not going home to change. "I don't think the world will implode, Cass. This is Ryan, by the way." While Cassidy and Ryan acknowledge each other, I bag the crocheted beret I just sold and hand over a receipt. "Have a nice evening."

"So here's my real question, Ryan," says Brooke, still sizing him up. "Are you man enough to hang out with my best friend?"

I'm ringing up another customer.

"News flash," Ryan says. "She was my best friend before she was yours."

Best friend? My insides go gooey for a second. I feel flattered and important. And maybe like I should change clothes before the party tonight.

"Touché." Brooke stays her course. "But I've been here the whole time."

"Good. That's important."

"Hmmm." She squints at him and then finally steps back. "You're a good guy?"

"I'm a good guy."

"Okay, I approve. You should come."

He looks at me.

"You should," I say.

I pick up the Magic 8 Ball from where Ryan abandoned it. While shaking it, I concentrate on my question: *Is my mother alive?*

Its reply: *Better not tell you now.*

||||| |||||

Heather and Cassidy's apartment above the Funky Nun still looks like they just moved in, although they've been here now for almost six months. Boxes still line the walls, some empty, some not yet open. This is one of the ways Heather and my dad are different. Seeing this place would drive Dad nuts—there's not a single room in this place that's completely put together.

I'm in the laundry room, looking through Heather's rejected samples, the designs she likes but doesn't think will sell. The stock has always been accessible to Cass and me. Because most of the stuff is so out-there that it's not even in the same solar system as my style, I don't usually consider the prototypes when I'm looking for new clothes.

But my sister insisted I find something more exciting to wear tonight, and while ordinarily I would've brushed her off, Ryan did agree to meet us there later.

Cassidy suggested a little extra effort tonight couldn't hurt, and maybe she's right. I mean, nothing is going to happen between Ryan and me. But still.

Besides, I was such a bitch to Cass earlier that I figure I can offer peace through a Cassidy-approved outfit.

Kismet licks my ankles, my elbows, the floor I walk on as I move from bin to bin. "Poor girl," I say. "You miss me, don't you?"

She jumps up on me, even though Cassidy and I spent weeks at puppy boot camp with her to avoid this type of bad behavior. But I scratch her ears so she knows I miss her too. I never minded the jumping, anyway.

Get another dog. Yeah, Dad. As if any other dog could take Kismet's place.

"Okay," I say. "Let me find something to wear, and then we'll play."

I pull a bin off the shelf.

Kismet wedges her head under my elbow and peers into the bin with me.

I yank out a pair of capri pants—stretch denim with turquoise pom-pom fringe along the cuffs and yellow bandana-type print rimming the pockets—and hold them up. "Should fit," I say to my dog, "and not too crazy, comparatively speaking." I peel off my leggings, toss them into the dirty clothes hamper, and step into the pants. They're a touch snug, but they'll do.

I drape my hoodie over the edge of a box and go to work looking for a shirt to wear over my standard white tank top. But my dog's patience is wearing thin. She nudges me with her cold nose and drops a soggy tennis ball at my feet.

"Go get it, Kissy." I toss the ball out the door, open another bin, and sift through outlandish jackets and fringe-adorned cardigans. After a few seconds, I hear my dog nosing around in the hallway; it sounds as if she's getting into something.

Sure enough, when I go to check on her, I find her with her face buried in a box. "Did the ball land in there?" I crouch next to her and open the box. The ball is resting atop a nest of linens. Great. Clean sheets, and they're covered in Kismet slobber.

"Are you about ready?" Cassidy calls up the stairs.

"One sec," I call back.

I take the top layer of sheets to the laundry room and drop them in the washer.

I open the door to the small laundry closet to retrieve the detergent. Just as I'm about to close the door, something catches my eye: a yellow-and-gray sleeve dangles from a box on the top shelf.

With one yank, the box falls into my grasp. I pull out a long-sleeved, cropped jacket with big yellow flowers on it— very vintage-looking—with pewter, daisy-shaped buttons.

Kismet appears in the doorway, looking guilty.

I slip on the coat. It's not my style. The print, for one thing, is far too busy for my solid-color-only fashion parameters. But the buttons . . . I feather a finger over one of them. "Daisies."

Kismet cocks her head and perks up her ears.

"My mom used to love this color," I tell her.

She barks, which I take as her attempt to tell me the jacket is the right thing to wear.

"Come on, Sam!" Cassidy's yell echoes up the stairs. "I've already locked up and everything."

"Just cleaning up after the dog!" And I'm wearing this god-awful jacket because I don't have time to find something else . . . and because all signs tell me I should.

Two minutes later I've started the washer. As I steer the dog to her crate in the next room, I see a bunch of Cassidy's old school projects strewn across the floor, spilling from an over-turned box. "Oh no. You've really been wreaking havoc, Kissy, haven't you?" I get Kismet settled in her crate, then return to the hallway to straighten up the mess. Working quickly, I gather Cassidy's kindergarten letter books—some with a few more teeth marks than they had before—and construction paper art projects.

Just as I drop everything in the box, something catches my eye. Peeking out from beneath the piles of paper is a fat envelope with my name on it, written in cursive across the top. Heather's writing.

I pull the envelope out of the box and then extract a stack of folded papers from it. A peculiar drawing sits on top: a storm with red rain, red puddles. A stick figure in the distance holds a flower-shaped umbrella and sprouts large raindrops of tears; a second figure lies prone, with *x*es for eyes and an enormous heart drawn at the center of its chest.

I leaf through the remaining papers. There are about ten of them.

Over and over again: red rain on a sunflower umbrella, a body on the ground, the heart.

My sunflower locket burns against my ankle.

Maybe the heart in the drawing isn't meant to be a heart in the biological sense. Maybe . . . maybe it's a locket.

||||| ||||| |

Ten of us sit around the bonfire in Brooke's backyard. The eleventh guest, Ryan, hasn't shown up yet. And considering that Brooke and Alex are engaged in a close conversation, and Cassidy and Zack haven't come up for air in three songs, I'm starting to wonder why I'm here. I know everybody else, but I can't think of anything to say, can't keep track of the conversations around me.

"Relax." The guy next to me nudges me with his elbow. I hear the laughter in his voice.

But it's impossible to relax when an envelope containing my gruesome childhood drawings is tucked into the inside pocket of this borrowed jacket.

Maybe I shouldn't have taken the pictures, but technically, they're mine. Even if I don't remember doing it, I created the awful scenes; I should be able to take them if I want to.

Before we left Cassidy's place, I went to the bathroom, I snapped a picture of the first drawing, and emailed it to Eschermann. I called him, too, and left a message about it, but I assume he's gone for the day. I'll have to wait until tomorrow to talk about it.

Why would I have drawn something so terrifying, and so many times?

Why would my drawings be mixed in with Cassidy's old schoolwork?

Does Heather suspect Dad knows something? Maybe she found the drawings and accused Dad, and that's why they separated. Or maybe she wouldn't have corroborated Dad's story in the first place, if the police had followed procedure and interviewed them separately.

I mentally repeat the story: Dad and Heather were out. I was supposed to be with a sitter, because Mom was leaving that day for a weekend trip to Georgia. Then I turned up at Schmidt's place, with no sitter, and Mom was gone. No one ever saw Mom again.

I can't remember anything beyond being absolutely petrified until Schmidt walked me home.

But where was Cassidy while Dad and Heather were out?

I was supposed to be with a sitter.

Where was Cass supposed to be?

Why doesn't anyone ask *that* question? Maybe Cassidy is the clue to testing the alibi. If Cass were with Heather, would she have been with Heather *and* Dad? Or was she at home with her mom, leaving Dad free to . . .

Shut up!

I spring to my feet and head toward the driveway. I just want to go home. I can't call Dad, though, because I'm supposed to be at the bowling alley.

I could walk, I guess. It's not that far.

But it *is* pretty dark.

It was a night like this that my mother told me sunflowers were the luckiest of all flowers, because they were optimistic, always reaching higher. I see the scene in my mind. Chocolate melted between graham crackers and roasted marshmallows.

Mom pointing upward, toward the tops of her favorite flowers.

Once I step onto the driveway, the floodlight censor trips, and I'm bathed in light.

There's a spot on the cuff of this jacket. Oh, no. The first time I wear this sample, and I've stained it. What is it? Salsa from the nachos we ate earlier? I scratch a nail against it, but it's embedded in the threads.

The rumble of an engine fills my ears, and I'm momentarily blinded by the headlights of a truck pulling into the driveway.

Ryan. Thank God.

I take a few steps toward the truck.

Ryan gets out of the car. "Hey, Sami."

I'm so happy to see him—he called me his *best friend*—that my pace quickens. Next I know, my lips are on Ryan's, my hand is on his cheek, and he's pulling me closer.

Open-eyed, we kiss, as if we've done it a million times under a million skies like this one.

We stare at each other for a long few seconds once the kiss ends.

"Sorry," I whisper.

"It's, uh . . ." Ryan bites his lower lip. "Yeah, it's okay."

I walk to the passenger side of Ryan's truck and get in. "Mind giving me a ride home?"

"No problem."

I shoot a quick text to Cassidy and Brooke: *Left for home with Ryan.*

Once we're on the road, I turn to him. "I'm sorry. I don't really know how that happened. I just—"

"It's okay."

"Let's just forget it, okay?"

"Sure."

For a few moments we drive in silence.

My phone chimes with a text from Brooke, telling me to come back. Two more come in quick succession.

I switch my phone to vibrate.

Ryan chuckles. "Forget it, Sam? *Forget* it?"

And I know what he's thinking: forgetting about that kiss might be impossible.

Impulsive.

Kinetic.

Thrilling.

That kiss was everything I'm not used to being.

And everything I can't afford to be. If I let him in, will it backfire? Will he judge us? How can he not? His uncle had no problem judging my dad. From what Dad's said, in the early days after Mom left, the worst of the rumors came from Schmidt. He made a painful situation that much worse.

So why I have an urge to unload the day's events on Ryan Stone is beyond me.

I stare out the window and see nothing but a black abyss of night.

But I imagine my mother's weaving her way through the darkness, touching down in all the cities on the map to reach me.

I feel incredibly close to her right now. I feel her out there, in the great beyond, with such intensity that it feels as if I could reach out and touch her.

It's almost as if . . .

I watch the little ghost on Ryan's rearview mirror spin and dance with every bump in the pavement, with every breath of this second-chance-summer wind.

. . . as if she's trying to tell me something.

"Sami?" Ryan touches me lightly on the elbow. "You okay?"

She's growing more and more vivid in my memory. More real than she's ever been. Dimensions of her are carving out of my mind, details beyond her favorite lucky numbers. It's as if she's strategically placing clues in my path.

"I think she'd dead," I admit. There. I've said it. I don't know how I feel.

"Aww, Sami." He grasps my left hand, gently squeezes it, lets it go.

"I think she's dead, and I think I saw it happen, or at least I may have seen her body." I turn toward him. "Do you know what happened that day?"

He raises his eyebrows. An invitation.

"When Dad and Heather came home that evening, no one was there. I was supposed to have a sitter, but I don't remember having one, and in any case she wasn't there either. They assumed I was with Mom, that she'd left with me. And hours later, your uncle brought me home, saying he found me in his basement. And I was afraid of him."

A street lamp illuminates him as we pass beneath its beam. He licks his lips and gives me a nearly imperceptible nod.

"And for the life of me, I don't know why I would've been in his basement. I just can't remember anything about why I went over there, what I could've been doing there for so long."

"Sami, my uncle didn't find you in the basement that day. *I* found you. *In the passageway*. We were playing in the tunnel. We weren't supposed to be in there, and he yelled at us. *That's* why you were afraid of him that day."

I process this. "You found me."

"Yes."

"Do the police know that?"

"I'm sure my uncle told them, but they never interviewed me back then. I was already back home by the time the report was filed, and—"

"You said we were playing. Did we have plans to play that day? A playdate?"

"I don't know. I don't think so. I heard you in the passageway. You were crying, I think. I went in to get you, and I tried to make you laugh."

A fuzzy memory filters in. "You had sidewalk chalk. You were drawing on the walls."

He grins. "Yeah. But my uncle didn't know where I'd gone. Eventually he came looking for me, and we got in trouble. He put a lock on the door after that."

And we stopped playing together, too, after that day.

"You asked why I stopped coming to visit." He pulls up to the curb in front of my house. "I stopped coming because, frankly, that day changed things." He puts the truck in park and shifts to face me. "My uncle wasn't always the grumpy old man of the neighborhood. Your mom's leaving was a turning point for him."

Her *leaving*. Not her *death*.

"Maybe a shift in the way he viewed humanity," he continues. "I mean, think about it: either your mother walked away and cut off contact with everyone who cared about her—including you, and you meant the world to her—or something bad happened to her. Any way you look at this, there's no happy conclusion."

"I used to think my mom was hiding in your uncle's loft. And then you found her things. Do you think that's too much of a coincidence?" I take a deep breath. "Now, understand that I live with the pressure of suspicion on my dad. I know how that feels, so when I ask this question, it isn't because I think it's probable. It's because I need to rule out anything that's impossible."

"You're asking if I think my uncle had something to do with your mom's disappearance." He gives my hand another squeeze. "No. But maybe I'm too close to be an effective judge of that."

Have I been too close to my father to be an effective judge of *his* innocence?

"And forgive what I'm going to say now because I don't know if he's right or wrong: my uncle's pretty convinced your dad knows something."

I sigh. "Everyone is." And now I'm starting to be part of *everyone.*

There's a light on in Gram's motor home. Dad's bustling about inside the house, and it's early. It's only a matter of time before one of them peeks out to see me in a parked truck with the guy I just kissed. And it's been so long since I've seen Ryan, and he knows things I don't remember. *He found me in the passageway.* I feel like if I let him drive away, he'll be gone . . . along with everything he knows.

In a split second, within a breath, I decide: I'm going to trust him.

With my free hand, I pull the envelope from the inside pocket of my jacket. "I found this at Heather's."

He drops my hand to take it from me and pulls out what's inside. He looks at the pictures by the light of the dashboard, then turns on the dome light to look more closely.

"I don't remember, but I must have drawn them when I was little. Heather had them stashed in an envelope in a box with Cassidy's school projects."

After studying them for a few more seconds, he hands the stack back.

"That's why I'm starting to think . . . that something happened to Mom, and I saw something. But how could I have forgotten seeing something like that?"

"You could've blocked it out. Kids—people—can do that with traumatic experiences. And if you saw something and don't remember it, it's not your fault."

"But all these years, I've been defending my dad and blaming my mom, and—"

"You were six."

I shut up.

"Six, Sami. You were just a little girl. You have to give yourself a break."

It's been suggested before. But it's tough to separate me—just a girl—from the rest of my life.

"Anyway, I have chocolate covered graham crackers. And some incredible late-season strawberries. You hungry?"

"Actually . . . " I can't help laughing a little. "Famished."

卌 卌 ||

Ryan walks half a step behind me through our backyards, from his Uncle Henry's place to mine. "You got quiet fast."

"If she hears us"—I indicate toward the dark motor home in my driveway—"she might wake up, and then she'll come out."

It's not even ten thirty yet and my curfew is eleven, but I'm nervous about the consequences of what I've just done. I told Dad I was bowling with Cass and Brooke. My approaching the back door with Schmidt's nephew—*anyone's* nephew, but particularly Schmidt's—probably won't go over well.

"Hey." Ryan's whispering now.

I look over my shoulder at him.

He leans against our carriage house, right next to the door with the three-paned window, so I stop walking too. "We learned some good things tonight," he says.

"Such as you don't know how to shuffle cards."

"Such as you make a mean smoothie."

"Anyone can do that with the right berries. But you . . . you play a mean piano."

"And you're going to read *Gatsby*."

"Definitely." Mom's book is the only object from the box Ryan found that I stashed in my backpack to take home tonight. The rest—along with the envelope of my crazy drawings—is still at Schmidt's house. I left another message for Eschermann, telling him we'd found a few things he might be interested in seeing. Hopefully, he'll meet me at Schmidt's tomorrow morning.

"I'll let you catch up to me," he says. "We'll read it together."

I cross my arms and shiver. It's a warm night for this time of year, but it's still chilly when the breeze blows.

"Shit, I left my jacket in the kitchen."

"Well, it was getting in the way during the marshmallow experiment."

I laugh. "Note: marshmallows roast better outside than inside over a gas stove."

"Maybe we need some longer chopsticks."

"Maybe."

"Want me to run back for your jacket?"

"No, it's all right. I'll get it tomorrow morning."

He holds my gaze for a couple of seconds. It feels good to be back in his life, good to have plans to see him tomorrow, if only because I'm going to meet Lieutenant Eschermann at Schmidt's place.

"You know if you need anything, all you have to do is call me. I can get here pretty fast."

If anyone else had said this to me, I might have bitten his head off. But Ryan somehow doesn't imply all the negativity in *why* I might need him; he only emphasizes that it's *okay* to need him.

I nod. "Duly noted. Thanks." I take a few steps toward my house. I should probably get inside before Dad or Gram hears me talking to someone out here.

"Hey."

"Yeah?" I dawdle near the walk.

"For what it's worth . . ." In the darkness, I hear more than see his smile, and I hope he can't see the blush I feel creeping into my cheeks. I still can't believe I *kissed* him. What was I thinking?

"I missed you, Samantha."

I don't know if I'll ever be able to explain this to him, but I know that when I remember tonight, it won't just be the kiss that I think about. It'll be what we did after we left Brooke's—playing rummy, eating s'mores. He gave me a vacation from the chaos. Even in the wake of everything coming to light—Trina Jordan, my drawings, the box of Mom's stuff—he allowed me to be Samantha Lang, normal sixteen-year-old girl, instead of Samantha Lang, daughter of woman-who-disappeared.

"Thank you," I say.

"Good night."

"Night." I'm pretty sure he's watching me walk into the back door. It feels good to have him in my corner.

The moment I enter the house, the stench of something medicinal meets my nostrils. Something alcoholic.

Instantly, the warm and fuzzy feelings I conjured during my visit with Ryan dissipate. A prickly sensation crawls up my spine.

My father hasn't had a drink in years. His marriage to Heather was contingent on his sobriety. But now that Heather's out of the house, could he start drinking again? Especially with everything coming to light about Trina—is it enough to push him off the wagon?

I remember how different Dad used to be when he was intoxicated. Vacant, paralyzed, like he had one foot in the grave.

Just thinking about it causes my chest to tighten.

I enter the kitchen to see my grandmother seated at the island. Instantly, the mood of the house shifts another decibel toward doom.

My dad is standing at the sink. His lips are thinned into a line, a sure sign he's angry about something.

I try to study him for any signs he's impaired, but I can't tell from this distance. I suppose there's a possibility I smell something else. A cleanser, maybe. Or a topical astringent. But it doesn't smell like rubbing alcohol.

"Samantha." Gram opens her arms and smiles without showing her teeth. "I thought you might've stopped in after school. Aren't you ever home?" I lean in for a halfhearted hug but quickly shrink away. It's *her*. She's what I'm smelling. She smells like alcohol. I should've known she'd be half in the bag an hour after she arrived.

Still, I recall more than one occasion when both Gram and Dad were slurring before it even got dark outside. I wonder if they'd had a drink together. My eyes are on Dad, who hasn't said a word yet.

I linger on the fringes of the room, ever-conscious that the father I thought I knew may have been nothing more than smoke and mirrors. But all the same, he's the only father I have. I loved him when he was drunk; I love him still. But can I love a man who may have killed my mother?

"Do I smell alcohol?" I ask.

"I was cleaning out some clutter," he says. Which doesn't really answer my question.

"Hungry?" Gram asks. "I could whip up a quick burger." There's a slight slur to her words. "I learned a trick during my visit in Nashville. Just add a little jalapeño to the ground round. Gives it quite a kick."

I practically gag with the thought of animal fat oozing around the carcass on the plate. "I don't eat meat."

"What do you mean, you don't eat meat?"

"Mercy . . ." My father attempts to intercept the conversation. He's always called her by a version of her first name, and I guess I do too, considering her given name is Gramercy.

I remind my grandmother: "I don't eat anything that used to have a face."

"Worms don't have faces. So you would eat worms but not beef? Those cows are bred to be burgers. You need meat."

"No, I don't."

Gram sighs. "Like her mother."

The tension in the air is thick. Although I won't meet her eyes, I feel her stare hovering on me, her disappointment hemming me into a corner.

Again, I detect the stench of an alcoholic beverage. And it's not just coming from Gram. It's wafting over from somewhere else in the kitchen, though I don't see a drink anywhere.

I look around, and I catch sight of a blue bottle cap on the countertop near the sink, some logo emblazoned on it, like a neon arrow: *drink me, drink me*. I dart over and pick up the cap. "Where did this come from?"

Dad replies, "Vodka. I found a fifth under the sink and spilled it."

My grandmother swears under her breath. "Wasteful."

"Why did you have vodka under the sink?"

"*I* didn't."

Is he accusing *me* of stashing vodka? But before I can deny it, he holds his hand out, palm up. "Phone."

The hum of the ceiling lights, turned to the dimmest setting, fills the space.

"What?"

"Phone, Samantha."

I pull it out of my pocket. Place it on the island between us. He scoops it up, proceeds to tap and swipe at the screen.

"So . . . what? You're just going to look through my phone?"

I haven't seen him this tense, this angry, in a long time. Maybe part of me forgot that he could get like this. It was easier to block it out than to wonder . . .

My father's secret first wife may have died in a ditch.

My mother is missing without a trace.

"You turned off the ringer."

Because I kept getting texts that I didn't know how to answer. "Sorry. I forgot about that, but—"

"I couldn't find you tonight, and you weren't doing what you said you'd be doing."

"That vodka wasn't mine, if that's what you're getting at."

"Don't use that tone with your father!" Gram says.

I barely give her a glance. "My friends and I don't drink. You can still trust me, Dad. Same as always."

"Trust has to be earned," Gram pipes in. "Are you listening to me?"

I ignore her. The way I see it, this is none of her business.

Dad's still worrying over my phone. "So who were you with? I know you weren't with Cass."

Gram shakes her head and says, "Your father is going through enough right now, young lady."

He turns on her. "Mercy, I need a minute with my daughter."

Gram doesn't push back. She reserves all her aggression for me. "I guess I could use a smoke before bed." She already has one out of her pack and in her mouth. "We'll talk more about this later, young lady."

Young lady. The very term crawls under my skin, like so much about my grandmother.

"G'night." Gram stops to hug my father, albeit briefly, on her way out the door.

"Good night, Mercy."

"Vegetarian," my grandmother mutters over her shoulder. "Just like her mother." She disappears out the door.

"She's drunk," I say.

"Yes, she is, but that doesn't mean you should disrespect her."

"Maybe she doesn't respect me."

"We're not discussing your grandmother right now. We're discussing you." Dad pockets my phone. "Where were you tonight?"

I can't speak. I'm too stunned by his actions. *He's keeping my phone.*

"Samantha?" He narrows his gaze at me. "You said you were going bowling with Cass and Brooke."

"I started with them, but . . ." Do I tell him the truth that I was uncomfortable because Cass and Brooke were playing tonsil hockey with their respective other halves, and I was there all alone stewing about recent developments? "I couldn't, Dad. I just couldn't *be* there."

"You could've called me."

Tears burn down my cheeks.

"How'd you get home?"

"Neilla—Officer Cooper—she dropped me off at Schmidt's place." It isn't a lie.

"I know." His lips are a thin line again. "I spoke with Ken Eschermann. But that was at four o'clock."

"You called Eschermann?"

"He called here. Said he couldn't reach you on your cell. And now we know why. You'd turned your ringer off."

"I'm sorry about that. I was going to turn it back on. I just forgot."

"You forgot."

"Yeah."

"I allowed you to go out tonight, despite everything going on," he says slowly, "because I figured you could use the time with your friends. But when I couldn't get ahold of you, I texted Cassidy, who told me you left for home at seven thirty."

I open my mouth to reply, but nothing comes out.

"Seven"—his fist comes down hard on the countertop—"thirty!"

I take a few slow steps toward the staircase.

"I have a call you made *to the head detective*, Sam! A text from Cass that says you *left over three hours ago*! And you're *not answering* when I call or text! What do you think was going through my mind? How do you think it looks when I have to tell Ken Eschermann that I *don't know where you are*?"

"I'm sorry."

"Where were you?"

"I was . . ." Can't tell him I was at Schmidt's place. "With a friend. In the neighborhood."

"You'd better not be saying what I think you're saying. You came in through the back door. I didn't hear a car pull up."

He knows. And after years of being in control, years of practicing restraint, he finally cracks. His eyes are full of pure rage.

"That boy's uncle went on television, Sami. He broadcasted terrible, terrible things about our family! And you! You're over there doing God-knows-what with his nephew!"

"I was playing rummy and eating s'mores." I keep backing toward the staircase.

"I'm not an idiot, Sam. Don't treat me like an idiot."

All I need is for Dad to see a text come through from Ryan. "Can I have my phone?"

I count the seconds it takes for him to draw in an audible breath: six and a half. Almost seven. He's just as long with the exhale. "You can have it back tomorrow."

"So, you're going to read through my text messages?"

"Am I going to find something I don't want to see?"

"That's *my* business. *My* personal business, Dad. I don't go through your phone."

"Are you hiding something from me?"

"Are *you* hiding something from *me*?"

"God *damn* it, Sam!" His fist comes down on the island countertop again.

I flinch.

And then I run for the stairs.

Once my hand lands on the railing, I'm sprinting up the steps, counting in my head. After the ninth stair, I lean left to follow the bend and nearly trip up the remaining seven. I catch myself, preventing a face-plant, with palms against the hardwood floors. A twinge of discomfort registers. One of the floor planks has splintered, the one that continuously creaks when we walk over it, and a sliver of wood lodges in my left index finger.

I catapult into my room and lock the door behind me and sit on my window seat. I stare out into the night, inhaling the cool air. The exterior lights on Schmidt's back patio are golden orbs against dark sky. The light waxes when the tears in my eyes grow fat. If I were still the six-year-old girl my mother left behind, I might imagine she's traveling to me by magic bubble.

All she has to do is make a phone call—*hey, this is Delilah Lang, I've just arrived in Madagascar or Kazakhstan or Antarctica or insert-remote-location-here, please leave my family alone*—and we'd get some peace.

And I used to believe that might happen someday.

But now I'm not so sure.

I pull *Gatsby* from my bag and open it to page 117. I press the book to my chest, as if I can absorb my mother's essence through her handwritten annotations.

The image comes to me: I'm running down the street, golden and burgundy leaves arching overhead, and Mom's on the other side. Just have to reach her, just have to get to her, and everything will be fine.

Everything will be fine.

Except that suddenly, the image shifts to my running through a dark, enclosed space. It's getting narrower, and the ceiling closes in on me, and it's getting harder to breathe, and I can't get out, and . . .

I close my eyes and try to conjure the scent of my mother— had she worn perfume?—but it's been so long. I can't remember any scents beyond the wafting of burning leaves and cookie batter.

Suddenly, I'm very tired. I breathe deeply. In . . . and out. In . . . and out.

I drift in the numb melancholy hanging in this room, in this house.

The dark is as dark as it's ever been.

Everything is still.

Dad's talking to his phone, recording his plan for tomorrow.

He's speaking softly, but I concentrate on what he's saying in order to gauge where he is in the house.

Walking up the stairs, I surmise.

Nearing the landing.

Closing the distance between us.

He passes my door.

Passes the door to Cassidy's old room.

His words are indiscernible, just a hiss of whispering. And then I hear the name: "Heather."

I freeze. Listen more closely.

"Nothing happens."

My blood runs cold.

"Nothing," he says again.

Heather.

Did I hear him right?

Trina Jordan-Lang—gone.

Delilah Maxwell-Lang—gone.

Heather Solomon-Lang . . .

If anything happens to her . . .

|||| |||| |||

I see her in my mind: a woman pushing against walls that hold her captive, fighting for her freedom.

It's *me*. I'm the one pushing, gasping for breath.

I'm not breathing.

Not breathing!

I try to fill my lungs with air, but I can't. It's as if I'm suffocating, as if I've used up all the air on earth and there's nothing left to sustain me. I push against the walls, panicked breaths escaping me in quick darts. The frame of the room shatters, the wood cracking and breaking, leaving splinters inches from my face, from my heart, ready to stab, ready to pierce and puncture.

A motor revs. The place is about to be bulldozed over, and they don't know I'm inside.

"No!" I sit upright and knock my head against the window. Rubbing the spot of impact, I concentrate on the feeling of air entering my lungs and attempt to gauge my surroundings as I awaken.

Ah, yes, this is where I slept last night. On the window seat. And clutched in my hands? F. Scott Fitzgerald's masterpiece.

My eyes are puffy from crying, and now they're crusted with sleep, too.

Vrmmm, vrmmm.

I turn toward the sound.

Ryan is outside, perched in a dying hickory. There's a thick white rope tied around one of its branches, and the other end of the rope dangles all the way to the ground. He's lodged between branches about two-thirds of the way up, almost at the same level as my window. A chainsaw hangs at his hip until he engages it and presses it to the branch with the rope tied around it.

The lawn will look bare without that tree, but I'm sure I'll eventually stop noticing the gap where it used to be. Just like I rarely think about the absence of the sunflowers that Schmidt used to grow near his barn.

Vrmmm, vrmmm.

The sound of the chainsaw throbs in my left index finger.

That's right. The splinter.

I pick at it with my teeth. Maybe I can pull it out.

Outside, the branch separates from the tree and it swings, suspended with the tethers tied in a pulley-system to another branch and to a bolt attached to the hayloft door.

I watch, chewing at the splinter in my finger, as Ryan climbs down the tree, lowers the branch to the ground, tethers another branch, and repeats the process.

He moves so expertly that I wonder if, in addition to being homeschooled, he's some sort of lumberjack in Kentucky.

A knock on my door startles me. I practically jump out of my skin.

"Sami?" My father speaks through the door. "Sami, I'm sorry about last night." He sounds exhausted this morning, but calm. Collected.

"Sam? Can I come in?"

When I feel for the shard of wood in my finger, I can tell it's bulging now, fighting against the forces that keep it confined in my skin.

"Are you in there?"

"Yes."

"I shouldn't have lost my temper. But you understand the amount of stress I'm under, don't you?"

I find a pair of tweezers in a drawer in my desk. I press the embedded edge of the splinter with my thumb until I feel it poking out the other side.

"And through it all," he continues, "I have to keep you safe. I have to think in terms of your best interest."

Finally, I squeeze out enough of the splinter that I can grab it with my fingernails. As tender as it is, as much as it hurts to yank on it, I know it'll feel better once it's out of my skin.

"Come on, Sami. Open the door. Please."

I pull the splinter free, suck at my fingertip. The faint metallic taste of blood meets my tongue.

"Okay. We'll talk after my workout?"

I don't reply.

Dad's footsteps are steady as he descends the stairs.

I shove my hair back from my face and bind it with a hair tie into a messy ponytail. Shed my capri pants with the ridiculous pom-pom fringe—so not comfortable to sleep in—and slide on some leggings.

While I'm sure I look like hell warmed over, I know I don't have much time. For all I know, Gram could already be downstairs, standing guard at the door, ready to shove pork sausage in my face.

With a little hesitation, I enter the hallway. Dad's workout jams rise up two stories from the basement.

I brush my teeth and splash some cold water over my face. It's all I have time for. I even leave the crust of mascara under my left eye.

I sneak down the stairs and through the kitchen to the mudroom, where I grab my running shoes.

I don't put them on here because I'm paranoid about time.

With one eye on Gram's motor home, I walk in bare feet through the breezeway—eleven steps, then seven—and into the carriage house. Once in the dark confines, I let out a breath. If she saw me, I'm pretty sure she would've poked her pointy nose out her door.

Unseen, I escape out the carriage house door, following a path I walked yesterday. To Schmidt's place.

I near the now-empty flower beds where the sunflowers used to grow. I pause there, out of the way, and allow the cool, dry soil to squish between my toes.

Ryan descends the tree like one of those monkeys in a rainforest, hand over hand, foot over foot, ready to lower another branch to the ground. He catches my glance and gives me a nod.

"Morning, Sami." He jumps to the ground, covered with sawdust. "What happened last night? I texted, but—"

"My dad took my phone."

"Oh." His hands rest at his sides.

"So I didn't get your message."

"You'll see it later, then."

"You're taking a tree down." Apparently, I'm the queen of obvious commentary this morning.

"It's dying." He points up at the branches. "Other trees are losing their leaves, but this one hardly had any to lose. It's struggling, and rotting in places. Probably won't survive the winter. Best to take it down. It could do some real damage if it fell on its own. Could take down another tree, or a power line. Hell, it could smash through a window or land on a roof."

"How'd you learn how to do all this?"

"It's trigonometry." He shrugs.

I look up at the ropes, tied to three distinct objects. Triangles. "I guess it is."

"You want some coffee or something? Tea? Cocoa?"

"I was going to go for a run, but sure." I'm already following him down the brick walk, cold beneath my feet, despite the bright sunshine trying like hell to warm it.

Last night we came in through the back door, directly into the kitchen. Today, he leads me to the front. I spot a rolled-up newspaper lying on the front stoop, pick it up, and glimpse the headline: *Evidence Continues to Point to Local Professor.* It dizzies me for a second, although if I'd thought about it, I probably would've anticipated this.

Of course there would be a story in print.

Ryan opens the door, and we enter.

The front entrance hall is impressive: two stories tall, with a high-hanging chandelier.

Ryan takes a seat on the edge of a long wooden bench and starts to unlace and remove his work boots. Following his lead, I place my shoes under the bench too.

The hardwood floor creaks beneath my bare feet when I follow him into the dim maze of rooms, past a pale blue space with the grandiose piano—the type with the lid propped open—and the window seat. I peek at another room I've yet to see—dark paneled walls, bookshelves from floor to ceiling spanning the walls astride a stone fireplace. Every inch of the shelves is packed with books, but there isn't a television anywhere.

We pass through an arched hallway to an enormous dining room. A photograph snaps in my mind, something like déjà vu. When he presses against a swinging door, another image flashes—me following my mother through a door like this one.

Eventually, we wind up in the kitchen, where we were last night. It seems like a long time ago. "So what'll it be?" he asks.

"Just water's fine right now, thanks."

Even though I don't want him to see the headline, I tell him, "I brought your paper in."

"Hmm?" He pulls a mug and a glass from a shelf. "Oh, thanks. Would you mind just tossing it in the burn bin?"

There's a brown paper grocery bag near the basement door, filled with papers.

"I'll use it as kindling."

Jeez, the guys on this property will burn anything.

"I mean, who reads actual papers anymore?"

I shove the paper in with the others. "Your uncle?"

"Not even him. He just hasn't cancelled it yet. Call it a nostalgic habit he doesn't want to admit he quit."

I sit on what has become my favorite barstool in the kitchen, over the back of which my cropped yellow jacket is still draped. "I started *Gatsby* last night."

"Yeah?" He slides a glass of water on the table in front of me and turns to the single-cup coffee maker. "What do you think so far?"

"I think I understand why my mother must have read it so many times."

He nods. Then he turns toward me, leaning against the farmhouse sink, and frowns a little when he looks at me. "Sami . . . are you all right?"

I'm so worn out that tears creep into my eyes again. "Honestly?"

"No. Lie to me."

I almost smile. But this is nothing to laugh about. I was actually *afraid* of my father last night. I swear he was talking himself out of doing something to Heather! *Heather: nothing happens.*

And then today, he seemed like himself again.

Had I imagined it? Or . . .

"Lieutenant Eschermann called me back last night, and when I didn't answer my phone, he called the landline, looking for me."

"Oh."

"So my dad's pissed, and not just because he had to tell a cop he didn't know where I was last night, but because I was with *you*. Did you know your uncle was interviewed on TV? Apparently he said some not-so-nice things about my dad, and *that's* why my dad doesn't want me here. So he took my phone, and now I don't know when Eschermann's coming, or even *if* he's coming, and I don't even know if my dad's going to let me out of the house to talk to him because I think I'm grounded, and I'm not even supposed to be here but I sneaked out." I take a breath. "So I might be stuck in the house for God knows how long, with my father, and my grandmother who basically hates me. And I can't exactly talk to the cops about this stuff in front of my dad. I mean, the stuff you found in the loft? Sure. But these drawings?"

"So let's call the cop now," Ryan suggests.

"I already left him a message yesterday."

"And he returned the call. Get him over here now. He'll come. He'd be crazy not to. Finding your mom is probably the biggest case of his career, right? He'll come."

Eschermann is sitting on the bench in Schmidt's foyer. He's wearing jeans and a worn Chicago Blackhawks pullover. I'm glad he came alone. Sometimes when he brings an entourage, it's uncomfortable. I don't think I could've spoken so freely with an audience.

And Ryan, even though he knows everything except the bit about the passport and the theory tying my mother and Trina Jordan to the Jane Doe in Georgia, graciously went back to lopping branches off the half-dead hickory to give us some privacy.

"I'll send these over to one of our child psychologists. They should be able to tell us what they mean, or if they mean anything at all." Eschermann bags the envelope stuffed with my drawings—it's all evidence now—and tends to the box. "Can you tell me where you found this?"

"Ryan found it up in the barn," I say. "By the old wine cellar, he said."

"Huh."

"Schmidt thought you'd taken everything of my mother's before."

"We did."

"Don't you think it's weird? That's where I thought my mother went, and all these years later . . ."

"We did check the barn, Sam," Eschermann says. "Your mother had been keeping some things in there, Schmidt said. So we looked. And we checked the whole house. We cleared Henry Schmidt almost immediately."

"Then how did you miss the box?"

He looks at me the way I've seen him look at my father

a hundred times: a deadpan, no-emotion stare. "I don't know. Maybe it was put there sometime *after* the search. Maybe it was overlooked. But the important thing is that we've got it now."

"Do you agree it's proof that what my dad said is true? That she'd planned to go home to Georgia?"

He nods. "And I also agree that if she'd actually gone to Georgia, she would've taken these things. Obviously if she'd gotten a job at an institution of higher learning, we would've been able to trace her. Maybe she decided to work as a cashier. I don't know. But this paperwork tells me she intended to strive for more."

I agree.

"You see what I mean, Sami. There's too much coincidence surrounding your mother's case. Either she left in a real hurry, or she left against her will. The kind of mom she was . . ." He shakes his head. "She never would've stayed gone this long otherwise."

"But Schmidt . . ." It feels rather like sacrilege to outright accuse him in this house. Maybe that's why I'm nervously pacing through the magnificent foyer. "He and my mom were friends, right? What if they were *more* than friends? What if he loved her, and didn't want her to go, and there was some sort of accident?"

"It's a valid theory."

"Okay, so—"

"But there are others perhaps even more viable. We cleared Schmidt ten years ago. We haven't yet cleared your father, and we haven't yet cleared your mother in the Trina Jordan case. And I still have a sneaking suspicion that Heather may recant her alibi. If she does, Sami, you should be prepared for things to get intense for a while."

"You know, I've been thinking about that too." I stop pacing and match his deadpan expression, as best I can. "If Heather and Dad were together, Cassidy had to have been with them. There was nowhere else for her to go. So Cassidy can confirm they were together, or maybe she won't, but either way you'll know, even if Heather doesn't recant."

"Cassidy was with her biological father that day."

It hits me like a football in the chest. "That's impossible."

"No, it isn't. I'll show you the footage of the interview, if you'd like. She specifically states, on camera, that she was with her father."

"Yes, it *is* impossible, and I'll tell you why. Cass hasn't seen her biological father since forever ago. Did you interview her biological father?"

"He was in Kuwait at the time, but the record checked out. He was deployed after your mother left. In the area at the time of her disappearance. He could've stopped for one last visit with his daughter."

"Could have. But wouldn't have. The guy could be next door and wouldn't think of stopping in to see Cass. So you're trusting what a six-year-old said. And if she said she was with her dad, she said it because someone *told* her to say it. Or maybe she meant that she was with *my* dad. I don't remember a time she didn't call him Dad, or refer to him as her father."

"Worth another round of questioning, then, Sam."

"Of course it is. You question me over and over again. Why don't you pester Cassidy with this stuff? She's just as in the thick of it. He's her father too. Dad and Heather were together. They weren't married right away, but they've known each other—they've *loved* each other—most of their lives."

"I'll talk to Heather and Cassidy this afternoon, then."

"Thank you."

"I should get you home, so your dad doesn't start worrying again like he did last night." He peels the latex gloves from his hands, now that he's done handling evidence. "And you should know better than to let him worry, Sam. A simple phone call next time, a text, anything, all right?"

"Yeah. I know." I turn toward the kitchen. "I'll just get my jacket."

I retrieve it from the kitchen, stop for a second to put my water glass in the sink, and return to where Eschermann is waiting for me.

"Sam."

I sit down on the bench and pull my shoes out from under it. "Hmm?"

"Where did you get that coat?"

I look up. Eschermann is pulling another pair of latex gloves over his hands. "Heather's," I tell him. "It was in a box of samples. Why?"

"A box of samples? At the Nun?"

"No, in Heather's apartment."

"I'm going to need to take it."

"Why?"

"You know I can't tell you that, Sam."

Slowly, I straighten.

Allow Eschermann to take the coat.

"There's a stain on the left cuff," I say. "I thought it was the salsa from yesterday, but it wouldn't wash out when I tried."

"Looks like an old stain to me."

In hindsight, I should've known then that the jacket wasn't a sample. It looked worn even before I put it on. And as quirky as Heather can be, the jacket is more out-of-style than retro. But even if the jacket isn't a sample, it must be Heather's. At least I assume so. It was at her place.

But so were my creepy drawings.

And if Lieutenant Eschermann wants this jacket, that must mean that he somehow suspects . . .

Puzzle pieces form in my mind. I maneuver them, turn them, try to make them fit.

All these years, Eschermann has been assuming that Heather's been covering for Dad. But what if Dad's been covering for Heather?

‖‖‖ ‖‖‖ ‖‖‖‖

I'm locked in a staring contest with my father.

Neither of us has spoken for at least thirty seconds.

My phone sits on the table between us.

I know the fate of my phone rests on the outcome of this conversation. But I'm so irked, and confused, that I'm not sure I can be as respectful as I'm going to need to be to play this right.

"Let me tell you a little bit about the state of worry you put me in last night." He clears his throat and folds his hands on the table. "Imagine not knowing where your daughter is. Calling her, leaving her messages. Texting her, without reply. Imagine meeting up with your wife—"

"You saw Heather?" This is highly irregular since the separation. "Why?"

"And she hasn't heard from you, or Cass. No one knows where you are. Imagine how that made me feel."

I want to turn it around on him, tell him that's how I feel *all the time*. Like no one wants to tell me anything, like even when he tells me something lately, it's not true, so he may as well not tell me anything.

"She hadn't heard from Cassidy since school got out, you closed the Nun early, and you had a migraine."

I wonder how he knows that.

As if he's reading my mind, he says, "The nurse at school called Heather yesterday."

"I caught it in time. Before it got bad."

"Spent most of the day in your guidance counselor's office?"

I shrug.

"So why, if you missed classes, were you out last night, let alone out where you weren't supposed to be?"

"Why, if you and Heather are getting a divorce, were you calling her to talk about me?"

"Tone."

I refrain from rolling my eyes because I know that'll only get me in hotter water.

"We touched base," he says, "to see if either of us had heard from either of you, and when we decided neither of us knew, we drove past the bowling alley. Venture a guess as to whether the Jeep was in the parking lot?"

I don't say a word.

"After that, we grabbed a sandwich at the Madelaine. We tried the finder app on your phone and Cass's. You have to get better about leaving that option on."

We turn it off so they don't know we're not bowling.

"Cassidy said she left a note for Heather," I offer. "I didn't think—"

"Heather isn't my priority. You are."

"I *was* playing rummy!" I can tell by the way he's looking at me that he doesn't believe me. "I think I deserve a little trust in the matter."

"How do you expect me to trust you when you don't tell me the truth?"

I yank out my ponytail. "You want to get to the truth?

Let's talk about the truth."

"Yes. Let's do that."

"Were you really with Heather the day Mom left?"

I know I hijacked the conversation, and I know he can't be happy about it.

His brow furrows. "Of course I was."

"You swear to God? You swear *on my life*?"

"Yes, Samantha."

"You're not lying."

"No, I'm not—"

"Because recently, you've been a liar."

"*You* lied to me last night."

"Okay, I lied. But I didn't lie about an ex-girlfriend who happens to actually be my ex-*wife*, and who happens to have been missing even longer than Mom. And I didn't try to minimize the issue with my daughter, only to find out the entire story was broadcast in the commons of her school."

"You didn't tell me that yesterday."

"It was a shitty day, all right? And that's why I couldn't stay with Brooke and Cassidy. I couldn't *deal* with their normal world last night, all right? Because it's just another reminder that no matter what I do, it's impossible for people to know me without judging us, and it's impossible for me to open up to anyone because I *know* they're going to judge us even if they take the risk to know us well. And even if I try to set the record straight, there's enough information out there that makes me look like a liar, so it's still impossible for people to trust me. I mean, what kind of life do you think I'm going to have when this is constantly hanging over me?"

"I'm sorry we're in this situation, Sami. But I didn't create it. I'm just trying to survive. Same as you."

"And what happened with you and Heather? If you *love* her, if you're having dinner at the Madelaine, why the divorce?"

For a moment, he doesn't say anything. "The stuff with your mom . . . okay, we'll talk about it. But what happened with Heather and me . . . it's none of your business."

"You know how bad it'll look if something happens to Heather, right? You know no one will believe you if—"

"What are you talking about? What's going to happen to her?"

I take a deep breath. "I heard you recording your day last night. I heard what you said about Heather."

"What did I say?"

"You said her name and 'nothing happens.' Why would you have to tell yourself that?"

"Sami . . . no. I never said that, Sami."

"You're lying again. I heard you say it."

"Sami."

I look up so he knows I'm listening, but I avoid looking him in the eye.

"I didn't say what you think I said. I wasn't even recording my day. I was talking to your grandmother. Now that she's here, she has questions about the divorce, but I'm not going to tell her either. Heather and I agreed: it's no one's business. So what you heard was my telling Mercy nothing happened with Heather."

Okay, so maybe I misunderstood what I heard.

Amid the awkward silence, I feel for the torn skin on my finger where the splinter went in. I clear my throat. "If you won't tell me what happened with Heather, will you at least tell me what happened between you and Mom? Everyone says you're the only father Cass has ever had. Well, I've started thinking Heather's really the only mother *I've* had."

"That's not true, Sam. Delilah will *always* be your mother. And she was . . . she was wonderful with you. She was wonderful with me."

"So what happened? Is Cassidy right? Was Mom cheating on you?"

"Henry Schmidt was not—"

"I don't just mean Schmidt. I mean, with anyone."

My father shakes his head. "No." He unclasps his hands, but only for a second. "It was my fault. *Me.* I'm the one who cheated. Not your mom. Me." He holds my stare. "With Heather."

I'm dumbstruck for a breath. He lied about that too, then, all these years. "I always thought you and Heather got back together after the divorce."

"I never wanted you to know. Especially after your mom left. I needed you to love Heather the way I knew Heather loved you."

I push away from the table, feeling as if a thousand jolts of electricity just shot through me, and I get to my feet.

If my dad and Heather had a relationship before he divorced Mom, maybe they had reason to want her gone.

"Sam, I never meant to hurt your mom. My affair with Heather is one reason my drinking got out of control, one reason—"

"Does Eschermann know?"

"He knows Heather and I have been involved for some time. He knows we've known each other since we were kids."

"That's not what I asked. Does he know Heather's the reason you and Mom divorced?"

There's a long silence before he says, "When you don't have anything to hide, you don't hide anything."

121

So Eschermann does know.

"I answer every question Ken has," Dad says. "Because I want to get to the bottom of this, same as anyone else. Maybe even more. Find out what happened. Get closure. Bring her back for you, if that's possible. That's all I've ever wanted."

"I always assumed you were glad she's gone," I say.

"Why?"

I shrug. "You were divorced."

"She didn't trust me anymore after she found out about Heather. And we couldn't live together anymore, it's true. But she's still your mother."

I'm gravitating toward him. "But you never missed her."

"I did. And I missed her for you."

"You did?" I reach for his hand. Tears well in my eyes.

"You don't remember those early days?" he asks. "Waiting at the window for her to come?"

"No." But as I say it, glimpses of staring out into the rain, or maybe through tears, flash in my memory bank. Snuggling against my father's chest. Waiting. "Well . . . maybe. Bits and pieces of it."

"There were days I thought you'd never forget, that you'd never get over losing her," he says. "You were so sure she was still nearby. Schmidt's barn. The passageway connecting our carriage house with Schmidt's house. It never occurred to you she'd leave the neighborhood."

We're silent a moment. "I caught you trying to get into the passageway once. You were so convinced . . ."

That, I remember: *you must never open this door.*

He's practically whispering now. "No father wants his daughter to grow up this way."

Sure, he's said these words before. But I think I believe

him for the first time in a long time.

"One good thing came from her leaving. I finally got my act together. It took a while, but I was finally committed to being a better dad, committed to you. I sure as hell didn't want you growing up like this. Cops at the door every time a lead develops, neighbors talking, reporters camping on the lawn—and still never hearing from her, never knowing." He brings a hand to his eyes. He's slumped over a little, and I think . . . maybe . . . maybe he might be trying not to cry.

His efforts to hide his tears from me only intensify my own urge to bawl.

"One parent gone," he says. "The other under suspicion. I don't know how you do it."

No longer strong enough to stand, or maybe just lacking the desire, I lean against him. I believe him. I believe what I've always believed, despite the human remains in Georgia, despite Trina Jordan, despite what I think I heard last night. "We make do," I remind him.

For a moment, I breathe him in. I flip through photographs in my mind until I settle on one that brings a warm memory: Dad trying to teach me how to throw a baseball.

You've heard people say "throw like a girl." Girls don't throw any differently than boys, okay? You just wind back, power through, and release the ball when you can't reach any farther.

I realize I've reached for him my whole life. And he reaches back every time.

The chime of the doorbell echoes through our house.

I look out the window.

Eschermann is standing on the porch.

꤀꤀꤀꤀꤀ ꤀꤀꤀꤀꤀ ꤀꤀꤀꤀꤀

The sunlight is uncomfortably bright on the front porch.

Lieutenant Eschermann produces a burrito-rolled ELPD baseball cap from his back pocket and presses it atop his head. "Take a walk?"

The scent of peppermint wafts from him; I see he's just popped a stick of gum into his mouth, and he's offering one to me.

I take it.

Side by side, we descend the porch steps in silence.

Eschermann says nothing all the way down Kenilworth, nothing when we hook a left onto Charles. The lake is straight ahead now. If I listen closely, I can hear the waves rushing up on the shore. In my mind, I see lakes on the map. Mom would have liked to live near water. How many lakes can there be in this world? Too many to count. There's no way to check the perimeter of every one of them for a woman who loves to bake cookies and has questionable taste in music.

A scenario plays out in my mind: she's on a sandy beach, building castles, wearing that navy blue bikini . . . the one with the white polka dots. I can practically feel the grit of the sand accumulating under my fingernails, practically hear the laughter of children in the periphery, calling to her: *Mom!*

But this isn't a warm, comforting memory. This is my mind conjuring someone else's reality, imagining other children who can call to her and get an answer.

Could my mom have a whole other life by now? Other kids?

The scent of burning leaves meets my nostrils. I imagine the soft crackle of flame meeting twig.

My mother loved this time of year, loved the changing of the scenery. I wonder why she never minded the death of it all. Summer is dying. The leaves . . . they're dying. They're most beautiful right before they fall.

I close my eyes, and a picture of her materializes in my mind too. Beautiful. Right . . . before . . . she . . . fell. Fell into nowhere, fell into nothingness.

"Samantha, where did you find the jacket?"

"Heather's. I told you."

"In a box, you said? Where was the box located? Hidden? Out in the open? Was there anything else in it?"

I look at him out of the corner of my eye, but the sun is too bright, and because of the way he's positioned, he's backlit. I can't read his expression.

"Sami, this is important."

There's a sense of urgency in his voice, when I normally hear only determination.

I'm acutely aware of the sounds of his footsteps, and mine, on the pavement: his *shalep* to my step.

"The box was in the closet in the laundry room. On the top shelf. But I wouldn't say she was trying to hide it. It was right there for anyone to see."

"Any particular reason you chose to wear it?"

"I don't know. I was in a hurry." We're turning left onto Reston, onto the block populated with only a few houses—among them, Schmidt's—turning away from the lake. I look for one last glimpse of it on the horizon. "It was my mom's favorite color."

"It looked like something your mom might wear?"

"I don't know about *that*."

"Anything else in the box?"

"I . . . I don't know. Maybe."

"Do you remember your mother ever wearing the jacket?"

I stare at him. "You think it's Mom's?"

"I didn't say that."

Eschermann pulls his mobile phone from his pocket. "Bear with me, Sami. I have to . . ." He's dialing. "Yeah, it's Eschermann. I'm going to need a warrant to search the Funky Nun. Mmm-hmm. And the residence above it."

Warrant?

My insides are twisting again, wringing like a wet rag, trying to squeeze everything out of me. I feel like Eschermann is pinning me into a corner.

Am I incriminating my dad? Heather? Should I be talking this freely about things I know nothing about?

Eschermann hangs up and looks at me again. "Sam, I have to ask you to—"

"No, no." I'm backing away from him. "I'm not saying anything else without my father here. Or . . . or a lawyer. Or *someone*. Anyone who cares about—"

"I care about you, Sami."

"No you don't! You care about solving this case. And for what purpose? So you can retire? Run for mayor?"

"Calm down, Sam, all right?"

I don't know how to calm down under these circumstances. It feels as if a black hole has opened beneath my feet and it's swallowing me. It feels as if there's no one on earth I can trust.

"I want to go home." But even as I say it, I wonder if home is far enough away. I wonder . . . I wonder if this is how my mother felt right before she left. Disoriented and alone, as if she didn't have a friend in the world. She knew about Heather. Maybe she knew Schmidt liked her too much. Maybe she even knew about Trina. I wouldn't blame her for disappearing, if this is how she felt.

"I'll take you home," Eschermann says, "but first, I need you to calm down. Sami, listen."

I try to calm down. I listen.

"I need you to think hard about what else you saw in that box."

My fingers tremble as they wipe away tears. "I really don't think there was *anything* else in it."

"Just a jacket in a box. Nothing else."

"And if the jacket *was* my mother's, it's another piece of her. It should be mine. I should be able to wear it. It should be with me instead of at the station in a sealed bag. If it's my mother's—"

"No. Sami." He sighs heavily. "The jacket you were wearing . . . it matches the description of a jacket Trina Jordan's wearing in one of the last known photos taken of her. I think that jacket belonged to Trina Jordan."

He may as well have thrown a brick at my chest. "What?"

"I took it to the station and compared it to the description. But maybe it was a mass-produced jacket. Maybe they sold it at Target, I don't know. The label's been cut out, so I won't know more until I send it to the lab."

I don't know how to respond to that. Why would Heather have Trina Jordan's jacket? It doesn't make sense . . . unless . . .

Unless Heather was involved in Trina Jordan's disappearance. Or my dad was involved, and Heather somehow ended up with the remnants.

Not Heather.

Heather couldn't have done anything . . .

She's the only mother I have, and she wants what's best for me. Always.

Except that lately, she's been different. Lately, it feels like she and Cassidy don't believe in Dad anymore. It seems so unexpected, so unnatural after all the years that Heather stood by him. Is it a cover? Are they throwing shade at Dad to hide something Heather did, or to hide something she knows?

I look up into the canopy of gold and auburn leaves above us; the colors blur through the tears accumulating in my eyes.

"My dad didn't do anything wrong," I burst out, because I've said it so many times for so many years that it's become its own kind of comfort mechanism. "I know all of this looks bad. I know that. But he wouldn't . . . he isn't capable. And I don't know how all this connects to Heather, but . . . you know Heather. You know she wouldn't do something—anything— like . . ." Like what? Murder? Transporting a body? "And if she did, why would she have kept the jacket? Why keep something like that for ten years? When it's only going to make things look bad for her later?"

"That's what I'm going to find out."

"You think they're guilty of something."

"It isn't my job to decide. But there've been some more developments in the Trina Jordan case, and if this checks out—"

"What developments?"

He gives me that look again, the one that tells me I don't want to hear what he has to say. "For one thing, Trina Jordan's social security number resurfaced earlier today in a small town in Georgia."

Momentary relief. "So she's alive. You found her."

But that relief—if she isn't dead, Dad can't be accused of killing her, Mom can't be accused of killing her—is instantly replaced with panic: if Trina's alive, that means my mother has no reason to be hiding.

"More likely, her information was simply sold. Happens all the time. Identification gets separated from the body of a victim, someone picks up a wallet, sells the ID on the black market after enough time has gone by."

"So she's probably dead."

"Probably, but we don't have proof of it. That's the other development. Test results showed that her DNA didn't match Georgia's Jane Doe."

"You sent my DNA to Georgia," I say. "To test it against the body."

"I'm sorry to have to tell you this, now that Trina Jordan is ruled out . . . yes. We've decided to run labs to see if there's a DNA match to your mother."

My gut goes hollow. It's not like I didn't know this was a possibility, and nothing's changed. Not really. "What about the passport application?"

Eschermann holds my gaze for a second, long enough for me to realize that the way Trina Jordan's social security number surfaced could be the same way my mother's information was used to obtain a passport.

"Oh."

But I can't wrap my head around this. I've spent so many years dismissing the possibility. Until someone shows me definitive proof that my mother's gone—*dead*—no one can convince me it's true. Even if part of me thinks it might, just might, be possible.

"Point is," says Eschermann, "Trina Jordan is presumed dead now, even though she isn't the Jane Doe. And if that jacket checks out, it's another connection between your father, Heather, and the case."

I have nothing to say in response. So I run.

|||| |||| |||| |

I turn and bolt down Reston. Footfall after footfall brings me closer to Schmidt's door, closer to Ryan.

It's all an illusion. The closeness I felt with my mother last night . . . a lifetime with Heather, with Cass . . .

I quicken my pace, as if racing against the route on the map. There has to be a quicker way, a faster path out of here.

"Samantha!"

I trip up the front steps of Schmidt's house, and this time I can't catch myself before I fall and scrape my knee. But I don't care about that, about the stream of blood I feel trickling toward my ankle. I yank on the bell pull.

"Sami." Eschermann is on the brick walk leading to Schmidt's door now, about ten feet behind me.

"Stop it," I say through tears. "Please, just stop. Do you understand the position you're putting me in? You're putting me in the middle, putting me between my parents, between Dad and Heather, even, and I—"

"Sami, if the DNA is a match to your mother, we have to find out how she ended up in Georgia. You don't remember. But someone must."

"Maybe Henry Schmidt knows! He had some of Mom's

things! Here! And this is where I thought she'd gone!"

"Henry Schmidt has given us permission to search the premises again. He's cutting his vacation short to be here. He's cooperating."

Finally, the door opens, and everything is silent. No one says a word. Not Ryan, dusted with the remains of the hickory; not the cop behind me, trying to do the best and the worst things for my family at the same time; and not me, with tears streaming down my cheeks.

I think Ryan heard us. Heard *me*, accusing his uncle of having something to do with my mother's disappearance.

It feels as if time has stopped.

My throat feels like cotton, as if it's closing up on me, as if I may never speak again.

I take in a sharp breath, only to find my gum sticking in my throat.

My throat constricts another inch, I feel I might choke, and my knee burns where I scraped it.

I slip into the house, ducking under Ryan's arm and booking it down the arched-ceiling hallway, through the serving pantry, to the kitchen.

"Sami?"

I can't tell which of the two insists on following me, but I don't turn around to acknowledge either one. *Get rid of the gum.*

I find the garbage, spit it out.

Water. A neat stack of plain white dishes occupies the sink. I grab a glass from the drying rack and pull the lever on the faucet. For a second—just a hiccup, really—a sense of relief washes over me. Easy does it, I tell myself. Tackle one problem at a time. Job one: drink.

I fill the glass and drink from it.

Ryan comes up behind me and slaps something cold and wet into my hand. "Your knee."

It's a wet washcloth. "Thanks."

"Tough morning," Eschermann says when he enters the kitchen.

I don't know if he's confirming the fact to me or attempting to explain my strange behavior to Ryan, and at the moment, I don't care. I press the washcloth to my knee and get slammed with a sense of déjà vu . . . weird; that keeps happening in this house.

"I can imagine," Ryan says, but he won't look at me. "Can you excuse me a second? I was about to shower when I heard the bell. I'm covered in dead tree."

"Of course," the lieutenant says.

"You can just"—Ryan glances at the floor—"let yourselves out when you're finished."

"You okay, Sami?" Eschermann asks when Ryan's gone.

I'm inside a shrinking triangle, my father at one corner, one dead ex-wife at another, and my mother at the third. And I just called out the uncle of the guy I kissed last night, all but accusing him of knowing what happened to my mother.

I focus on wiping the blood off my knee, nodding one of the biggest lies I've ever told: *Yeah. I'm fine.*

Closing my eyes, I imagine I'm a little girl again, weaving around the hickories, my mother chasing me, laughing. Tickling my belly when she catches me.

And then, like the hickory Ryan's felling, she's gone. Just like that. But I'm feeling she's still here, somewhere, if I could only find her.

Like her using the passageway to escape.

Like her hiding in Schmidt's barn.

I'm gravitating toward the back door now.

It was so long ago, but I feel the same urgency now, the same insistence I felt as a kid: I have to know if she's in the passageway. I have to know, have to know, have to know!

"Samantha?"

I stop in my tracks when I hear Eschermann behind me.

Numb, I turn toward him.

"Sami, I know you're worried, but—"

"Understatement."

"—but ultimately, we're getting closer to the truth, closer to the end. At this point, it's just a jacket. Circumstantial at best, unless there's any incriminating evidence in the threads."

I think of the stain on the cuff. "Like blood?"

He nods.

"Okay." I flinch, blinking away the glaze in my eyes, and picture the pushpins marking towns in my mind. They're comfortable distances from the edge of nothingness, over which I'm about to plunge.

Water rushes through the old plumbing in this house—the sound of Ryan showering. And as much as I want to stay—at least to apologize to Ryan—"I should get home."

"I'll walk you," Eschermann says.

This time, we take the long way home, past the empty front porch swing—that's where Schmidt read *Huck Finn* to us; I remember now—and completing the loop from Reston to Jefferson to Kenilworth.

"Does Cass know about the jacket?" I ask.

"If she doesn't yet, she will soon, but do me a favor. Don't talk with her, or anyone, about it. Not until I have a chance to discuss it with Heather and your dad. And maybe not even then."

There's another TV network van on the parkway. We're going to have to walk past them. Sweat beads at my temples, and I impulsively grab Eschermann's sleeve.

"It's all right," he says. "We're just going to walk past them. Don't say anything, and I'll make sure they don't ask any questions."

We navigate through the small sea of intruders, their eyes boring into me. More than once, Eschermann holds up a hand to ward off somebody's attempt to start a conversation. Soon we're standing on my doorstep, and my father is quick to open the door and usher me inside.

"Chris?" Eschermann's voice stops my dad from closing the door on his face.

"Yeah."

"That development we discussed a few days ago. I'm going to need you to come in to clarify a few things."

"Does it have to be today?"

"I can take you away in cuffs, or you can come quietly in your own vehicle. The arrest won't stick—we both know that— but you don't want to walk past the camera looking like a felon, do you?"

Suddenly, my own heartbeat deafens me.

He just threatened to arrest my dad!

"I'll be right behind you." Dad's still sweaty from his work-out, but he doesn't even ask if he can shower first.

"I'd prefer to follow you."

The next thing I know, my phone is in my hand and my father's keys are in his.

And then he's gone.

|||| |||| |||| ||

My grandmother takes off as soon as my father leaves. She mutters something about going to the station to support her son, pecks me on the cheek, and tells me not to go anywhere.

When I was little and Eschermann would call Dad in for questioning, I'd wait with friendly officers who'd play with me while my dad was in the hot seat. I'm much more comfortable waiting out the ordeal in my own house, and I have to admit I'm glad Gram will be there for my dad when the questioning is over. Now that Heather's left, I feel like he's dealing with everything on his own, and he's about to crack with the pressure.

Cassidy and Brooke have parked in front of Schmidt's house and walked through the yards to come to me. They came as quickly as I texted, and they're now sitting at the breakfast table, scarfing down the burritos they brought with them, while I'm picking at the one they've designated as mine—brown rice, green salsa, avocado, lettuce, red pepper, extra cheese. No tomato, no meat. Good friends are like that. They know what you want on your burrito, and they bring it to you without even asking if you're hungry.

I am, but I can't seem to eat.

I scroll through my phone. Dad left all of the messages

unread. If it was a test of trust, my father passed.

I stop on a message Ryan left last night: *Good friends, good times.*

I send him back a smiley face and hope it's enough to rebuild the bridge I think I just burned by pointing the finger at his uncle. I wonder if Ryan is out of the shower yet, if he'll reply. Maybe I'll make a batch of Mom's snickerdoodles and bring them over to formally apologize later.

"So." Brooke nudges me with her elbow. "You kissed that guy last night."

"How'd you know?"

"Matt Darcy saw."

"Great." If I'd known we had an audience I probably wouldn't have done it.

With everything going on since last night, I've hardly thought about the kiss, but the energy of it revisits me now. "What was I thinking?"

"What *were* you thinking, because if it's half as interesting as what I'm thinking . . ."

Cassidy lets out a chuckle while leaning over her phone. It's hard to tell if she's laughing at Brooke or at something Zack said via text.

Brooke looks at me—"I fear we have lost her forever"—and takes an enormous bite of her burrito.

"I think you're making a mistake, Sami," Cassidy pipes in, still tapping keys on her phone. "That guy won't even be here next week."

"It's not like that," I say. "We used to be best friends."

"Yeah?" Finally, my sister looks up at me. "Then why the drama of the kiss?" She abandons her half-eaten burrito to lean back in her chair. Her text alert goes off again.

"I wasn't doing it to be dramatic—"

"And then you left. I mean, we're trying to be there for you, and you leave with some guy you hardly know."

"In what way were you trying to be there for me? You were submerged in Soccer King."

"She's right about that, Cass," Brooke says. "You were no more available than I was."

"How was I supposed to realize that she would throw herself at some random guy the moment we turned our backs?"

"He's not *random*!" I snap.

"Cass, come on," sighs Brooke. "It was just a kiss. Get off her already."

"We're her friends," Cassidy says. "We're *supposed* to get on her about this stuff."

"Fine," Brooke says. "If that's what friends do, I'll get on you: why are you wasting time with Zack? He's gone next year."

"Not valid. At least I might have a date for prom. I'm investing in something here."

"I hate to tell you this, Cass, but my brother may be well past this by the time prom rolls around. He's a flaky guy."

"Wanna bet?"

"Will you *shut up* about guys, and prom, and all the rest of this bullshit?" I shove my chair away from the table. "We have bigger issues to deal with right now."

Cassidy stares at me. "Look, just because I choose to ignore the *bullshit* with your mom's case, it doesn't mean I don't care about it. But I can't let it consume me like it does your father."

"*My* father? Since when isn't he ours?"

"You know what I mean. But to be honest, Mom and I were talking, and this other girl . . . it doesn't exactly scream *innocent*, you know?"

I cross my arms. I don't have time to think about this betrayal, to process the idea that Cassidy—and apparently Heather too—could suspect my dad. Little does my sister know that the case is about to take a turn . . . and land at the Funky Nun. Or maybe she and Heather do know that. I wonder again if Heather is suddenly changing her tune about my dad because she's trying to divert attention away from herself.

There are only two scenarios in which Heather would start accusing Dad of being responsible: if she knows he's guilty, or if she's guilty herself.

I snap out of this train of thought and focus on Cassidy. "I agree that everything looks pretty weird," I tell her. "That's why I want to find out the truth. And to do that, I need help." Cassidy's standoffish expression doesn't change. I glance over at Brooke. "I need to look through photo albums. I need to see if there are any pictures of the jacket I was wearing last night."

"Why?" Cassidy asks as Brooke is saying, "I'm game."

I wasn't supposed to mention it. "I don't know. Eschermann won't tell me, except that it could help Dad if I find any pictures of it."

"Well, you won't," Cassidy says. "Mom wouldn't wear it."

I shrug and hedge my way out of it. "I know, but we at least have to look."

Cassidy's phone twinkles again with a text alert. She doesn't break eye contact.

"Go ahead and answer it," I say.

She seizes the phone. "I have to. He's leaving for practice in twenty-four minutes, and he'll be at the soccer field all day."

"Ball is life," Brooke mutters with a roll of her eyes. "That's why I date the slightly-off guys who hang out at poetry slams."

"Go to Zack's game," I say.

"I have to work at one thirty," Cassidy says. "So I can't do much to help you past lunch, anyway, and it's not because I don't care. It's because *someone* has to work at the Nun."

"I work," Brooke says.

"Rarely."

"Sami's in crisis right now," Brooke says. "You might want to prioritize."

Cassidy slams her phone down. "You're telling me about crisis? I know crisis! I lived through it with her! But, Sami, at some point you have to examine the coincidence of a few things: your mother disappears ten years ago, right around the same time cops find remains of a woman who might be Dad's ex-wife."

I stiffen, tempted to tell her, even though Eschermann asked me not to, that Trina isn't the Jane Doe, and that Heather's about to be as thick into this quicksand as Dad.

Before I can speak, though, Brooke says, "You know what, Cass? Go to his game. If he's your priority today, despite everything going on, go. I'll handle the Nun alone."

"You hardly work while you're there!"

"Come on, you love being in charge. You *like* running around with fitting room keys, getting customers different sizes, all that stuff. I just let you do what you like."

I'm already on my feet, making my way toward the photo albums on the bookshelf.

"Whatever." Cassidy offers Brooke a middle finger salute along with her words. "I can help as long as I'm here. Let's make the most of the next twenty-four minutes."

I pull photo albums from the shelves, hand one to each of my friends, and set one aside for me. Just as I'm about to collapse into a sofa to flip through the pages, I allow myself to look upward, to the highest shelf, where hardcover books line the space: Melville, Twain, the Brontë sisters, Hemingway . . .

They're the only items Mom put here that remain where her hands last touched them. Many of the books are first editions, which perhaps is why Heather and Dad left them there when they cleared my mother's footprints from this house.

I pull *Moby-Dick* from the shelf—a decade of dust comes with it—and press my palm to the cover, as if it's a Bible. Imagine my mother's hands touching this book, turning its pages.

The binding is worn; threads dangle from the spine. Mom was always reading, and although I don't remember her cracking the hardcovers, I wonder if she may have annotated any of these books the way she did *Gatsby*.

I open the cover, flip a few pages.

My eyes meet with a piece of copy paper, thinner than the stock we keep in our printer, older maybe, folded in half. It falls open in my hands.

Nobody's Fool is typewritten in Courier and centered along the top, in a header, followed by a dash and *by Delilah Lang*. At the far right corner, I see a page number: *64*.

Page sixty-four. That means pages one through sixty-three should be somewhere too.

"What are you doing?" Brooke asks.

"I just found . . ." I leaf through a few more pages and find another typewritten page. And another and another. I turn the book upside down and gently shake it. More pages fall out.

"Sam?" Brooke's beside me now.

"Look at this!" I say.

She picks up a photo that's fallen from between the pages of the book.

I push Melville back onto the shelf and pull down *Wuthering Heights*.

Shake, shake, shake.

More pages filter out.

I hand a Tolstoy to Brooke, who's too short to reach the top shelf, and grab another for me. There are typewritten pages hidden in these books too.

"What are you doing?"

I hear Cassidy over my shoulder, but I can't spare the time for eye contact. "Get a book," I tell her.

"Sami." Brooke nudges me with an elbow. "Look." She hands me a candid picture of my father, standing opposite a dark-haired woman in a short, willowy sundress. The woman is reaching for him, as if in the moments after someone snapped this picture, she would be touching his face.

Brooke flips the picture over. There's a date scrawled on the back. Quick math tells me I was almost five when the picture was taken.

Got to be Heather. More pages fall from the book I'm wiggling. *Nobody's Fool by Delilah Lang* heads each of them.

"Cass, is this your mom?" Brooke asks.

Cassidy gives the snapshot a glance. "I don't think so."

Of course it's Heather. Although the woman's face isn't discernible, there's no mistaking that long, dark, wavy hair, or Heather's mile-long legs. Given the title of the manuscript, Dad's admission he cheated on my mother with Heather, and the fact that the pages and this photograph were stashed inside books only Mom read, I'm guessing Mom might have known about Heather all along and wanted to prove they weren't fooling anyone.

Brooke and I share a glance.

"I know my own mother, okay?" snaps Cassidy.

"Sam, your dad was a stud," Brooke says.

"Ew," I say.

"I'm not saying *that*," Brooke says. "I'm saying it speaks to the appeal, you know? Think about it. Heather's gorgeous. Your mom was gorgeous. And this chick, whoever she is, is gorgeous. Don't tell me you've never wondered . . ." She shuts up, but I hear the words she's yet to utter:

How does a man with *two* exes and a drinking problem get a woman like Heather? And how does she agree to marry him?

I take the picture from her grasp. "Focus."

Soon, the three of us have shaken out over one hundred fifty pages of what appears to be a manuscript, or at least part of one, hidden in the hardcover books no one ever touches. "Your mother wrote a book." Brooke's eyes are wide. "This is *amazing*."

The three of us are sitting on the floor now, with scattered papers surrounding us. We're arranging the papers by number.

I remember the clickety-clack of the typewriter keys. Despite the fact that we had a computer back then, Mom wrote the old-fashioned way. That means this is likely the only copy of her work. And the fact that she hid it tells me she didn't want anyone to see it.

It's like finding a diamond in the midst of river rock.

It's precious. Rare.

"What are you going to do, Sami?" Cassidy asks.

"I'm going to read it tonight."

"Well, *duh*," Brooke says. "Are you going to tell your dad? The cops?"

"Of course."

"And what about this?" Brooke retrieves the photograph from where I set it aside on the end table.

"I'm going to ask Dad if it's Heather."

"It's not my mom," Cassidy says immediately.

"Do me a favor," I say. "Ask your mom when she and Dad got together."

"Which time?"

Valid. "Ask her if she was ever with my dad while he was married to my mom."

"No! Sami, we know they started up again after the divorce."

That's what we'd always been told, but I know the truth now.

"What?" Cassidy says.

I want to tell her what I know.

But a worm of jealously eats its way through my heart. Dad has always loved her mom more than he loved mine.

A knock on the back door startles me. Who could it be? Gram wouldn't knock. Any members of the press would come only to the front door, as would Lieutenant Eschermann or his police force.

"Sami? You home?"

I recognize Ryan's voice—the drawl.

"Ryan! Come in." I rush to the mudroom and let him in. He smells of Irish Spring and nondescript hair product. "Hi."

Brooke and Cassidy are behind me now, obnoxious onlookers over my shoulder. "Hunky farm boy!" Brooke says instead of hello.

He half smiles at her, half shakes his head. "Sorry to barge in on you, but I found this in the yard when I was raking. Is it yours?"

Something dangles from his hand. He holds it out for me.

"You're the only person besides me walking through the yard lately—well, you and your friends. I found it alongside my barn while I was raking the leaves out of the flower bed."

Where the sunflowers used to grow.

The object snakes into my hand.

It's my locket! I run my thumb over the heart shape, find comfort in the sunflower shape engraved into its surface.

I can't believe I almost lost this locket! It's unspeakably precious to me, and I allowed it to come loose from my ankle.

"Thanks." My gratitude slips out ineptly, in a half-voice.

"No problem."

He lingers there for a few breaths before tapping his fist against the doorjamb. "Well, I have a lot of work to do, so . . ."

"Yeah," I say. "Thanks."

"Later."

"Hey. Ryan."

"Yeah."

I look over my shoulder at my best friends, who wait intently to see what I'm about to say. A silly smile is plastered to Brooke's face.

"Let's just . . ." I follow him out the door and close it behind me. "Listen, I'm sorry about what I said earlier."

"When?" He squints through the late-morning sunlight and wets his lips. "What'd you say?"

"On the front porch of your uncle's house. I said—"

"Oh, that." His gaze travels to something behind me. "Listen, I get it. The thing about my uncle—he's Socratic, you know? Doesn't take information for granted. He'd respect that you're considering every option. You're wrong, from my point of view, but if I were in your situation, I might risk being wrong too, just to put the theory out there."

"So . . . we're good?"

He touches my arm. "Of course. I'll see you later."

He gives me one last glance before he makes his way

through the yard toward his uncle's place. The locket practically burns in my hand.

I return to the family room, where Cassidy is pulling her jacket over her shoulders. "I have to run to the Nun."

"I'll be by later," I say.

Brooke is straightening piles of paper. "Cass, I *said* if you want to catch the game, we'll cover."

Cassidy hugs Brooke. "Thank you, thank you, thank you! But you have to go *now*, okay? Mom was very adamant about my being there before she left."

"You don't trust us?" Brooke asks.

"You and Miss Serially-Ten-Minutes-Late?" Cassidy shakes her head. "No."

As Cassidy is on her way out the door, I prop my foot atop the coffee table to loop the chain of the locket around my ankle. I push my sock down and out of the way.

The locket is still on my ankle. This one . . . it must be my mother's.

||||| ||||| ||||| |||

My fingers close around my mother's locket, which is still dusted with dirt around the clasp. Maybe it had been in Schmidt's flower bed since she took off ten years ago, but it seems rather coincidental Ryan would come across it today, of all days. Could it mean she lost it recently? Wouldn't it make more sense that it slipped off her neck yesterday or today?

I open the clasp with some difficulty, parting the two halves of the locket. The left side is empty, but on the right, a picture of a young man and a newborn baby—Dad and me— fills the concave space.

The photograph mesmerizes me for a second. There aren't many pictures of Dad and me, and I wish I had this one enlarged to poster size because it depicts adoration. We're in profile; he's kissing my cheek, and I'm wearing a frilly little cap. This picture proves my mother did love my father once upon a time. Why else would she have put this picture in her special locket?

And now that the locket has turned up . . .

I just want to see her again. To feel safe in her embrace. To tell her I've never forgotten her. I'll forgive her, no matter why she left. We'll get through it.

"We have to call Eschermann." I reach for my phone. "I have to tell him about this locket. It has to mean Mom's been here, right? I mean, how else would it get here?"

"Sami, wait." Brooke grabs my arm.

But Brooke doesn't understand because she doesn't know about the passport application, and I can't tell her!

"If she came all this way, if she was in your backyard, she wouldn't have left without seeing you."

"Then how do you explain this?" The locket is warm in my hand. "Ryan just found it. *Today*. Are you telling me it's been in that flower bed for ten years, and it just now turned up?"

"Maybe. Or maybe it was in the box Ryan found, and it fell out of the box when he brought it inside."

"You don't understand." I'm near tears. I feel them building in my eyes, in my nose, in my throat and lungs. "My mother never took this off. She wore it every day, and she was wearing it the last time I saw her. I haven't seen it since."

"Think about that, Sami. *Think about that.*" Brooke's got me by both shoulders now. She squeezes a little, forcing me to catch my breath. "She *loved* you."

I stare at her.

"Is it more likely," she says in an even tone, "that your mom came home recently and didn't see you? Or that this locket recently fell out of a box?"

I take a few steps backward on trembling legs.

"And if she always wore the locket," she continues, "that means one of two things."

"Either she left it behind when she left me," I say quietly.

"Or it wasn't her choice to take it off," Brooke concludes. But she doesn't say what I know she's thinking, either: that maybe my mom no longer has a neck around which to string it.

Lose-lose.

The dogs alerted behind the barn.

"So the question is . . ." Brooke begins to stack books. "Why is this locket here, when your mother isn't?"

I pull my hair back into a ponytail and secure it with the hair tie currently restricting circulation around my wrist. "Brooke?"

She raises a brow.

"My dad admitted to me that Heather's the reason he and my mom split."

She nods slowly, and I can already tell the wheels in her head are turning.

"So are you thinking it means your dad's lying about other things?" Brooke asks. "Or are you worried he has motive?"

Both.

But I play it safe: "I'm starting to think Heather might know something. She was my dad's alibi ten years ago. And . . ." But I refrain from mentioning the jacket.

"You have to talk to her."

"Just come right out and ask her if she thinks my dad had something to do with my mom's disappearance?"

"Let's go to the Nun now—get her talking, see what she volunteers *without* your asking a direct question."

It's as good a plan as any.

////

The twin lockets strung around my ankle rub against each other and against my ankle, as if symbolizing Mom and me, together again after all these years.

I look more closely at the photograph we found in Tolstoy: Sunflower stalks in the background tell me this picture might have been taken in my backyard, within view of Schmidt's house. And the woman looks like Heather, although her face is only partially visible.

Slipping the photo in my jeans pocket, I approach the Funky Nun. The scent of incense overwhelms me before I even step inside. Heather has made a new sign with brightly-colored tempera paints and a scrap of wood and propped it in the window:

☺ *Open for Fashion Consultation. Not Open for Questioning* ☺

I wonder if she'd been bombarded with reporters this morning. Or maybe Eschermann paid her a visit.

When we enter, Heather looks up from behind the counter, where she's hand-sewing a screen-printed, custom tag into a garment. "Where's Cass?"

"She's at Zack's soccer game," I say.

"We switched shifts," Brooke explains. "And Sam's here to help."

Two customers, both girls I recognize from school, browse the racks. One of them is perusing the bottles of holy water, and the other is glued to the crystals.

Heather's dark hair is gathered atop her head in a ball, and tiny, octagonal-framed glasses are perched on the bridge of her nose. "What do you think?" She holds up a black shirt with bright pink, gauzy ruffles on the sleeves. "I made matching bell-bottoms too."

"Are flares still in?" I busy myself with straightening a rack of tie-dyed scarves.

"Not flares." Heather bats away the word with a hand, as if it were hanging in the air. "Full-out *bell*-bottoms. Isn't it fun?" She's holding up another item, made of the same black and pink fabrics. "Try this on." She stands up and tosses the ensemble at us. One piece lands on me, the other on Brooke.

"Mine!" Brooke claims both the top and the bottom, which is just as well. I'm not here to acquire more quirky prototypes from Heather's stash.

Heather pulls the glasses from her face and fixes her gaze on me. "How you holding up, Sami?"

Brooke slides behind the counter and gives me the go-sign.

The girls at the back corner of the showroom are whispering. When I look at them, they avert their eyes.

"Actually . . ." I lower my voice. "Can I talk to you for a few minutes?"

"Brooke, you're on duty?" It isn't really a question as much as a command. Heather picks up her ever-present cup of Madelaine Café's iced tea, leaving a circle of sweat on the fabric square she was using as a coaster, and leads me to the office at the back of the shop, which stores all sorts of fabric, from tweeds to chintz. It's grossly disorganized. A sewing machine sits on a table on the far end of the room. It's the only item in here without a thin layer of dust.

The scent of incense is stronger in here. Heather sits first on a secondhand chair, and I follow her lead, choosing the chair that used to be in our living room.

"Lots going on, huh?" She pulls the clip from her hair— "This business with Trina Jordan . . ."—and shakes her curls free.

"Did you know my dad had been married before he married my mom?"

"Married?"

I wait it out.

She fingers a worn spot in the arm of the chair. "I always suspected he'd married her, but I didn't know for certain until I read the article yesterday morning. It was annulled, you know, which means, technically, that it never happened."

"Except that it did. And he never told either one of us." I decide to strike now. No need to beat around the bush. "Did you know he was married to my mom?"

"Of course I knew—"

"When you started sleeping with him, I mean."

She averts her eyes.

"He told me," I say, before she considers denying it. I take out the photograph I recently found. "And today, I found proof of it."

She takes the picture with trembling fingers, studies it, flips it over to see the date Mom scrawled on the back. "Where did you find this?"

"With some of my mother's things."

"Oh, God."

"I guess I'm wondering," I continue, "if you were involved with him during his relationship with Trina, too, and maybe he didn't want you to know he was married to *her*, so that's why he never told you about her."

Heather takes a deep breath. "I knew he'd been engaged in college to a girl who'd died in an accident, but Trina . . ." Heather trails off, still staring at the photo.

Perspiration breaks on my palms, at my temples. "What girl in college?" I wonder why Lieutenant Eschermann never mentioned this third girl—or rather the first?—who met an untimely end. "What was her name?"

"Lizzie. Lizzie . . . Dawson, maybe? She died in a car accident, Sam. You don't have to worry about *her*."

Implying that I do have to worry about the others?

And if this girl died while she was dating my father . . .

It's too much of a coincidence. If three women disappear-slash-die and my father is a common thread connecting them, it must mean something. No one's luck is that bad.

Carefully, I say, "It's just that—I'm realizing that there's so much I don't know about him. And if he even has secrets from *you*, when you've known each other most of your lives—does anyone really know him?"

I watch her profile. She's staring out the window and bringing the straw to her lips for a slow sip of tea. "This picture was taken before your mother left."

"Mm-hmm."

She hands the photograph back, her face grim. "This isn't me."

"It looks like you."

"Be that as it may, Samantha, it isn't me."

In a way, she's confirming my worst fear: that Dad is a mystery to all of us. That he may have lied, not just about Trina, not just about when he started seeing Heather, but over and over again. And if he's capable of that, what else is he capable of?

I call up pictures on my phone—selfies Brooke and I took before all the guests arrived at her house last night. Obnoxious poses of us pointing to oblivious Cassidy and Zack getting kissy in the background. "I borrowed a pair of pants from the samples last night."

"The pom-pom fringe. Cass told me."

"Did she tell you I borrowed a jacket too?"

"You're welcome to anything in those bins. You know that."

"I sort of think I shouldn't have borrowed this one." I hand over my phone and watch closely as her eyes widen.

"This jacket wasn't in the samples boxes." She's flipping back and forth between the pictures. "Where did you find it?"

"In a box in the closet. Cass was rushing me, and Kismet drooled on some clean sheets—"

"You put them in the wash."

I frown. It's hardly the point I want to make. "Yes."

"Thank you."

I won't let her sidetrack me. "Heather, where did you get this jacket?"

"I found it."

"Where?"

She lets out an exasperated sigh. "In the passageway."

The passageway between our carriage house and Schmidt's house. The passageway my dad told me to stay away from. "When?"

She's staring at me, as if weighing the possibility I'll just forget all about it.

But I can't back down. "Please."

"A long time ago."

"The last day anyone saw my mother?"

"Thereabouts."

It feels as if the wind has been sucked from my lungs. It's true, then. This jacket might have something to do with my mother's—or Trina's—case.

"I found this jacket," Heather says, "lying across a box. One of your mother's. She was packing her things, getting ready to head out of town."

"So it *is* my mother's jacket."

"I assumed it was." She wets her lips before continuing. "And your father assumed she'd left for good."

"As it turns out, she did."

"No, Sam. Left for good *with you*. She was taking the trip to find a place to stay in Atlanta—permanently—with you."

My heart both aches and warms at the same time. I hadn't known this—that she was going to take me with her. I just thought she was moving down there on her own. "I was supposed to go." *She was going to take me with her,* I think again. But something changed her mind.

"Not *then*. She was going to come back for you once she'd found a place. But when your father and I came back that day and Delilah was gone and most of her things were gone, her car was gone, and *you* were gone, we assumed the worst: that she'd taken you *for good*—she had sole custody of you, it was well within her rights—but we didn't have a chance to say good-bye to you."

"Why didn't I know this?" I wonder aloud.

"Your father didn't want you to know she'd changed her mind. He thought it best to let you grow up thinking this was the way things should be."

If I were Dad, would I have done the same? Or would I have told my kid the truth?

Heather continues: "He was angry with her—*really angry*—when he thought she'd left with you."

"And later, Schmidt brought me home."

"And a few weeks after that, when she still hadn't turned up, he was really angry with her for leaving you behind. We've told the police. I can't tell you how many times we've told—"

"What about the babysitter?"

She eyes me for a second. "She was gone. We assumed Delilah had released her."

"No, I mean, who was it?"

"I don't know, Sam. The police have asked that too, but I wasn't involved in decisions like that back then."

"And the jacket?"

155

"We thought she'd be back. I washed it—it was filthy, covered in dirt, like she'd been rolling around in a flower bed—and set it aside for the day she came back. There was a box or two left behind . . . and *you* were still here . . . so I assumed it wouldn't be long . . . but she never came. And some weeks later, the police started asking questions. They dragged the lake for her car—they didn't find it, but given the nature of the first fiancée's accident they thought they should—but by then, I'd already washed the jacket, and I was afraid it would look like I *intentionally* washed the jacket, but I was just trying to be nice. Call it a guilty conscience or over-compensation for my role in their divorce, but I was just trying to be nice."

"So you hid it."

"I knew the jacket wasn't going to prove anything about where Delilah went, so I kept it packed away. I'd vouched for your dad. I'd washed the jacket. *I was sure she'd be back.* And Ken Eschermann—he was already hinting I'd been *lying* for your dad—"

"Were you?"

"No!"

"So why'd you dig up the jacket now? After all this time?"

"I *didn't*, Sam. I moved out of the house. It must've gotten mixed up with my things." She sighs. "I was shocked when I opened the box and saw it."

Still, I wonder what she was going to do with it after all this time.

Heather stands and heads toward the door. "I have to go. I have an appointment. But if you want to talk more later . . ."

"Thanks."

"You'll let Kismet out before you leave?"

"Yeah."

"And if you want to keep things easy for your father"—she pauses at the doorway—"delete the pictures of that jacket."

Wouldn't it make things easier for *her* if news of the jacket never reached Eschermann?

A chill darts up my spine. Maybe I've been wrong.

Heather isn't solely covering for Dad.

Dad isn't solely covering for Heather.

They *both* know things they're not telling.

My phone buzzes with a text alert. It's from Ryan: *Call me asap. Found something I think you'll want to see.*

‖‖ ‖‖ ‖‖ ‖‖

Ryan found pictures of my mother in a shoe box at his uncle's place.

Dozens of them.

Appropriate photos, he'd said, but the number of them is alarming.

Brooke is going to drop me off there once we close the Nun.

Closing time can't come soon enough. Reporters have gathered outside the shop, deciding to harass Heather now. One reporter even posed as a customer and started asking questions, but Brooke managed to get her out the door before she got any information. We locked the door after that. Brooke is straightening the rack of holy water, and I'm reading my mother's manuscript.

The phone's been ringing off the hook with requests for comments too. The phone in the shop, as well as Heather's landline upstairs.

Every few minutes, one of the phones wakes Kismet from a dead sleep and gets her so riled up that she starts wagging her tail without regard for what she might hit with it . . . including me and the stack of manuscript papers on the counter.

Based on the pages I've managed to read, *Nobody's Fool* is a thriller about a woman whose marriage is on the rocks. When she accuses her husband of cheating, he turns it around on her and makes her think she's crazy. And no one believes her when she thinks the mistress is threatening her life, either.

"It reads like fiction," I say. "But considering everything we know—"

"You're wondering if it's autobiographical." Brooke goes to work on aligning the vials of sand now.

"I hope it isn't." My hands are numb, and I'm feeling a little lightheaded. "But it's naive to ignore that possibility." I inhale for eleven and lower myself to Heather's chair. Kismet takes the opportunity to jump into my lap, as if she's still twenty pounds of vanilla-colored fur instead of ninety pounds of dog. Her tongue is like wet pink velvet against my cheek. Exhale for seven.

"You think Heather is involved in all this," Brooke says. "You think she's the mistress your mom was writing about."

"I think . . . it's plausible that Heather and my dad coordinated their versions of what happened, or what didn't happen, and this may be the closest I ever get to hearing my mom's version."

Heather washed and hid a jacket, which was stained with something that might have been blood on the cuff.

Dad has lost three ex-girlfriends/wives, though only one is confirmed dead.

Dad and Heather had been in love most of their lives. Is it possible that Heather is responsible? That she got rid of Mom so she could have Dad all to herself?

If she did—or even if my mom survived a fraction of the horrible experiences she wrote about—it means I've been loyal to the people who destroyed her life.

I let Heather in.

I trusted her.

I allowed her to take my mother's place.

And she might be the reason my mother's gone.

"Listen." Brooke snaps her fingers in front of my face.

I shake free from the glaze.

"I have a date with Alex tonight. But I'm going to cancel and hang with you."

"Don't do that."

"He'll understand. And I'm sorry, but Cassidy's been far too casual about this whole thing. I mean, the report about your dad and this other woman who disappeared, the manuscript . . . and she's at a friggin' soccer tournament? She's in the thick of this too, you know, whether she admits it or not," Brooke says. "I know this has been going on a long time, and maybe you get desensitized to the drama after a while, but this is new drama. There's no reason she should be worried about watching my brother kick a ball around at a time like this."

I chew on my lip. "Do you think it's possible she's being this way because she knows something we don't?"

"Like what?"

"I don't know. Something Heather told her but hasn't told me. You notice she called him my dad today, when for years, she's called him Dad and referred to him as our dad. Maybe she knows something that's making her want to distance herself."

"You're suggesting that Cass knows something that could incriminate your dad or Heather, and instead of telling us—or the police—she's just decided not to think about it? Just back off from everything?" Brooke doesn't look convinced.

"All I'm saying is that she's not acting normal. But I guess everyone seems suspicious to me at this point. It's hard to think straight when I just found out that the police are working on identifying a dead body who might be my mom."

"Oh, Sam." Brooke's been chewing at her thumbnail, but she pulls it from her mouth when I say that. "You never told me that."

"Forget it," I say. "Forget I mentioned it."

"Impossible."

"It could be nothing. It's far away. But they think they should rule it out, so they're testing the DNA to see if it matches my mom's."

"It sounds like you're the one who knows something Cass doesn't," Brooke points out.

The phone's ringing again.

"God, I can't be here anymore. Let's just go, okay?" I turn to gather the pages of Mom's manuscript and shove them in my backpack.

The phone has only just stopped ringing, but it's making a racket again. Even though Brooke rarely answers the phone when she's on the clock, she must have checked the caller ID because she says, "Sami. It's the cop shop."

I pick it up. "Funky Nun. Samantha chooses joy."

"It's Lieutenant Eschermann. Has Heather come by the shop?"

"No. She had an appointment at two, and we haven't seen her since."

"Right. That appointment was with me."

My heart flutters. Her appointment was with the police?

"She never showed," Eschermann says. "I've tried her cell phone and her landline at the apartment. The shop phone's been busy—"

"It hasn't stopped ringing. But Heather's not here. She left just before two."

"Well, she's not here at the station. Her car is in the lot, but she—"

"So she's *missing*?"

"In that no one seems to know where she is, yes. Have you talked to Cassidy? Maybe she's with her mother."

"She's at a soccer tournament. Have you asked my dad if she called or texted him? Since, you know, he's right there at the station."

"Well, that's the other thing, Sam. We released him. He left the station at about one forty. And if you're telling me Heather left the shop just before two . . ."

Oh no.

"Sam, no one's seen your father since then. He isn't at your house, he isn't on the NU campus. I spoke with your grandmother. Neither of us can get him on the cell either. Have you spoken with him?"

"No."

"Do me a favor. Try to call him. Maybe he'll answer a call from you." He pauses. "Sami, with the developments in the case, I asked your father not to leave town. As a courtesy to me."

Evidence must be building against him. "If you told him not to go, he won't go." But if he isn't innocent, maybe he would.

"Under normal circumstances, I don't think he'd go without *you*. But Sam, he might have reason to keep Heather from speaking with me."

The world whirls around me. "Do you think he . . ." I can't even say the words. "No, no, no. He wouldn't. Not Heather. Why would he do something to Heather?"

"Why Delilah, in that case?"

But it's different. He and Mom were divorced. He and Heather had dinner last night. Their divorce isn't final. Their lives have overlapped longer than any other relationship Dad's had. "Maybe they're just having coffee. No one knows they're not just sitting at the Madelaine—"

"We do, actually, know they're not sitting at the Madelaine. Or at any other restaurant in the area."

That means they're out looking for them. That neighboring police forces are out looking for them. I feel raw, exposed, as if everyone knows, as if everyone's judging.

Someone on the outside presses her forehead to the glass and peers into the shop.

I do a double take.

Caramel hair. Blue eyes.

I see her surrounded by sunflower blossoms.

Mom?

I drop the phone.

卌 卌 卌 卌

I blink, and she's gone.

Just wishful thinking. Something I created at that moment to make myself feel better, to help me get through it all.

No different from my childhood theories about my mother's escaping to Schmidt's place. Illusions, nothing more than fairy tales, dropped into my head like Candy Land daydreams.

But it's time to grow up. Time to realize what's really going on—what's been going on—since the day my mother disappeared.

In all likelihood, my mother has not spent the past ten years on one endless carefree road trip, and there's a good chance people close to me, people I trust, know what happened to her.

I'm staring out the window of the Funky Nun, staring at the people gathering on the Walk. I look for my mother among them, although I know I won't see her face. If she were here—if she were anywhere—she would have come for me by now.

She's gone.

Replaced with the lens of a camera.

Zeroing in on me.

"Shit!" I instinctively duck behind the counter, where I curl into my own embrace, hidden.

I hear Brooke talking with Lieutenant Eschermann on the phone, but I can't concentrate on what she's saying.

My forehead rests on my knees, and my arms crisscross over my head. Heather's creations drape around me, and for a moment, I feel safe.

Safe, like when I was playing in the sunflowers, their radiant warmth and happiness surrounding me. I relied on those flowers, I realize now. They were dependable. Sprouted up alongside Schmidt's barn and grew, grew, grew all season long, while other blossoms came and went—the tulips, the daffodils, the roses.

Schmidt stopped planting them several years ago, right around the time I began to notice days could pass without my thinking of my mother at all, without my pondering her absence or whereabouts. When she truly became *gone* to me.

I wonder if that's when she became *gone* for him too.

It's not that I could ever forget her; I may have learned to live without her, but there's a void carved permanently into my soul. A void no stepmother can fill, a void my father can't come close to sealing, a void that tells me to trust no one because the one person I trusted more than anyone else on this planet—the person I needed more than anyone—left me.

I know even my dreams about her coming back one last time and taking me into the passageway—however vivid—weren't real, either. Those dreams, those visions, are my mind's way of remembering her. Just a kid's way of dealing with something she can't possibly understand.

Like the drawings I found at Heather's place: stick figures attempting to make sense of a senseless situation.

Brooke crouches on the floor before me. "We have to go. That cop wants to meet us at your place. He has a warrant to search the Nun and he's sending evidence techs over here—he doesn't want us getting in their way."

"Is the camera crew gone?"

"No, and there's more than one now, but I closed the curtains over the window."

At this, I snap back to the present.

"We'll have to be quick getting to the car," she says. "I'll go out the front and drive around to the alley for you. No one's looking to have a word with *me*. As far as they know, I just work here."

I hear the hum and click of Heather's printer-slash-copier. *Hummmmm, click. Hummmmm, click.* "Are you *copying* something?"

"Well, yeah. I told the cop about your mom's manuscript. He wants to see it."

I look at her; she's the best friend ever, but she's crazy. "If Eschermann wants to see it, it's evidence. And you're *copying* it?"

"You deserve this piece of her, Sami, and if we turn it over to the cops, who knows when you'll be able to read the rest of it."

"Heather didn't make it to the station."

Brooke shakes her head. "Doesn't sound like it."

Her car is in the station parking lot, but she never made it in for her meeting. My dad was released at the same time, and they're both unaccounted for. My stomach is turning somersaults. "What could have happened to her?"

"I hope she's okay." I know Brooke is trying to calm the stormy waters right now, but the fact of the matter is, *nothing* is okay at the moment. One of two things happened to my stepmother:

Knowing evidence was starting to mount against her, she took a train out of town. That's how I'd travel, if I needed to disappear. By train. No identification needed. Just pay cash for your ticket, and you're literally gone.

Or . . . knowing she had evidence against him and was about to blab, Dad took her somewhere. Either to talk her out of spilling the beans, or . . . or to do whatever he might have done to Trina, to my mom. And maybe even to the girl he knew in college.

I think of what Eschermann told me at the station the other day: *Your father has a third ex-wife now, doesn't he? Anything happens to her, and we won't be able to call it a coincidence.*

And I think of Dad in the hallway the other night: *Heather—nothing happens.* Maybe he really said what I thought I heard. And maybe he's changed his mind since then.

"We have to reach Cassidy." I'm positive she won't answer Eschermann's calls because she won't recognize the number, and particularly because she's busy watching Zack. And I know the brand of nonspecific that Eschermann uses in his messages. He'll ask her to return the call. Either she'll put it off, assuming he's calling for information about my mother, or she'll call back instantly and hear that her mother is, for lack of a better word, missing.

That kind of news, I know firsthand, should come from someone close to you.

"It's my fault." I'm texting my sister now. We have to go to the soccer fields, or if the tournament is over, we have to go wherever Cassidy might be with Zack. "If something's wrong with Heather, it's my fault."

"That's ridiculous, Sami," Brooke says. "How is any of this—"

I hold up a finger to delay Brooke's commentary, just until I finish the text: *Have to talk to you. 911.*

She returns: *Heading to the Madelaine with Z. Meet us there.*

Me: *Come home instead. Important. 911.*

Heather left the shop, but she never got to the station.

And it's my fault.

Because I protected him all these years. I defended my father, even when the case against him looked grim and foreboding.

I believed in him when I should have believed in the truth.

HHT HHT HHT HHT
I

Maybe my father waited outside the station for Heather to arrive.

Maybe he lured her into his car. How difficult would it have been? They had dinner at the Madelaine Friday night. All he had to do was tell her he was worried about me or Cassidy, and she would've walked right into his trap.

That's where my imagination hits a brick wall. I can't imagine what might have happened next because I can't imagine Dad doing something so sinister. But that doesn't mean I don't think he's capable. Not that long ago, I would've insisted otherwise, but knowing what I know now, it's hard to think he isn't.

But it's so unlike him. This is my *father* I'm talking about. The guy who put me on a pony and jogged at my side throughout the entire mile-long trail ride when I was nine. The guy who transformed his basement gym into a strobe-lit slumber party tent when I was twelve.

That guy couldn't have done even a tenth of the things crossing my mind now. Could he? But it seems Heather's been wiped off the face of the earth . . .

If only we knew what had happened to Mom, or to Trina, we might be able to piece together a scenario that might help us find Heather now.

But if Jane Doe Georgia isn't Trina Jordan, and even if she turns out to be my mother, I still won't know how she died because Eschermann *can't disclose*.

Then I have a flicker of an idea:

The first girl. Dad's college fiancée. She's confirmed dead. If I could learn what happened to her . . . even if the police ruled it an accident . . .

I click open the browser on my phone and search for *Lizzie Dawson accident.*

"What's going on out there?" Someone's banging on the back door of the Funky Nun—Kismet stirs—and Cassidy's voice carries in from the back foyer. "It's like Strawberry Fest all over again with the traffic and the cameras."

"You like strawberries?" says Zack, who's with her. "Dipped in chocolate?"

Brooke and I share a glance. We're about to shake her world to the very core, and Zack's talking aphrodisiacs.

"Cass . . ." I lead Kismet, already leashed, toward the back door where my sister is sitting on a stool, taking off her ridiculously high-heeled pumps. "Don't take off your shoes."

"We have to go." Brooke grabs her brother's elbow and attempts to steer him back out the door. "Cass, have you heard from your mom?"

Zack pulls away. "First you say we have to come here. Now, we can't stay? Do you know how hungry I am? We ordered a pizza."

"We have to go." I sniff over the threat of tears. "The police are bringing in a team of techs."

"What for?" Cassidy unbuckles the other shoe and slips it off her foot. "What do they think they're going to find here? It's not like Mom knows anything about this mess."

"She might," I say.

Cassidy gives me a dramatic roll of her eyes—"Doubtful"—and reaches for Zack's hand; he pulls her to her feet. "We ordered a deep dish pepperoni, and a small cheese for you, Sam."

"They have a warrant, and your mom . . ." I blink away tears. Hold it together. I can't just blurt it out. *Your mother is missing.* "Cass, listen. The jacket I wore the other night? It isn't a sample."

"I could've told you that. It was in the Goodwill box. My mom was going to give it away. She never does that with her samples."

Heather was going to give away the jacket? But why? If it had turned up after all these years and she truly had nothing to hide, would she have tried to lose it in a sea of donations at the Goodwill? Untraceable and lost to us forever?

"It matches a jacket Trina Jordan used to have."

"Trina Jordan?" Finally, Cassidy straightens. "Then why would my mother have it?"

"I don't know, but she did. And I wore it, and Eschermann saw it, and the whole thing sort of snowballed."

Something dark and unrecognizable passes over Cassidy's face. "Why'd you wear it in the first place?"

Before I can explain that I felt it was somehow connected to my mother and that it was her favorite color, she continues: "Unless you knew it looked like something that girl would've worn—"

"*What*?"

"—and you were trying to put my mom in the same sticky situation your dad always finds himself in! God, you are unbelievable, you know that? Whatever trouble your dad's in? He's in it on his own. Why do you think they separated? Because Mom can't handle the bullshit of it all!"

171

None of this matters right now, this blame game. What matters is finding Dad and Heather. *God, let her be all right.*

"I know how much this stresses you out!" A line forms between Cassidy's brows as she's screaming at me. "But if you were smart, instead of throwing Mom in front of a moving train you might think about saving her the trouble. I mean, where do you think you're going to go, when the cops finally pin all this on your dad?"

When she says it—*your* dad—her lips flatten to an angry line.

"And he's going to. That cop is determined to sink him on this."

I wipe tears on my sleeve. "Cassidy."

"I never used to believe anything people said either. What do they know, right? But you have to admit this stuff with this other girl . . ." She sighs and shakes her head. "It's too much coincidence not to have some element of truth in it. And it doesn't look good."

"Cass," I choke out through tears. "Heather never made it to the station for her two o'clock appointment."

"What?"

"Have you heard from her?"

"I've texted, but . . . she hasn't been texting back."

"If you don't know where she is, she's missing."

Her cheeks wash a tint whiter than they were a second ago. "What?" It comes out in a whisper. She goes sort of limp against Zack.

"She was supposed to meet with Lieutenant Eschermann. Her car is in the lot, but she never made it to the appointment. No one's seen her since she left here."

"Where's Dad?"

"I don't . . . Cass, I—"

"Where is he?" She's screaming again.

"They released him at the station." I take a deep breath and add, "Right before Heather got there. Her car is at the station."

She springs out of Zack's arms and lunges at me. "What did he do with my mother?"

I fall back against the wall—Kismet yelps in surprise—but only when Cassidy's hands meet my shoulders again do I realize she shoved me.

Brooke is instantly between us. "Stop it!"

"If you hadn't been defending him for so long, insisting he was innocent, maybe he wouldn't have been out there—"

"I know, I know." All I want to do is wrap Cassidy in a hug and remind her we're in this together, just like we've been in *everything* together for as long as we can remember. But she's looking at me as if I'm the devil's spawn.

And maybe I am, considering the missing—dead?—women in my father's wake.

"We have to find her," I say. "And we have to get back to the house. Eschermann's meeting us there. He'll help us find her."

"I'm not going anywhere with you." She's backing away from me now, treating me like a disease she'll catch if she gets too close.

Another consequence. In insisting on Dad's innocence, I've risked Cassidy's trust. How long has this been building, this rift between us, this suspicion on her side, without my noticing?

Brooke turns to her brother. "You and Cassidy go in the Jeep. I'll take Sami."

I tighten my grip on Kismet's leash and start toward the back door, toward the back alley where Brooke parked when she moved her car.

Cassidy grabs for the leash. "You're not taking my dog."

I yank back on the leash, maintaining possession. "No. I'm taking *our* dog. She can't stay here without Heather, and neither can you."

"Mom's coming back," Cassidy says. "She has to *come back*."

I understand. She wants to believe it will happen.

I used to believe my mom would come back, too.

||||| ||||| ||||| |||||

||

Now that word is spreading about the Jane Doe, news crews from even downstate are amassing, overtaking our little town. Well-dressed field reporters saunter down our sidewalks saying things like, *In a decade-old missing persons case, authorities may now have a lead. And that lead points to Northwestern University economics professor Christopher Lang.*

And they know where we live.

"It's like a circus over there," Brooke says as we near my street.

"Keep driving," I say. There are too many troops gathered in front of my house to brave parking in the driveway. "We'll park one block over."

I glimpse Gram's motor home in the driveway as we pass. I wonder if she might know where Dad and Heather are, even if she didn't admit it to Eschermann. And if she knows, maybe she'll tell me. If I'm pleasant and respectful toward her, maybe she'll treat me as an equal and talk *to* me instead of talking *at* me. If she's really here to help, as Dad claims, wouldn't she *want* to talk to me?

I reach out with a text: *Coming home from work. Talk soon?*

She doesn't instantly reply, but I'm not surprised. She

carries her phone in her purse, so she might not see my text for a while.

When we get out of the car, we hear a rhythmic *chop, chop, chop* of an ax hitting chunks of tree trunk and branch.

Brooke is texting her brother, warning him to park around the block and walk through Schmidt's yard when he and Cassidy get here.

I have Kismet by the leash, but she's still difficult to control in the midst of all the craziness—the splitting of wood, the murmur of voices coming from the street side of my property—so I sit on the ground with her, petting her, calming her down as best I can before we cut through the lawn to my house.

Ryan is in the side yard, near the bonfire pit, chopping hickory branches on a stump. He balances a hunk of lumber, swings the ax up and over, and brings it down hard, splitting the branch in two. Two more swings and hits, and the branch is quartered. He sweeps the pieces off the stump and repeats the process with another section of tree, then begins to gather the remnants in a wheelbarrow.

As he's rolling the wood away, he catches my glance. "Hey." He lowers the wheelbarrow and wipes his hand over his forehead. "Did you want to see those pictures?"

Oh. The pictures.

Of my mother.

With everything else going on . . . well, it's not like I forgot, but . . .

"Are you all right?" he asks.

"Not really."

"There's a lot going on right now," Brooke tells him. "Maybe now's not the best time—"

"No," I interject. "I want to see the pictures."

"That lieutenant is coming," Brooke says.

"Why don't I meet you at Sami's, then?" Ryan suggests. "Give me a minute to get cleaned up, and I'll stop by."

Kismet lets out a ferocious growl, followed by a few angry barks. She yanks on her leash.

"Kissy!" I yank back.

The dog is straining toward the house, where an invasive news crew is inching farther and farther up my driveway. I glance back at Ryan. "We'd better go in. See you in a few minutes."

We won't be able to go in through the front door without being in direct view of some of those cameras. We'll have to cut through the carriage house and into the breezeway.

"Samantha!"

Stupidly, I turn toward the sound of my name, only to be blinded by the spotlight of a camera.

I quicken my pace.

Soon I'm power-housing toward the carriage house door: painted lavender against the slate gray of the building, with a small window divided into three narrow panes at the very top.

I lead Brooke and Kismet inside and close the door behind me with a soft click.

It's dark in here. I hate it.

After a glance at the door in the floor—still there, still shut—I reach for the wall to guide me to the breezeway.

The voices of the reporters on the driveway and on the street in front of the house are muted, but I know they're still there, homing in on us.

I hustle us through the breezeway and into the house. In the kitchen, I pause.

A paper cup with a bend-straw and lid sits atop the island.

The Madelaine Café's logo is plastered to the side of the cup, and there's lipstick on the straw. A shimmery pink.

"Sam?" says Brooke. "You okay?"

I point to the straw. "That's Heather's signature lip color. She was here."

"Maybe it's someone else's drink."

"Whose? It's not mine, and no one else lives here."

"Your grandmother's, maybe?"

"She doesn't wear lipstick. At least not that shade."

And if the cup is Heather's, it means she didn't go directly to the police station. She stopped here first. The last place Mom was seen? Here. The last place Heather was known to be, now that we've found her cup in the kitchen? Here.

Mom's car disappeared with her.

Heather's car is at the station. But no one saw her there. And anyone with a license and keys can drive a car and park it wherever he wants to.

Kismet whines, perhaps sensing how tense I am.

Trina Jordan went missing. So did her dog.

If Heather took off of her own volition, she would've taken Cassidy with her, even if she didn't take Kismet.

And the same is true for my mother. She wouldn't have left me. I know that now. I was supposed to go live with her in Georgia.

Heather has information. About the jacket. About the creepy things I drew as a kid. About whatever else she's been hiding about what happened the day Mom disappeared. And she had an *appointment* at the station to disclose it all. It's not like the other times, when Eschermann called her in. She chose to go.

And come to think of it, even if Dad really thought Mom must've taken me with her *for good*, wouldn't he have called the police anyway? Immediately? Her leaving with me wasn't the plan. There was supposed to be a babysitter. Mom was supposed to have gone to Atlanta, scouted out a home for us, and come back for me.

See you Wednesday, Samantha-girl.

She *did* say good-bye. She wouldn't have left me alone to wander to Schmidt's place. She thought she was leaving me in good hands.

And whoever she left me with knows what happened to me that day . . . and likely what happened to Mom.

"I can't handle this." I pace the kitchen. "I mean . . . what more can possibly happen today? Heather being gone is one thing. But now, having evidence that she was *here* before she disappeared? How much more am I supposed to handle?"

"As much as you have to." Brooke grabs my wrist.

I stop moving for a second.

"You're asking *why you*?" Brooke continues. "Well, why *not* you? You don't want to be special, don't want to be singled out. Well, if nothing bad ever happened to you, *that* would single you out."

I guess that makes sense. But I still feel as if an abundance of bad has happened to me. When do I meet my quota?

"We'll get you through this," she says. "However bad it gets."

"And I'm just supposed to sit here and wait for everything to work itself out?" A breath later, I know what to do. "You know what? My dad has secrets. He has this ex-wife, this ex-fiancée . . . Hell, he won't even tell me why he and Heather are getting a divorce! We know he has secrets."

Brooke's subtle nod proves she's at least willing to see where I go with this.

"So why the hell am I honoring his privacy?"

She follows me through the house and down the stairs to the basement, where Dad's private lair is located. I pass his free weights and punching bag and head to the room Dad uses when he's working and needs to spread out. I click the switch on his desktop monitor, and it flickers to life.

"He'll have it protected by password." Brooke takes a seat in Dad's swivel chair.

"So we'll try everything we can think of." I pull books from his shelves. Mom hid a nearly-complete manuscript between the pages of books. Who knows what I might find here, in Dad's library?

"Sam, he didn't shut it down."

It seems like forever ago, but I remember he left in a hurry this morning. I took a walk with Lieutenant Eschermann; Dad must've come in here before his workout. Then I came back, and he left for the station.

"Or maybe Heather was in here." Brooke clicks on his browser history.

Would Heather have known his password? Maybe. Maybe not. But it makes more sense that she would've left the computer on, not Dad.

"Search Lizzie Dawson." I shove one book back onto a shelf and pull another down and begin to leaf through it.

"Wow," Brooke says. "Lizzie Dawson comes up in his search history."

I'm looking over her shoulder now at countless social media profiles of women of all ages named Lizzie Dawson, Elizabeth Dawson, Libby Dawson. None of them looks dead.

I take over the keyboard and search "Elizabeth Dawson accident."

Nothing overwhelmingly helpful hits on that cue, either.

But either Dad or Heather was recently searching for information about Lizzie.

"It was before we were born," Brooke says. "Maybe none of the articles are digitized. Let's try his name too."

The back doorbell chimes.

Ryan is here with the pictures he found.

"Get the door," she says. "I'll let you know . . ."

But as I walk out, I catch a glimpse of a long list of search results with an old headline at the top: *Local Student on Trial for Vehicular Homicide.*

‖‖ ‖‖ ‖‖ ‖‖
‖‖

"Here we go." Ryan hands over a shoe box; it's heavier than I expect, labeled with a hastily scrawled *D*. I set it on the table in front of me and lift the lid. Suddenly I'm nervous and excited and scared all at the same time.

My mother is staring up at me.

Slowly I sift through the piles of snapshots, the scenes coming alive in my mind.

As the years have stretched like miles between us, I've allowed her to become more and more a mix of indistinct memories, but as I hold these mementos in my hands, vivid recollections return to me in a sweep of emotion:

I smell the marshmallows and hot dogs on the bonfire.

I hear the far-off echo of Def Leppard coming from Schmidt's speakers.

I feel the nip of cool night air at my cheeks and the warmth of the fire emanating from the stone ring in the middle of the flagstone patio.

And I see my mother laughing, her skin glowing a russet orange, reflecting the fire. Her eyes, blue like mine. Bright, vibrant. Her hands on my cold cheeks: *Do you know what you are, Samantha-girl? You're the best part of my life.*

I blink away tears. For a moment, she was here. One blink, and she's gone again.

I can't rewind time. Can't hold her any more tightly than I did at that moment. But as I sift through the photographs in the box, glimpses of her come back to me:

Mom on the beach, smelling of coconut oil and sun.

Mom setting a picnic lunch in the backyard, just because.

Mom with a box of homemade cookies. *Happy Valentine's Day.*

Mom reading a book, her glasses perched on the end of her nose, as she's lazing on a chair in Schmidt's library.

I look down at the memories I've recovered. Snapshots of Mom's calming yet somehow contagious smile scatter over the table.

"There are hundreds of them."

"Yes."

"Where did you get these?"

"Attic. I was talking to my uncle, and he said—"

"Why does your uncle have so many pictures of my mother?"

He nibbles on his lower lip for a second, and his brow crinkles up. "I talked to him earlier, and he hinted that he knew her well. Better than anyone, maybe."

I don't remember Mom and Schmidt being close enough for him to take this many pictures, and I don't know if that's because I was too young to understand or because there was no relationship to understand, period. What if it was all in Schmidt's head? What if Mom was being neighborly, and Schmidt assumed they were something more?

I focus on the picture of Mom in Schmidt's library. She isn't looking at the camera. She's intently focused on the pages in her hands. It's almost as if Schmidt was enthralled with her image, as if he wanted to preserve the way she looked at that moment.

It wasn't as if she was dancing, or singing, or modeling an outfit. It wasn't a special occasion, like Christmas or a birthday. Why else would Schmidt capture this moment, of all moments, on film? What about my mother in this pose spoke to him? I can't understand it, unless . . .

"Your uncle was in love with my mother."

Ryan shrugs. "I don't know about *that*, but—"

"Look at the sheer volume of these pictures, Ryan." My voice cracks with either frustration or determination, or maybe a little bit of both. "My father doesn't have this many. *I* don't have this many. Your uncle says he knew her well. But what does that mean? Were they sleeping together?"

"Sami." Brooke calls up from Dad's den, where she's still on Lizzie duty.

I focus on Ryan: "Tell me what you know."

"I just know what I picked up on when we spoke, and it sounded like—I don't know—like she *mattered* to him."

"More to him than he mattered to her?" I ask.

"Maybe."

I take more pictures from the box. Mom on the Lakefront Walk. Mom under the hickory trees. Mom beneath the sunflowers.

Is it possible, if Schmidt loved my mother and she didn't love him back, that he wouldn't have wanted her to leave?

Maybe he tried to stop her from going.

Where was I when Mom was gone?

Henry Schmidt's place.

And where did I think Mom had gone?

Henry Schmidt's place.

And where had the dogs alerted?

Behind Schmidt's barn.

Is it possible Mom and I went to Schmidt's so she could say good-bye, and Ryan and I started playing, and something happened? An accident, maybe. He didn't mean to hurt her, but he did. Or maybe it was calculated murder.

I was gone for hours before Schmidt walked me back home. I was afraid of him.

Maybe I was afraid because Schmidt yelled at Ryan and me for playing in the passageway, like Ryan says.

Or maybe I was afraid of something I'd *seen* in the passageway. The dark passageway that used to haunt my dreams when I was little. The passageway I pushed out of my mind eventually until I forgot I had even been there with Ryan.

"I used to think she was there, at Schmidt's place, hiding in one of the rooms. I thought maybe she'd gone there through the secret tunnel that connects the house to our carriage house," I say.

"Mm-hmm." Ryan keeps his gaze pinned to me.

"And we were in there the day she disappeared." I narrow my eyes at Ryan. "I have no recollection of how that happened." I know Eschermann thinks I've repressed things. That's why he wants me to be hypnotized, but Dad won't let him. Maybe because Dad doesn't want me to be traumatized. Maybe because he doesn't want me to remember something that will implicate him.

But for now, I'm focusing on Schmidt, not my father.

"I'll ask him about it—*you* could ask, if you want—when he gets home," Ryan says.

For a second or two, I'm frozen with the possibility of having a conversation with the man who might be responsible for my mother's disappearance. As I'm grappling with this, Brooke enters the kitchen, her eyes wide. I know immediately that whatever she learned from her Internet research won't make me feel any better.

I turn back to Ryan. "When does your uncle get home?"

"Tomorrow. Maybe the next day."

"I thought he was coming home early."

"He is. But it takes a while to drive from Florida."

"He drives all the way to Florida?" Brooke asks.

"Uncle Henry won't fly."

New information my brain has to process:

Would someone take a detour through Georgia—perhaps to bury a body—on the way to Florida?

When I close my eyes, I see stick figures with *x*ed out eyes, hearts—or lockets?— and a smaller figure in the distance, sad.

Was I trying to draw something I'd seen but forgotten?

Schmidt.

Heather.

Dad.

Who holds the key to the secret I desperately need to unlock?

But if it's Schmidt, why are Dad and Heather gone now?

And while ties abound between Dad and Heather and Trina Jordan, there are no ties between my father's first ex-wife and Schmidt. He couldn't have had anything to do with Trina Jordan's disappearance . . . could he?

Are these pictures of Mom pieces of this puzzle? Or are they just photographs of a woman loved by a man?

I pick up another stack of photos and look at them one at a time. In each, she looks comfortable. Happy. Not like someone who feels threatened. Still, I'm unnerved by the number of them and by the fact that some of them appear to be candid, as if he'd taken them without her knowing.

And then I see it at the bottom of the box, peeking up at me from beneath pictures of my mother in various states of contentment: a road map.

I pull it from the box and unfold it on the island.

It's a map of the United States, and certain towns are marked with tiny green asterisks. I know this map. It's an exact replica of the one I see in my mind whenever I'm anxious. It's the map that calms me down.

"This map." I can't formulate words beyond these two. But a misty memory flutters in:

Mom and me, sitting at a table with this map spread out in front of us.

And I feel her here, my mother, as if it hasn't been a decade since she last stood in this house.

"Sami?" Brooke says. "Did you hear me?"

Although I haven't heard a word she's said, I'm nodding because I *am* listening . . . to the memory.

Mom: *One more and we would've been lucky.*

I look to the markings on the map, count them—seven total. There's a map spread on the table, and she's marking it with a thick green marker. All the places we're going to stop to picnic amidst the sunflowers along the way.

Along the way to Georgia.

I brush my finger over the mark at a small town at the outskirts of Atlanta. This town had been our destination. There were only six stops until she marked this one. Six isn't lucky.

Well, I guess we're going to have to add another stop to make it lucky.

Unless Atlanta counts.

Yes, yes. Atlanta counts. Our final stop. Seven places total, seven places we've never been together, but seven places we'll see.

And we'd wanted to see every town on the whole map together.

"She was supposed to take me with her," I say. It was supposed to be a journey shared with me. Dad had me for a long weekend while Mom found a place for us to live in Atlanta, and after that, Mom and I were leaving. For good.

How different would my life have been, if she'd made it back for me?

I circle Atlanta again with the pad of my finger.

There's a body near this town. It was in the ground. And then in the morgue. And now, my blood samples might prove that Mom got to where she wanted to go, one way or another.

The letters of recommendation and job applications—in Schmidt's house. And now the map and these pictures.

"Why does your uncle have this map?"

Ryan looks at me with serious eyes. "I don't know. I can call him right now. You want me to call him?"

A thread of fear weaves into my system. The thought of speaking to him when I'm wondering if he might've dumped my mother's body . . .

But Ryan's already dialing.

"Hey, Uncle," he says, casual as can be. "I found the box of pictures you told me about."

Brooke and I look at each other. Ryan had been *looking* for them? Schmidt *told* him to look for the pictures?

"Yeah, yeah. There's a map in the box. I'm here with Samantha, and she has some questions about it. I'm going to put you on speaker."

I grip Brooke's hand. I'm about to talk to the man I've

been avoiding for ten years. The man who publicly accused my father of killing my mother.

Ryan puts his phone on the countertop. "Uncle Henry?"

"I can hear you," comes a voice from the speaker. "Samantha Mary?"

I soften a little. Mom sometimes called me by my first and middle names. "Hi."

The background noises tell me he's driving. "You have some questions?"

As suspicious as I was three minutes ago, I figured I'd fly at him with guns blazing, but his patience, his tone . . . "Mr. Schmidt." I swallow over uncertainty.

"You can call me Henry. You're not a little girl anymore."

"Henry?"

"Yes."

"You have a lot of pictures of my mother."

"Yes."

"Why?"

"I was in a photography class at the college where she taught."

"Oh . . ."

"I used to take pictures of my gardens. She suggested I take the class, and she was a willing subject for portraits. There should be quite a few pictures of you in that box, too."

I'm looking through another stack. There *are* some pictures of me . . . me and Mom.

"I'd like to keep a few of them," he says. "But you're welcome to keep some of your favorites too."

"Thank you."

"Of course."

"There's also—there's a map in this box."

"Yes."

"How did you get it?"

"She left it at my house."

"The police might want to see it."

"The police *have* seen it. I turned it over to them ten years ago, and they returned it after they looked through it. I've been holding onto it, thinking you might want it someday, but you've been pretty distant until now."

"Why did she have the map at your house?"

He doesn't really answer the question: "We used to spend a lot of time together. You, your mom, and me."

Ryan clears his throat.

"And Ryan," Schmidt adds. "When he was in town."

I suppose she must have left things at his place from time to time. I sink into the memory again, counting destinations on the map. Eating chocolate-covered grahams.

"Seven stops," I whisper. "Eleven, seven."

"Your mother's lucky numbers," Schmidt says.

"Yes."

"It's a biblical verse," Schmidt says. "Ecclesiastes, chapter eleven, verse seven."

Brooke already has her tablet out and Bible app up.

"My mother read the *Bible*?" For the most part, I've grown up without religion. I don't recall ever setting foot inside a church.

"Your mother read *everything*."

Brooke pushes the tablet in front of me. I read the verse:

"Oh, how sweet the light of day, And how wonderful to live in the sunshine! Even if you live a long time, don't take a single day for granted. Take delight in each light-filled hour, Remembering there will be many dark days."

It's my mother's philosophy.

I rewind time to the day Mom and I were sitting at the worktable in Schmidt's kitchen. *Seven stops is lucky.* Apparently, that luck didn't serve her well.

If she had actually gone to Georgia, she would've taken her map. Just as she would've taken her job application materials. Just as she would've taken me.

"Were you . . . you know . . . Were you involved with my mother?"

After a long, drawn-out sigh, he says, "Things weren't good, Samantha, between your parents." Again, he didn't quite answer my question.

"Because of my father's affair."

"So you know about that."

"Dad told me. And I found a picture of him with another woman before they were divorced."

"Your mom needed a friend. She'd left her life behind in Georgia, her parents had been gone a long time . . . She needed refuge, somewhere to go when things were tough."

"I used to think, right after she disappeared, that she was hiding at your house," I say. "I was so sure that she'd come out of your house one day."

"Well, she stayed there a few times after your parents' divorce was final, when they were sharing the house. He'd drop in to see you, and she'd drop in to see me."

I wonder, again, if she chose to stay there because he was a friend, or because he was more to her. He seems like a nice guy. Nothing like the ogre my father insists he was. Could my mother have found a companion in him? "She was planning a trip to Georgia."

"Yes."

"To get ready for a move there."

"That's right. But she'd promised to come back every fall."

"For the bonfires."

"You remember the bonfires." He chuckles.

Of course I do. Lately it's hard to forget those things. "She was going to take me with her?"

After a long pause, he says, "That's how I know something happened to her. She was gone, but you were here."

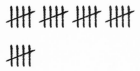

After Ryan leaves, I go back to Dad's office and read the article Brooke found.

Lizzie Dawson's car was run off the road by a larger vehicle. She and her fiancé—my dad—had just had an argument. Dad later admitted as much in court, when he was tried for vehicular homicide.

He was acquitted due to lack of evidence.

This is too much to take in. He was tried but acquitted. For lack of evidence. That makes it sound like there could have been evidence if they'd only found it, not that he was actually innocent.

I tell Brooke to go home. I just desperately want to be alone.

////

When Lieutenant Eschermann finally arrives, Cassidy is his reluctant companion. The tension between us is as thick as morning fog on Echo Lake, and to make matters worse, Gram joins us too.

Kismet alternates lying at my feet and Cassidy's, as if proving her loyalty to each of us spans beyond the issue now dividing us.

The one positive development is that Eschermann's team has managed to keep the news crews off the lawn and off the street, so they're a safe distance from the house now.

Eschermann tells us, "We reviewed security cameras at the station. Heather got into Chris's car willingly, but I can't prove she stayed willingly."

I can't bear to look at Cassidy. "My dad's in enough trouble, right?" I say. "So why would he take Heather?"

Eschermann sighs. "Let me tell you something about crime. There's an element of panic in being found out, and when that threat is imminent, even the most rational criminals risk getting in deeper, if it means evading consequence." Even though Gram and Cassidy are both in the room, I feel like he's talking just to me. "Whoever pulled off the disappearance of Delilah Lang is smart. After all these years, do you think he's going to take a pass on protecting himself? Say if someone knows something and she's about to disclose, do you think he's going to let her walk into the station?"

I take a deep breath, wait for the towns to pop up on the map in my mind, watch the roads connect into perfect little triangles.

Eschermann leaves us to our own devices while he coordinates with his team. Gram gets busy in the kitchen, kneading something that looks like dough, but she's not the type to be making bread.

Cass and I sit on opposite ends of the living room.

I'm looking through the photo albums, continuing the search for a picture of someone in the yellow jacket I wore.

So far, I haven't found anything as intriguing as Mom's manuscript, which interrupted the search for the picture the first time around.

"I'm not here because I want to be, you know." Cassidy speaks in a low voice, I assume so Gram can't hear. "I'm here because I don't have a choice. Eschermann doesn't want me at the apartment alone, and there was no chance in hell he was going to let me go to Zack and Brooke's for the night."

"Okay." I study pictures of Dad and Heather. Me and Cassidy as little kids. We were fast friends, instant sisters, even if it did take our parents an age and a half to tie the knot. But she may as well be a stranger to me now.

Silence falls between us for a spell—a dark, brooding awkwardness that chews at the air—until she speaks again: "While we were waiting for the evidence team at the Nun, I started reading your mom's manuscript."

I busy myself with straightening a photo that's loosened from its adhesive, just so I can avoid looking at her.

"I know what you're thinking: that she was writing about my mom. But Mom had nothing to do with it."

"Okay."

"Don't you want to know how I know?" She leans a bit closer. "Because that's *not my mother* in the picture we found. If you look at it closely, you'll see the hair is curlier."

I suppose she's forgotten the curling iron wasn't invented yesterday.

"And the mini-dress," Cass says. "Mom's not a fan of the empire waistline. High-waisted miniskirt? Sure. With the right top. But a dress like that does little to accentuate the female form. Mom wouldn't have worn it."

"It was so long ago. She might've worn it back then." Although in all the pictures I'm now perusing, Heather's style has remained pretty constant.

"Please. Fashion sense is fashion sense."

I could tell her—again—that Dad admitted their affair and Heather didn't deny it, but where would that get me at this point?

"Whoever that woman was," Cassidy continues, "she's your key. She's the reason your dad did whatever it was he did to your mom. And my theory? He was cheating on *my* mom too. Why else would they suddenly split, after they stuck it out for so long? Why else wouldn't they tell us what happened between them?" She takes a deep breath, stuttering over budding tears. "And now history's repeating itself."

"Cass." I bite on my lip for a second in deliberation. Will anything I say satisfy her? "Dad *loves* Heather. He just said it the other day."

"Well, maybe love is making him do irrational things. How many women are we talking about now, Sam? How many times does this have to happen before—"

"Stop!" It's more of a hiss than a word. "Do you think it's coincidental that my mother wrote about a mistress plotting to get rid of a wife—when Dad admitted to me that he and Heather were together before my mom filed for divorce? And before she finished the book, to tell us how it all turned out, she disappeared?"

"Are you blaming my mother for whatever happened to yours?" She's shaking her head at me, a look of disdain crossed with disbelief on her face.

"I'm not blaming anyone. I'm saying Heather knows something."

"And he's trying to shut her up. And you can't even acknowledge—"

"Cass, you're right, okay?" I pause. "If I had to blame any-one . . ." I reach for her across the cocktail table—she has to listen—but she pulls away when my fingers graze her elbow.

197

"Cass, if I had to point my finger at anyone right now, it'd have to be Dad."

I match Cassidy's stare, second-for-second. *See me*, I pray. *See me instead of Dad. We're sisters. Divorce or no divorce. Sisters, no matter what.*

"I don't want to believe it, but I *do* see, Cassidy. I *do* see that there's a lot of evidence now. A lot to suggest I've been living a lie—that *he's* been living a lie—and that, postcards notwithstanding, my mother is *never coming back*. Heather's the only mother I have now. I'm going to do whatever I can to help find her. But it won't help to jump to conclusions."

I take the next photo book off the table and start to look through that one.

Wait.

I look more closely at a photo. It's Dad, holding a newborn baby.

But the date at the top of the page . . . I wasn't born for another four months.

That baby isn't me, but her hat is familiar.

I open the second locket strung about my ankle and compare the pictures. The same frilly hat appears in both.

I peel the picture from the page and look at the back of it. C & C is written on the back. Chris and Cassidy?

"Cass?"

Just as she looks up, Eschermann and Neilla come in from the back porch, where they'd been talking. I can tell by the way he's looking at me: he has bad news to share.

My throat constricts, and my gut tumbles.

Gram sees the cops from the kitchen doorway and rushes into the living room to hear what they have to say. I glance at Cassidy, and for an instant, it feels as if we're on the same team again.

"We found Chris's car down Cuba Road," Eschermann says without preamble. "Way past Route 12. He's been in an accident."

"Dear Jesus." Gram brings her hands immediately to her heart. "What happened?"

"No witnesses to speak of, so we can't be sure. But it looks like he lost control and ran off the road."

Ran off the road. I just read those words in the article Brooke found about Lizzie Dawson.

"Is he all right?" Gram demands.

"He wasn't at the scene, ma'am. We're combing the records of area hospitals to see if he might've been brought in."

"But he wasn't in the car." My relief at knowing he probably walked away from the accident is quickly replaced with fear that once he's found, he's going to be facing some difficult accusations and hard-to-ignore evidence. I wonder if he's coming home at all, in that case, or if he'll go straight from the hospital to a jail cell.

Eschermann turns to my sister. "Cassidy?"

She looks up when the lieutenant says her name.

"Can you identify this item?" Eschermann is walking toward her, holding out his phone, which she takes.

As soon as she looks at the image on the screen, she starts sobbing. "My mom's keys."

I perk up. This is good news. A clue to finding Heather!

"Where did you find them?" Cassidy asks. "Did you find them in Dad's car?"

"Thank you, Cassidy," Neilla says.

"Did you find them in Dad's car?" Cassidy screams again.

Eschermann presses his lips together and sort of looks away before he answers with a staccato nod and a clipped "Yes."

Dad and Heather are definitely together. Normally, this might comfort the daughters of a missing couple, but it only fills me with dread.

"But she wasn't there?" Cassidy asks. "The car was wrecked, but she wasn't there either?"

"The responding officers found her purse in the brush not far from the wreck. It must have been thrown from the car. Her cell phone was in the purse."

Neilla says, "The last call of record from Ms. Solomon's phone was to 911 around twenty after two. The call disconnected before the dispatcher could get the nature of the emergency."

So she could've been calling to report the accident, but she also could've been calling because she realized my father was taking her out of town.

I imagine Heather's walking up the steps at the police station. Dad calls her over to talk. She's there early; she has time. She makes the mistake of sitting in the car. Dad suggests they drive around the block. Then he takes her away, on the road. He wants her to refuse to tell Ken Eschermann what she knows. She refuses and wants to go back to the station. But he's in the driver's seat and won't stop the car. She calls for help, but Dad terminates the call. They struggle over the phone, causing the accident.

Is that something my father could've done?

Eschermann lifts his chin, beckoning me.

I go over, look at his phone. I nod to confirm that Cassidy is right. Those are Heather's keys. But I see something in the periphery of the frame my stepsister did not. A bottle cap, labeled with a brand of vodka. When I look up at him, Eschermann gives me a knowing glance. He saw it too.

Dad was drinking.

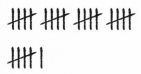

Cassidy curls up on the sofa. She hasn't stopped crying, and fittingly enough, Neilla is babysitting her. Maybe she'll cry herself to sleep, which would save me the daggers she's been shooting in my direction, but it'll also leave me alone with my grandmother and the police to weather the storm that's sure to rage on throughout the course of the night.

Lieutenant Eschermann and I move downstairs to Dad's office for one of our famous chats, which usually entails his trying to convince me of something, my denying it and calling it coincidence, and neither of us knowing anything more than we knew before the conversation began.

Gram follows us into the office and stands in the doorway with her arms crossed, listening as Eschermann and I talk.

"Henry Schmidt is right," Eschermann says. "He *had* turned those pictures over to us. And the map. Just like he said. She'd planned her route at his place."

"But why did she leave it behind, then? She would have needed a map to get where she was going."

"There's no way to know she didn't pick one up during her travels. Or maybe she had a photographic memory and a good sense of direction."

These are the kinds of explanations I would've spun out if you'd presented me with the scenario a week ago. But now, I can't take comfort in them. Too many variables. We can't draw a conclusion.

"So Schmidt wasn't hiding anything," I say.

"No," Eschermann says.

"I don't think we can be so sure," Gram interjects. "Those pictures—they're the mark of a man obsessed. And Samantha had been at his house the day her mother left."

"If we knew who Chris had hired to babysit her that day," Eschermann says, "we might know why Sam was at Schmidt's place, but it's only coincidence until I can prove otherwise."

"And you think his explanation makes sense," I say. "The photography course."

"It checked out ten years ago. He enrolled in a photography night class at the community college the semester before your mother left."

So he's just a guy who liked to take pictures. And my mom was his friend, so he took her picture.

"You can keep the pictures," Eschermann says. "Or return them to Mr. Schmidt."

"Actually . . . I know you have a lot to do, but maybe you could look through them one more time? Or maybe Neilla can? There are just so many . . ."

"It would make you feel better?"

I don't know if I can feel better until all of this is over. "Just to make sure we're not overlooking something. Like maybe we'll find one of my mom in the yellow jacket."

"Sure, Sam."

After another pause and a glance at my grandmother, I say, "I want you to know that I understand the obvious conclusion here," I say. "That in all likelihood, my father is somehow mixed up in all of this."

"Samantha!" Gram half-whispers, half-hisses my name.

Eschermann looks almost sad to hear me say it. I thought he'd be relieved finally to have me on board.

"You should be ashamed of yourself," Gram says. "I've never seen such a show of disrespect, such—"

"I don't want to believe it either, Gram! But Heather's gone, and considering what happened to all the other women Dad was involved with, we have to face the truth."

"You don't know the truth."

"Nor does anyone," Eschermann cuts us off. "Yet." He takes a deep breath and looks at me, not at Gram. "But we're getting closer, and that might mean dealing with some difficult realities. I'm here for you, Samantha. And Neilla is here for you. And the whole town is going to be here for you."

"My sister won't be." I glance up at the ceiling. I can still hear Cass crying in the living room above us. "If anything happens to Heather, I'll have no one."

"You'll have me," Gram says.

I snort. "I'll have you whenever you inconvenience yourself long enough to stop in and try to take over our lives. Why are you even here? Why do you show up at these random times and make everything worse?"

"I come when things are about to get ugly. I'm here to help, and in case you haven't noticed, young lady, I'm the only one—"

"You get wasted every night! How is that helping?"

"I do not get—"

"And you want me to do whatever you tell me to, you want me to forget my mother, you want me to excuse what Dad might have done! And I can't do that anymore!"

Eschermann cuts in: "Sam."

I turn to the lieutenant. "I defended him. I refused to believe what you were saying—what *everyone* said—and now it might be too late. Heather's gone now, and—"

"Samantha!" Gram shouts. "You shut your mouth!"

"Okay, enough." Eschermann is between us now, holding a pressed hand out to each of us, like a cop directing traffic. "Gramercy, can you give us a minute?"

With a huff, Gram stomps up the stairs.

Eschermann, once he's certain she's out of earshot, turns to me. "You do realize this isn't your fault, right? Whatever your dad may have done—"

"But I believed in him. And she's not coming back," I say. I don't even know which mother I'm talking about: Delilah? Or Heather? Or both? "How can I forgive myself, if she never comes back?"

"Sam. You've been doing what's natural. A little girl is supposed to believe in her father. You need to let yourself off the hook."

The only way that'll happen is if Heather's okay. There's nothing I can do about Mom, but if Heather doesn't come home . . .

"I'm going to find out what happened," Eschermann tells me, "I promise you. And however it turns out, we'll get you through it."

"Is there anything else I can do to help? Anything?"

"Now that you mention it," he says, "we found something else at the scene where your father's car was, in the brush."

What now?

"A postcard from Gatlinburg, Tennessee."

A postcard? A shot of adrenaline darts through me, carrying with it a renewed sense of hope. Quickly, though, I push past the hope and land on confusion. If my mother isn't coming back, she isn't sending the postcards. So that means someone at the scene of the accident was planning to send it on Mom's behalf—Dad or Heather.

"It's addressed to you with the same typed labels as all the others." He flips through images on his phone and then turns it toward me for a look: *11/7* is written in the message portion.

I meet Eschermann's stare.

"It's stamped," he says, "but not cancelled. It was never mailed, Sam."

"So someone local had it here?"

And it was found near Heather's purse. Thrown from Dad's car.

"There's a good thumbprint on this one. We'll run it through the system, of course, but as you know, that takes time. Did Heather mention anything before she left the shop? Anything of interest? Anything out of the ordinary? Was she, maybe, planning to go to the post office?"

He's implying Heather has been sending the postcards all along. And if she's sending postcards, it means she knows Mom can't.

"No," I tell him. "If she had somewhere else to go, other than the station, she didn't say. She didn't even say anything about coming here first, but considering the cup, obviously she did."

"Have you noticed anything missing? Something Heather left when she moved out and has been meaning to pick up, maybe?"

It could be anything. "Photo albums, maybe. But that wouldn't be so urgent that she had to stop on the way before seeing you, and anyhow, if that's what she came for, she left them here."

I take a deep breath. "Heather did say something. She said my father's college girlfriend died in a car accident. And Brooke found an article online. My dad was tried for vehicular homicide."

Eschermann nods. "He was acquitted."

"Only because of lack of evidence." I feel my eyes glazing over with another scenario: Dad and Lizzie argued. She left in a hurry. He followed her, but she refused to stop to talk to him. Things got out of hand . . .

"No one could prove that the car tailing Lizzie was actually your father's car. He had an alibi. One witness said it was a woman driving the car."

A woman.

"No matter who was in that other vehicle, Sami, the road conditions were to blame. They get an inch of snow down south and the whole state shuts down. That ice storm would've made driving rough. And Lizzie Dawson, with little experience driving in such a storm, was going too fast. It's unrelated to the other cases involving your dad. Trust me. I've studied the file to exhaustion." Eschermann palms the back of his neck, and his eyes are veined with faint red lines. I wonder if he's slept since Jane Doe Georgia blipped on his radar. "She wasn't the only one to die on the road that day. Terrible weather conditions, curvy roads. Recipe for disaster."

"But is it too much of a coincidence?"

There's irony in our sudden role reversal. Usually, I'm the one presenting possible scenarios of my father's innocence while Eschermann is trying to make me realize I'm being naive. Now, I think he's blind not to see what I'm driving at.

An uneasy feeling flips in my stomach. All these women, missing or dead. "I just think—Lizzie Dawson was the first. Maybe she sets a pattern."

"A jury didn't convict him," Eschermann says, as if he can read my mind and knows it needs easing. "You need to let it go."

But my father went through quite an ordeal to prove he hadn't caused Lizzie's accident. And no one thought to ask Heather about any motive she might've had to kill my father's first fiancée. "If Heather loved my dad back then, she could've followed Lizzie in Dad's car. She could've scared Lizzie into driving too fast. And maybe something similar happened with Trina, with my mom."

"Sam, you don't have to do my job."

"I don't mean to. I just want to help."

"And I appreciate it. But you can leave it in my hands. I'm going to take care of it."

"There's one more thing you should know about." I take the second locket off my ankle and hand it over. "Ryan found this in his uncle's yard. I thought it was Mom's."

Eschermann opens the locket.

"But I don't think the picture in this locket is Dad and me. I think it's Dad and Cassidy, which means this locket must be Heather's. We found it on the lawn—Heather could've dropped it when she came here earlier. And the photo means that Dad's been involved in Cassidy's life since she was a baby—way longer than I realized. What if Heather was jealous of my mom all along? And what if—she had something to do with what happened to Mom? If I saw something that might incriminate her, it would make sense that she's been hiding my drawings."

"Maybe." He's nodding. "But why keep them all this time, Sam? If she saw them as evidence of something she wanted to hide, she would've thrown them away by now. And looking at it from the other angle, if she thought your father was behind Delilah's disappearance, she wouldn't have let him around her daughter. She wouldn't have married him."

I suppose he's right.

"Sami, I spoke with a child psychologist. A few, actually. There's no definitive evidence that there's always a correlation between a kid's drawings and what a kid has seen. It's an inexact science, so anything a shrink might tell us about why you drew what you drew would be speculation. If we'd interviewed you while you were drawing, maybe it would've helped. But as it is, those drawings can't be used as a diagnostic tool."

"But the things I drew—"

"The only thing all three psychologists agree on is that the sad face on the smallest figure, as well as the distance you drew the child figure from the larger parent figure, denotes trouble and chaos at home. And we already know your life was chaotic at that time."

At the time? More like *all* the time.

"And you drew the parent with a big heart on the chest area, which showed that despite the chaos, there was love between you. But we already know that too."

"Then why did Heather keep the drawings at all?"

"That was something I'd hoped to ask her this afternoon."

Ominous shadows of the past dart in and out of my memories. Running through the sunflowers. Chasing me. But I'm lost, and when I come out from the flower bed, I can't find her. She's gone.

"I know you can't tell me everything, but Jane Doe Georgia . . ." I lower my voice. "Was there a locket found with her body?"

208

He narrows his eyes at me. "Why would you ask that?"

"My drawings. I think I drew a locket, not a heart. My mom never took it off." I scoot closer the box of pictures Ryan brought over earlier. "See for yourself. It would've been buried with her body. If there's a locket with the remains, we don't have to wait for the DNA results. We'll know."

But all Escherman says is that he can't tell me anything about the investigation while it's still ongoing. So it's yet another thing I can't get closure on. But do I want closure so badly that I'll risk hearing my mother is dead?

||||| ||||| ||||| |||||
||||| ||

Kismet lies in a big golden ball at my feet the moment I take a seat at the kitchen table.

"You need to eat." Gram places a medium-rare burger—it's bleeding into the bun—in front of Cassidy and a plate of sautéed vegetables in front of me.

It's a peace offering.

"I'm not hungry." Cassidy glances up at me, even though she must be talking to Gram.

"I know this is hard." Gram brings a basket of biscuits to the table. "But I'm sure those two are fine. They're at a hospital—they must be—and the police will find which one. When we know, we'll go to see them. I don't care if it's three in the morning, we'll go."

"Wouldn't we know by now?" Cassidy asks. "How long would it take for the cops to call all the area hospitals to see if they'd been admitted?"

I have to agree with her.

"Well, Heather's purse was thrown from the car. She didn't have her identification with her." Gram takes a seat at the table with us. "And for all we know, C.J.'s wallet got lost in the chaos too. It's possible they're unconscious and haven't been identified."

I barely register what she's saying. I get stuck on two syllables. *C.J.* It's Gram's nickname for Dad.

Whoever rented the box where the passport was delivered did so under the name C. J. Lang. I know Eschermann doesn't think Dad could've done it, but who, if not him? He couldn't have applied for the passport, that's true. But he could've rented the box.

Could Heather have applied for the passport? She has the same coloring as Mom, and after ten years, she could probably pass herself off as Delilah Lang. Could they be working together to cover up whatever unfortunate accident took place an eon ago? Maybe they know my mother is gone. Maybe Heather sends postcards to me out of guilt.

But neither of them has had time to go to Georgia, to apply for a passport, or to retrieve it from a box.

Say they *did* somehow get the passport. Could Heather travel as Mom? Officially get "Delilah Lang" out of the country? To Canada, maybe? Or Mexico? The authorities would then be looking elsewhere, not here. Heather could return by train, or bus, as Heather Solomon-Lang. Would she do that for Dad? To take the heat off him?

Gram continues. "Without identification, I'm sure they can't identify them right away. Especially if they're unconscious, and that's a possibility. The air bags deployed."

I ignore my grandmother, look at Cassidy.

"Dad is hiding my mom somewhere," Cassidy says. "He doesn't want her to tell what she knows."

"That's enough." Gram points a finger at Cassidy. "My son would never do such a thing. And you know that."

Now Cassidy's treating Gram to her stare of death. "I think he's already done it—and gotten away with it." She pushes her plate, with burger untouched, to the middle of the table. "And I'm not going to sit here and pretend it didn't happen. I'm going to bed."

"Maybe a little sleep will cool that attitude of yours," Gram snips. "Take a Tylenol PM."

Cassidy leaves the kitchen. I listen as she climbs seventeen stairs. Hear the creaking of the plank at the top of the stairs. One, two, three, four, five, six steps down the hallway. And the slam of her door.

"Your dad is fine." Gram does her best to smile at me, and clears Cassidy's plate. "Now eat something. You need strength."

"Gram?"

"What, honey?"

Honey. That's a new one from my grandmother, who mostly doesn't call me anything.

"You think Dad's innocent."

"I *know* he is."

I used to know, too.

"He's made mistakes, Samantha, but for the most part, he's just a man looking to be loved."

I push the vegetables around on my plate with my fork. "Do you think he was drinking today?"

"Absolutely not. He's survived some of the harshest accusations this world can throw at a man, and he's managed to do it without turning back to the bottle. That says something about his resolve."

"But if he's at the end of his rope . . ." I shrug a shoulder, leaving my accusation hanging in the air.

"Let me tell you something about the end of the rope. Do you remember the summer after your mother left? That detective was all over your father. Money was tight. Your father hired a lawyer and a private investigator, and he was hitting it pretty hard. Drinking a lot. So I came to stay for the summer."

The infamous summer in my memories, when I'd waited out a storm alone in Dad's basement den.

"One night we were watching television in the basement, and I followed your dad upstairs. He was in despair over not knowing what happened to your mother, over being the prime suspect in her disappearance. He was on the verge of ending it all."

I drop my fork. "What?"

"He had his keys in his hand. He was ready to drive into Echo Lake. And if I'd gone upstairs thirty seconds after I had, I would've been too late."

"He was going to . . ." I can't say the words, but they haunt me, all the same. Dad was going to commit suicide. "And you stopped him?"

She nods. "I watched him all night long."

All this time, I've been resenting Gram for abandoning me that night, and she was saving my dad from making an irreversible, a devastating, decision.

"Heather and I got him into a program the next day. And now, whenever things heat up, I come. Just in case it gets to be too much for him." So that's why she's here. She comes in case she has to stop something unthinkable from happening.

But now that Dad and Heather are missing . . .

Now that there's evidence of their driving off the road . . .

"But Samantha, I've never seen him that bad since then. And I would know if he was at that point again."

I wish I could take her word on that.

Gram won't admit it, but I know she must be wondering:

Is there a chance Dad hit the end of his rope today? That he aimed to finish what he couldn't finish when I was a little girl?

⊦⊦⊦ ⊦⊦⊦ ⊦⊦⊦ ⊦⊦⊦
⊦⊦⊦ |||

It's after midnight.

Cassidy must have taken the Tylenol PM, or she's working hard at not making any noise. I desperately want to talk with her about what Gram told me. Who else could possibly understand what I'm going through more than the girl who's going through it with me? But she doesn't see it that way. She thinks she's going through this *because* of me. Or at least because of Dad, and I'm an extension of Dad. And if I suspect Dad might've attempted to kill himself, Cassidy will only see it as Dad's bringing Heather down with him.

I texted Brooke a while back, but she hasn't replied. I sort of remember her parents coming home early before, and maybe they did it again. Maybe they came home when they caught wind of the turmoil in Echo Lake—old missing persons case, police exploring new leads—and realized she was at my house, when she should've been home. She's grounded, after all.

I text Dad. I text Heather. Of course, they don't reply.

I look out my window into the dark backyard. The window of the room Ryan was in last night is dark. But maybe he's up reading in one of the other twenty rooms in the place.

I text Ryan: *Awake?*

After a minute or two, he replies: *Sort of.*

I woke him up. *Sorry, go back to sleep.*

Ryan: *Want some company?*

Me: *My gram is downstairs. Probably shouldn't risk leaving the house.*

Across the way, a light illuminates one of the second-story windows in Schmidt's house, and Ryan's silhouette passes behind the blinds. A moment later, my phone buzzes with a FaceTime invitation. He wants to talk. Face to face.

My eyes are swollen from hours of crying, and I'm sure I look like death. Still, I answer the call. Ryan materializes on the screen, rubbing knuckles over unruly spikes of hair. Shirtless, yawning.

"Hello, Sami."

I sit on my window seat and trade glances at the screen in my hand and the glowing window in the nearby house. So close, but yet so far.

I turn my phone toward Schmidt's house—"I can see you"—and turn it back.

On screen, he looks to the left, maybe out the window to see if he can see me. "This is so much more effective than tin cans on strings."

"Does anyone really do that? Tins cans on strings?"

"I had tin cans on strings in my tree house, growing up."

"You had a tree house. That explains a few things."

"What does it explain?"

"I don't know . . . how you can climb all the way to the top of a hickory with a chainsaw at your belt, maybe?"

"Oh." He grins. "*That.*"

"Wasn't I supposed to visit your place when we were kids?"

"We talked about it, about your coming home with me for a visit. Before."

Before. My life is divided into before and after.

"You still can, if you'd like," he says. "Do you ride?"

"Motorcycles? No."

"Horses, fool."

I shake my head. "Just a pony when I was little. Once."

"Would you like to ride a horse sometime, Sam?"

"Yeah. Yeah, I think I would."

"We'll have to do that, then. We'll take you down to Kentucky while you're on break from school, and we'll teach you to ride."

"I'd like that."

"Any news on your dad?" he asks.

"No."

"Sorry."

A dull silence consumes us. I know he's tired. I should let him sleep.

Instead I blurt out, "Tell me about the day you found me in the passageway."

"You sure you want to talk about that?"

"No, but I have to stop pretending this isn't happening. I want to know as much as I can."

He clears his throat. "The week before it happened—I remember I was supposed to be heading home. I was visiting Uncle Henry for Halloween, I think. And we did the whole bonfire thing, the hot dogs, the s'mores, and trick-or-treating. You were dressed as . . ."

I join in: ". . . a ladybug."

"That's right." He scratches his bicep. "And I think I was some sort of superhero or something."

"Yeah. You were wearing tights."

"They might've been yours."

216

"Might've been."

"It was a good week, and a lot of it we spent together, you and me. I begged a few extra days out of the deal."

It's a warm memory. I glad we share it.

"And it's something that still eats at me sometimes . . ." He presses his lips together and gives his head a minute shake. "If I hadn't done that—if I'd been on my way back home with Uncle Henry that day, like I should've been—what would've happened to you? How would your life have been different? Would your mom not have found a moment to sneak away without you? Some nights, I kick myself for asking to stay. Maybe you'd be with your mom right now. Happy. And none of this would be happening."

"I think, lately, that it's more likely the opposite is true," I say. "If I hadn't had somewhere to run, somewhere I was safe, maybe I'd be with her, but I'm not sure she's *anywhere* right now. And Ryan . . ."

He finds my eyes in the FaceTime screen.

"My life *is* different because you've been part of it. I remember you now, remember my childhood with you. It's come back to me."

"Ditto." He smiles a little. "You were crying when I found you in the passageway. Bleeding from your knee."

So I must have fallen. I must have been running. "I just don't understand how it could've happened. One minute she was there—and the memory is so vivid—and the next, she's gone, and I can't remember a thing."

He pauses. "I'm like that with my dad. I remember the last great conversation we had—the last conversation he was really *Dad*, you know—but in the end, the details are fuzzy. The last words he said before he went, how he looked at the end when he'd been losing weight every day . . . Everybody says he wasn't more than skin and bones when he died, and this was a big man we're talking about. I don't have any recollection of him being thin and weak, and it wasn't because I wasn't there. I held his hand until he took his last breath." He rubs a knuckle over his right eyebrow. "I just don't remember him like that."

Neither of us says anything for what feels like forever. I'm just staring at him, and he's staring at me. His dad's dead. Here I've been carrying on about everything I've lost, and he never said a word about his father.

Something he said yesterday: *I was needed at home. Lots of land . . .* Was he needed at home because his dad got sick?

"I'm sorry," I say. "I didn't know."

"How could you have known? They don't put you on the news when your dad dies of cancer, you know."

I give him a sort-of smile. "Yeah."

"My point is I think it's okay that you don't remember whatever happened at the end because it sounds like it was probably bad, whether or not Delilah survived. It's okay to remember what you remember."

My last memory of her *is* pretty lovely.

"You know what?" He stands—I see it on my phone and in the window across the lawn. "I'm hungry."

"Me too, come to think of it." I hardly touched my vegetables, so I haven't eaten much since Brooke brought me a burrito, which I didn't finish. I don't think I'll be able to eat very much, but maybe I should try.

"Come have a snack with me. One thing I hate about being here when my uncle's gone: eating alone."

"I don't think I can get past my grandmother." I don't know where she's sleeping, or *if* she's sleeping at all.

"So go down to your kitchen for a snack, and we'll pretend we're together."

I open my bedroom door, and from where I'm standing, I see Cassidy's closed door, a barricade between us. There was a time we'd sneak into the same room, just so we could be together as we fell asleep.

With breath held, as if even breathing will stir her, I tiptoe down the hallway and turn left to get to the stairs.

Creak.

I freeze.

Wait.

No one awakens.

I carefully step down the stairs.

Kismet, who's been sleeping on the sofa, groans and stretches awake. Instantly, she's at my side, tail wagging.

Gram isn't anywhere. I peek out the kitchen window; lights are on in the RV. I wonder why she'd sleep in her motor home when we have extra beds in the house. But I guess I don't understand why she's living on wheels, either.

"So what's it going to be?" Ryan asks.

"Apples."

"Sounds good to me."

While he finds an apple in his uncle's kitchen, I take one from the bowl on the counter. So my voice doesn't carry up the stairs and wake Cassidy, I tiptoe down the stairs and into Dad's office to continue my conversation with Ryan.

"I just don't understand why, if they're at a hospital, we haven't heard from them. I mean, the police have to have heard, one way or another, whether they're at a hospital or not."

"You ever try to get information out of a busy hospital staff?" Ryan crunches on his apple. "It takes forever, even if you know for sure where your father is, what room he's in. I looked it up: there are four hospitals in the immediate vicinity. If the car was down Cuba Road, the ambulance could've taken them to any of the hospitals in the northwestern suburbs, too, which adds three hospitals to the mix. Plus it's the weekend. The busiest times for ERs are weekends and holidays, and it's been warm outside, which means more people are on the road. You'll get the call. It'll just take time."

I don't want to talk about it anymore. I can't talk about anything else, but I don't want to dwell on the what-ifs anymore tonight. Or ever. I just want to *know*. Once and for all. "So." I take a seat at Dad's desk, prop my phone against the desk lamp, and open one of his file drawers. "Tell me about Kentucky."

"What do you want to know?"

"Everything." I leaf through the files. Is Dad keeping other secrets?

"Well. That could take a while."

"Mmm-hmm." I pull out a file at random and look through its contents. Appliance manuals.

"There's a lot of land."

"So you said." I try another file. This one's full of information about Cassidy's Jeep.

"There's a stream at the rear of the acreage, and . . . the stables. We can house up to six horses."

"How many horses do you have?"

"The stables are full."

"So six."

"Yes, ma'am. But only two are ours."

As he tells me about paint horses and roan horses and Appaloosas, I continue to look through the records my father has kept.

I pull out the file labeled with our address. Inside is a plat of survey, which details the dimensions and location of our house, the carriage house, and the underground walkway to Schmidt's house . . . all the way to the property line.

My fingers follow the path I must've taken the day my mother disappeared. I wish I could remember.

I wish I were walking that path now, on my way to share apples with Ryan in his uncle's kitchen, just a normal girl sneaking out on a Saturday night.

I sink into it, try to put myself into the diagram, back in time, back to the day it all happened.

My eyes are getting heavy. I take my phone and the plat to the sofa on the other side of the room and lie down with it next to me.

"You're sleepy," he says through a yawn. "You should go back upstairs and get in bed."

"Not yet. Talk to me just a little longer."

"I'll talk to you until you fall asleep, if you want, but I think—"

"Would you?"

"Of course I will, but I think you should go to bed."

"I don't want to." I pull a throw from the back of the sofa and snuggle under it. Heather made this blanket. If I use my imagination, I can pretend this blanket is one of her hugs. I still can't quite wrap my head around the idea the woman who held me through my childhood nightmares could have had a hand in my mother's disappearance.

"If you fall asleep, I'm going to hang up. But if you need me again when you wake up, I've got the volume turned all the way up on my phone. I'll wake up."

"Thanks."

"In case I don't get to say it later: good night, Samantha."

"'Night, Ryan."

"What are you looking at as you fall asleep?" he asks.

"It's a map." I turn the camera to the plat. "Here's where I am. And here . . ." I trace the underground path with a finger. ". . . at the end of it, is you. And here . . ." I indicate an area just off the page. "This is where the dogs alerted. Where my mother was probably buried before my father moved her body."

"Oh, Sami."

"What's this?" I trace a dotted line that forms a square off the underground tunnel, past the property line.

"That's the old wine cellar under the barn. There's a hidden hatch in the barn floor, and a ladder. Another place to hide the liquor during Prohibition."

My mother's things were stashed behind the lathe near an underground cellar, Ryan had said. Could it be my mother was stashed there too?

||||| ||||| ||||| |||||
||||| ||||

I'm running through the secret passageway.

A minute ago, I saw my mother go in through the door in the floor of the carriage house.

And I see her up ahead.

Have to reach her, have to get to her.

I'm scared.

Something bad's about to happen.

"Mommy!"

Wait a minute.

That's not Mom.

Something's not right.

Not right.

Not right!

I jolt awake.

It takes a few seconds for me to orient. I'm in Dad's office. I fell asleep while Ryan was telling me about his favorite horse.

Beads of sweat dampen my temples. I know it was just a dream. A dream I'd had and lived through before. But unlike the other times I've had it, I know something's not right even after I awaken.

It's four in the morning. No one's awake but me. The house

is still and quiet, save the hum and rattle of the furnace as it kicks on.

I make my way upstairs.

The lights in Gram's motor home are still on. This must be hard on her, I realize. Dad's her only child, and his life has been a series of accusations and tragedy. No wonder she isn't sleeping.

Jack Frost touched every blade of grass last night.

Second chance summer is over, Mom.

We left the porch lights on, and the light in the carriage house gable, just in case Dad and Heather made it home in the middle of the night, but given the stillness of the place, I'm guessing nothing's changed. I check my phone. No call from Lieutenant Eschermann, no call from Heather, no call from Dad.

I wrap the blanket more tightly around my shoulders and think.

If Heather had called the emergency number and the call disconnected, and her purse was thrown from the car, why was her phone in her purse?

Does it make sense that if she'd been trying to make a call and the call didn't go through, she would've had time to put the phone back in her purse? If she and Dad had struggled over the phone, wouldn't the phone have ended up on the floor of the car, like her keys? Lost out the window? Wedged between the seats, maybe?

And if the call came in at twenty after two, it came long after she and Dad left the station, which means she probably wasn't calling when she realized Dad was taking her out of town. She would've called much earlier than forty-some minutes after she got in his car, if that was the case. She was calling to report the accident, which means she had to have been conscious after the accident.

Unless she didn't make the call at all.

I know it's early, but I call Eschermann, this time dialing his personal cell phone. It rings, rings, rings.

Voice mail.

"Lieutenant, it's Samantha Lang. I'm sorry for the early call. But Heather couldn't have made that call to emergency. The phone was *in her purse*. If it was an emergency and she had time to put the phone back in her purse, she would've tried nine-one-one again. Someone else called, put the phone back in the purse, and maybe even threw the purse from the car. Call me. I'm up." I hang up.

I look at the plat of survey again, at the square-shaped wine cellar beneath the barn.

If Eschermann hasn't been able to locate my father and Heather at a hospital, could it be because they aren't at a hospital at all?

Dad convinced Heather to take a ride.

What if he brought her here, to the house, and slipped something in her drink? Maybe he carried her to the passageway . . . What if he then drove the car out, crashed it to divert the police—have they looked anywhere but hospitals since they found the car?—called 911 with Heather's phone, and took off?

Then, we'd eventually find Heather, but he'd be gone with a decent start ahead of the police.

Kismet stretches herself awake and instantly starts nosing for me to take her out.

"All right," I whisper. "But let's be quiet."

I walk through the rear hallway to the mudroom, where I shrug on my jacket and slip on Cassidy's boots, which are at least a size too big.

Kismet and I exit. I can hear her paws crunching over the frosty grass.

I look up at Ryan's window, which is still dark, and then across the way to Gram's motor home, which is still ablaze with light.

A quick glance in the motor home window tells me that even if she's awake, she doesn't appear to be moving around. Maybe she fell asleep with the lights on.

Wait.

Cassidy's Jeep isn't in the driveway. I look up at her window, which is cracked open, but only by an inch or so. Did she sneak out to be with Zack? Or did she park the Jeep elsewhere? I'll look in on her when Kismet and I go back inside.

In the meantime, I shoot her a text: *Where are you?*

Kismet falls in place beside me but stays there only for a few paces before she darts ahead of me. She noses her way through the carriage house door, which couldn't have been shut all the way, and disappears into the carriage house.

"Kismet!" I'm still whispering. I don't want to wake the neighborhood. I follow her in, but she's nowhere to be seen.

I use the flashlight on my phone to pan the interior.

"Kismet!"

She pops up from the floor. Yaps.

I nearly drop my phone. The door in the floor is open.

My dog is already halfway down into the tunnel.

"Kismet, get out of there!"

But she descends farther down the stairs, farther into the passageway.

"Kismet!" I stand at the top of the stairs and whisper into the tunnel, but it's no use. She isn't listening.

Maybe she's trying to tell me something. Like . . . maybe Heather is in the tunnel.

I don't want to go in.

But I called Eschermann, and he'll be calling me back. I have my phone. If there's trouble inside, I can call for help.

"Kismet! Come on, girl. Come on out."

I hear her scuttling around in there. Playing.

I can either freeze to death waiting for her to come out, or I can go in after her. Lose-lose.

After a deep breath, I step onto the first step down.

I duck so I don't hit my head as I descend the remaining ten steep and narrow steps. Ten. Bad luck.

It's dark and dank, despite the single beam of the flashlight on my phone creating streams of light on the rocks-and-mortar walls, which bulge into the space at unpredictable intervals. The place feels like a dungeon.

And tucked into a niche, between the rocks of the foundation, is a vodka bottle, half-full. Dad's been drinking. He's just been hiding his liquor so I wouldn't know it. My heart sinks with the realization.

The scents of the underground passageway fill my nostrils—musty, wet earth, like the smell of the air right after wet leaves are cleared from grass. I close my eyes and I see a flash of the past:

I'm running toward my mother, golden leaves hanging over me. She's there, past the canopy of branches, waiting for me. But in a breath, the leaves morph to concrete. I'm running through the passageway, and I'm terrified. I feel as if I'll never get out. There's a shadow of a figure at the other end. Someone safe. Someone who's always taken care of me. Mom.

But when I catapult at her and bury my head against her body, the smells are all wrong, the feeling of her clothes isn't right. And the hands holding me . . . too strong, too tight! It's not my mom! I wiggle to get free, but the grip on my tiny body only constricts. Not Mommy.

In a flood, the memory rushes back to me.

I've been here, done this, before.

It wasn't a dream.

It *happened*.

It's not my mother.

Curly dark hair.

And whoever she is, she's running in the opposite direction, back toward the carriage house.

The memory slams into me, nearly knocks the wind out of me.

I gasp.

There's a flutter in my heart, like a warning not to go much farther. I imagine the walls caving in on me, the ceiling crumbling to rubble all around me. Trapping me. Suffocating me. Like I can't get out.

Like Jane Doe Georgia in a ditch.

The tunnel is barely wide enough for two people to walk side by side. It's cramped, and the space is only getting smaller and smaller.

Those dreams about being buried, not being able to get out. The drawings of the blood rain and the dead body in the rocks. The manuscript. The jacket. The picture of Dad with another woman. The images of Mom in Schmidt's box . . .

"Kismet!" My hissed whisper echoes in the space.

Is Heather in here somewhere? What else would entice the dog?

I delve deeper in, walking at a clipped pace, the space getting narrower and the ceiling getting shorter with every step. My hair grazes the top, as the passageway has taken me slightly up-slope.

My breaths are more like wheezes than effective respiration.

The path forks a little to the right, which I know leads to Schmidt's basement, but the dog stops here, pawing at the bottom of a door with large rusty hinges. A large iron handle practically taunts me, dares me to depress the latch. "What is it, Kissy? What's in there?"

I shine the light downward to see what's occupying the dog.

It's a caterpillar. A chunky, fuzzy caterpillar. The kind my mother used to collect from the trunks of the hickories and stems of the sunflowers.

Another memory: the caterpillar crawling over her fingers, as she told me what was going to happen to the creature once it built a cocoon.

In the corridors of my mind, I see mason jars filled with caterpillars spinning silk around their bodies. Cocoons stuck to sticks.

And then, the emergence of the butterflies, with their gorgeous, artful wings . . .

My fingers meet the old door and pull, but the door won't budge.

As the crow flies, the distance between our property and Schmidt's is about one hundred thirty-five feet. I've just walked about seventy feet, which means this door is about fifty feet past our property line. Which means this door is on Schmidt's property.

This must be the wine cellar.

My dream about her coming back to play one last time . . .

My obsession about her being in the passageway, or on Schmidt's property . . .

The dogs alerted behind this barn.

This is the wine cellar, and Dad had access to it.

Say a man loves a woman, but he's made a mistake with another girl. Say the woman he loves doesn't love him back anymore, but he wants to keep her close. Wants to keep *their child* close. Would he have stashed that child's mother in a hiding place? Could she have died there, a prisoner, before anyone knew she was gone?

Maybe Dad kept her here, behind this door, until he couldn't keep her anymore.

Until the cops caught wind of the fact that maybe she hadn't left town—that maybe she wasn't anywhere anymore.

Or maybe there was some sort of altercation and an accident. One bump in the wrong direction, and her head could've banged fatally against one of the rocks in the foundation.

I close my eyes and remember the last time I saw my mother. She was there in front of me. I didn't think I was alone when she left, but then I was running through the passageway. I thought I was running after her, but . . .

I never reached her. The tunnel curved, and I felt like I'd never get out of there.

And I never saw her again.

Kismet growls, then barks, and races back in the direction we came from.

I walk quickly behind her—as quickly as I can, anyway, but Cassidy's boots are slipping from my feet, and I can't run.

A moment later, the dog is out of sight, up the stairs.

Clank, slam!

The concrete tunnel reverberates with the sound, freezing me in place with the realization of what just happened. The door has slammed shut.

"No, no, no, no!" I trip toward the access steps, but I can already see the door leading to the carriage house is closed.

A few steps later, even the light emanating from the coach lamps and slipping through the cracks dissipates. Everything would be black, if not for the light from my phone.

I push and pound on the door, but it doesn't move.

I'm trapped!

"Help! Someone!" But no one comes.

Frantically, I redial the last number I called—Eschermann's. But my phone only buzzes at me. Call can't be completed. No service.

And, thanks to my hours-long FaceTime with Ryan earlier, I don't have much battery left.

I make my way toward the other end of the tunnel. "It's okay," I coach myself along the way. "I'll go in through Schmidt's basement. I'm not stuck here. I'm not going to freeze to death."

Something Ryan said, though . . . *he put a lock on the door after that.*

I won't be able to get in to Schmidt's house on my own. Worst case scenario, I'm in here for a few hours until the world starts waking up. I'll pound on the door until Ryan hears me.

And if he doesn't hear me?

Surely, whoever shut the door in the floor of the carriage house will put two and two together. *Samantha's not here. The dog was in the passageway. Guess I'd better look for Sam in the tunnel, then.*

Unless . . . unless it was a lure, a trap. Unless I'm in here because someone *wants* me in here.

It's only getting colder.

And my fists are raw from banging on Schmidt's basement door. What was I thinking? Ryan is two stories up. This door is at the back corner of the basement, and this house is enormous. Ryan won't hear me even if he's in the kitchen.

Shivering, I rock back and forth. It's so damn cold!

I close my eyes and look for the map in my mind.

There it is. Parchment. Veins of roads and rivers.

It's going to be okay.

But instead of towns popping up, it's trees. Trees, like the one Ryan recently reduced to a stump. Big, strong hickories that have been here longer than the roads.

I see leaves of the past slowly tumbling through the breeze, wafting on the wind until they settle on the ground where my mother's lying on her back, staring up at the sky, watching the clouds drift idly by.

You know what I think, Sami-girl? I think there are thousands of tiny fairies in the sky, and it's their job to keep the sky free from clutter. They're sweeping the clouds from the sky. And the days when it's cloudy—they have those days off.

Did my mother spend the end of her days stuck in an

232

underground prison, instead of enjoying the sky?

I don't want to be here one second longer, but I can't lose this memory, can't lose this moment.

Some fairies are better at sweeping than others. During their shifts, the clouds move more quickly across the sky.

I practically see her, lounging on that blanket, watching the fairies brush the dust balls from the sky. I'm cuddling at her side, and a book is tented on her flat belly. *The Great Gatsby.*

A sense of dread darkens me, and I can't think straight. My father couldn't have—*wouldn't* have locked me in here. Even if he did hurt Mom, he wouldn't do that.

Would Heather?

My mother, my father, Heather. Love triangle.

But Heather insists that wasn't her in the picture. I wonder why she'd deny it, when I told her Dad already admitted their affair.

What if there was more than one woman?

I force myself to look up, in my mind, at the woman I'd seen in the passageway that day. Force myself to look beyond the mass of curly hair.

But I can't remember her face. I can't picture anyone but Heather. Was it Heather I'd run into that day?

Or . . .

Curly hair. A face I've seen recently. Online. At the police station.

It's Trina Jordan!

Cassidy's right about the picture of Dad and that other woman, and Heather wasn't lying. It's not Heather. In that picture, he's standing opposite Trina.

And if my mom took the picture—it's her handwriting on the back—maybe she suspected Dad was having an affair with Trina.

But Dad denied it. He told me about his affair with Heather, so why would he lie to me about having a relationship with Trina? Maybe Trina was the one who didn't want things to be over. Maybe she pursued him, kept showing up uninvited. Could she have threatened my mother? Could she have been the inspiration for Nobody's Fool? Was Mom taking a picture to prove Trina wasn't going away? Could she have been in the passageway that day?

Wait a minute.

If I mistook my father's ex-wife for Mom that day in the passageway, it's possible Trina might pass for Delilah.

Would she, with lighter hair, be able to, say, apply for a passport with my mother's identification?

Pieces of the puzzle spin in my mind, and they're nearly clicking together.

Trina Jordan was married to my father. That means she was once—*duh*—Trina Lang. Could *Trina*, perhaps, be short for *Ca*trina?

Catrina Jordan-Lang.

C. J. Lang.

And if Trina isn't Jane Doe Georgia . . . maybe she's purposely stayed out of sight all these years.

Maybe because she did something she wasn't supposed to do.

Once the police connected Trina to my mother through my father, they put together a theory: Mom couldn't come home because she'd done something to Trina. Did they ever consider the opposite?

If Trina applied for my mother's passport, she knows my mother won't be needing it.

A jacket—which Heather assumed was Mom's, but which Eschermann believes was Trina's—was in the passageway.

There was a stain on the cuff of her jacket. Could've been blood. Was it my mother's blood?

I buckle from the inside; it feels as if my stomach is caving in, folding me in half. I drop to my knees.

All those years I spent waiting for her to come home—pointless. Stupid. I was looking to grasp onto something that had already slipped through my fingers.

The postcards flash in my mind like a slide show, mocking me. How excited I'd been the first time I found one in the mailbox. The stupid, naive hope those postcards had instilled in me . . .

I'd spent so much time, so many years, defending my mother, hating my mother, missing my mother—and if I'm right, if she's dead . . .

Grief balls in my throat, and fat tears roll in dollops down my cheeks.

But she never would have left me, and I should have known it. She was a good mother; she loved me.

I feel the memory of her warm arms around me, her lips pressing a kiss to my temple, as we stare into the flames of Schmidt's bonfire. Smell the charring hot dog on a stick. Hear her laughter.

In a flash, the memory is gone, replaced with the bone-aching cold of this cave.

A violent sob escapes from deep in my gut: "I'm sorry!"

I'm sorry, Mom. I'm sorry I doubted you.

I should've remembered the things she'd always told me—how could I have forgotten she'd promised to always be there for me?—should've believed in my mother's love for me, should've known better than to even *think* her capable of leaving me.

And now . . .

Heather's gone.

I can't explain that.

But if my theory about Trina is correct, it means Dad is innocent too. And over the past couple of days, I'd come to seriously doubt him.

I even told Detective Eschermann that I agreed with some of his theories.

God, what kind of daughter am I?

Or am I just grasping at thin air again?

I have to get out of here.

I'm putting pieces together with no one to follow up on it, no one to validate me or tell me I'm crazy for thinking such thoughts. I'm stuck here, screaming until my throat is swollen in this dank cold, banging on doors with raw fists.

Ryan won't answer the door at his end of the passageway.

Gram won't answer the door at hers.

And I can't stay here anymore! Not when I think I know what happened. Not when what I think I know can clear Dad's name, even if it can't find Heather.

Wait.

Think.

The wine cellar.

I concentrate, try to remember the details, the dimensions, on the plat of survey. If only that third door would open . . .

Maybe I'd be able to get out of here.

Ryan said the wine cellar is under the barn, and the box with my mother's things was tucked behind the lathe. If I could get beyond that door and climb up the wall somehow, using the lathe, maybe, I'll be home free.

The flashlight on my phone is starting to flicker.

How long have I been in here now?

It's just after five in the morning.

It's been only an hour, but it feels like ten.

I know things Eschermann has to know. I don't have time to wait for someone to realize I'm not where I'm supposed to be.

I kick at the door with the iron hasp. Rattle the handle.

Scream some more.

"Please," I say between sobs. "Please just open."

I take a deep breath and run at the door as best I can in the confined space. Of course, the door doesn't budge. I press my body against it, flatten my cheek against its old, splintering planks of wood.

"Please."

I brace myself against one end of the door and kick at the latch. Then I pull the boot from my right foot and slam the sole into it, chipping away the rust.

When enough has fallen away, I try again.

One last time, I grip the door handle.

Depress the latch.

Click.

I gasp.

Yes!

The latch budged. Now to work on those rusty hinges.

I clumsily get my foot back into the boot as I hold the latch down with one hand. The muscles in my hand ache with the effort, and the cold of the metal seeps achingly into my fingers. Still pressing on the latch, I bump against the door with my shoulder, again and again, until it starts to scrape against the ground.

Open a smidgen, and then a smidgen more.

With all my might, I ram into it, and it opens a few more inches. Another ram or two, and I should be able to get inside.

I shine the flashlight into the space but see nothing but a concrete shaft, not more than a four-foot square, muddied over time with dirt showering down from the earth-floor in the barn.

But there's a ladder.

My shoulders fall in relief, and more tears spring to life in my eyes.

I'm going to get out of here.

It's an old makeshift ladder, constructed with old lumber, and it doesn't go all the way to floor of the shaft. It stops about five feet up from the floor and butts against the ceiling, near the hatch in the floor in the barn. I shine the light into the corners. Ryan said he'd recently boarded something up to prevent critters from getting in here. Is there a chance I can snake through it myself?

Ryan will come out eventually to finish splitting the firewood.

I can hold onto the ladder and pound and scream on the hatch until he hears me.

I put all my weight behind one last thrust against the door, and it nudges open another inch or two.

I squeeze through, leading with a leg. One thigh through, hips through, torso and head through.

I did it.

The floor feels wobbly, almost spongy.

A split second later, I see why—I've been shoving the door against a buckled, rotted plank, the whole floor is rotted, and it's split now, and the floor can't hold—but it's too late to do anything about it.

There's nothing to grab hold of.

The ladder is across the shaft, just out of my reach.

And the floor is giving way beneath my feet.

And down I go, folding into the abyss beneath the cellar, landing against the rocks and mud and creepy-crawly creatures inhabiting the earth.

Crashing against old glass bottles.

Everything goes black.

卌 卌 卌 卌
卌 卌 I

Sit up.

Go on, do it.

Everything wavers in and out of existence, like the fade-out at the end of movies. Dizzy. Uncertain.

Wake up, Sami-girl.

My teeth chatter in the cold. I pull my coat more tightly around my body, but it's not enough.

Wake up, Samantha Mary.

I'm trying, Mom.

Mom?

I startle.

I gasp a breath but inhale only dust and dirt and musty air that smells like it's been cycling through this space for a decade.

"Okay, okay."

I draw in a deep breath. With the air come more particles of dirt, which I cough out. The gravelly breath I draw bruises my throat.

It's so dark in here.

I feel a tickle in my nose, an itch in my eyes.

A tiny speck of light, like a star in the sky viewed from the bottom of the ocean, beams in from the corner up there.

My chest tightens, as if the world is closing in on me, boxing me into a tiny cube, and while I know I'm lying still, it feels as if the earth around me is bobbing and swaying. Like I'm sealed in a box and tossed overboard a ship. Waves slowly swallowing me.

My wheezing breaths are the only thing I hear, aside from the ringing in my ears.

My head pounds, and I feel sort of nauseous.

Not a migraine. Please. Not now.

But the acute, rhythmic bleeping in my ears and the pain behind my eyes tells me it's already upon me, and I don't have my Imitrex.

"Okay, okay, okay." I don't know why I keep saying it, when things are very obviously not okay.

Instantly, the map pops up in my mind. I try to breathe through the pain and panic as towns bump up out of the paper, but it doesn't work this time . . . because I know Mom isn't in any of those places.

"Okay, okay."

Concentrate.

"It's okay."

Sit up, I tell myself, so you can stop choking on the earth.

"Okay."

One . . . two . . . three.

I push against the ground.

Slivered boards and dirt surround me.

The sound of glass clanking against glass fills the space when I move.

Wine bottles.

That's right. I got into the wine cellar, and the floor caved in.

One step at a time. I feel in the darkness for the perimeter of the space. Reach to the right, to the left. Feel the concrete walls.

Trembling. So scared, so cold.

On my knees now, then crouching on my feet.

Eyes starting to adjust to the dark.

Okay. Okay. I see the outline of bottles in the corner.

My finger grazes against something small, rectangular.

My phone!

Please, please, please let me still have battery left.

It's on red. Probably less than 5 percent.

No service bars. I dial anyway: 9-2-2. Back, back. 1-1. 9-1-1, Send. No signal, no transmission.

I punch a text—*help*—and I send it to all the contacts in my phone. Watch the blinking line—blink, blink, blink—until it tells me the message failed to send.

I pan upward. The ceiling is honing in on me.

I know it's just my eyes playing tricks. I know the room isn't shrinking—how could it?—but I can't stop feeling as if the space is dwindling to nothingness.

My fingers are shaking, but I manage to touch the App button on my phone. Find-My-iPhone app. No, no, not Angry Birds. Find-My-iPhone app. Fingers don't work when they're vibrating with the cold, and the light from the phone is wreaking havoc on my headache. Exit Angry Birds. There. Find-My-iPhone app. On.

Type out another text, describing my surroundings. Send. I know it won't work, but I have to try. I have to do something. I can't just sit here.

I shine the light again around the cubbyhole. Old dusty bottles, strung with cobwebs.

The passageway was used during Prohibition to bring alcohol to the main house. The wine cellar was accessible from the barn and the tunnel, and was hidden from the outside world. Who would've thought there'd be a cellar beneath the cellar? A hidden compartment inside a hidden compartment accessed through a secret path? I'm close to home, but my family may never find me. Is this where my mother had been too?

The dogs alerted behind the barn. The police searched the passageway. They dug up the grounds outside the barn, maybe even inside it. But what if they didn't search under it?

I have to get out of here.

The ladder . . .

It's at least ten, maybe eleven, feet from the ground. If I could get a running start, maybe I could jump and reach the lowest rung, but there's not enough space for that.

And say I do manage it, there's still the matter of the heavy panel enclosing the cellar. Do I have the strength to climb, scream, and pound until I make enough noise to be noticed?

My shoulder hurts from repeatedly banging into the door, and it hurts to sit, let alone climb, thanks to the migraine. I'm cold and damp and aching from the fall when the floor caved in beneath my feet.

They'll find me.

Of course they will.

But will I die of cold, of hunger, of thirst before they do?

My stomach churns. I'm going to throw up.

Second chance summer is over, Sami-girl.

I know, Mom.

I wrap my arms around my body, balled at the corner of this cell. Rock back and forth to keep warm. Stare up at the corner, where the star of light used to be, but see only dark.

How long have I been in here?

I check my phone, even though I know it's been dead for a while.

Dead. Like Mom.

The truth of that fact slices through me and pulls a raging sob from my sore throat. But I tamp it down instantly. Crying makes me want to vomit.

I can't just sit here and cry.

I grab a bottle and start scraping at the dirt walls around me, building up a mound of earth beneath the ladder. It's the only option I can think of.

Unless . . . unless my digging will cause the whole structure to avalanche around me, bury me.

I'll have to be careful.

I'm not breathing as much as wheezing now. I'm light-headed and dizzy, like the clouds must feel when the fairies sweep them away.

The dogs alerted behind the barn.

My mother was here once. She's the cocoon in the mason jar shoved under the porch. Lieutenant Eschermann was right. *Could be the body was moved.*

Trina moved her body.

Somewhere, there's a withered corpse of a butterfly enclosed and forgotten. I'm guessing she's in Georgia. I'm guessing she's now known as Jane Doe.

But this is where she died. Maybe not on this earth, but on the planks that caved in when I stepped onto them.

I saw her walk into the tunnel, but I never saw her walk out.

Or maybe someone shifted the planks to hide her body in the cellar beneath the cellar? What if, as I'm digging, I come across her, what's left of her?

I go limp with the possibility.

I have to do it anyway. I have to save myself. Unless someone hears me, I have to move the earth.

"Lieutenant!" I scream at the top of my lungs. "Neilllllla!"

My head pounds.

Vomit rises in my throat and I retch on the ground.

But I scream, I scream, I scream.

＃＃ ＃＃ ＃＃ ＃＃
＃＃ ＃＃ ||

The earth gets wetter the deeper you dig.

The wetter the earth, the better it is for packing, just like snow.

It's slippery, but if I form the slope just right, I'll be able to climb up the hypotenuse and reach the lowest rung of the ladder.

Mud is caked under my fingernails. It's probably in my hair, smudged under my runny nose, and maybe even lining my lungs by now. Cassidy's boots are ruined. My fingers hurt with the cold, and my throat must be redder than fire. I can't scream anymore.

But there's a spot of light coming through the hatch.

I want to feel that light on my face.

The battery in my phone is dead, so that tiny stream of light is the only illumination in this shaft.

I reach out to it, as if I can hold it in my palm.

But then, it disappears.

I *need* it.

"Please," I beg the fairies in the sky. "Brush the clouds away."

And the pinhole of light filters down on me again—"Thank you, thank you, thank you"—but only for a moment. And it's gone again.

My throat burns with my next sob. That light was going to help me get out of here.

It appears again, only to vanish with the next breath, then appear again.

Someone is in the barn!

And then I hear it: the repeated pounding, as if someone is banging a blunt object against wood.

Is Ryan splitting wood in the barn?

"Help!" I scream. "Help, help, help!"

But the sounds continue in measured cadence, and I don't have much of a voice left. Maybe he can't hear me above the noise.

I wait for a break in the rhythm.

"Ryan!"

But before I get it out, the pounding starts again.

It's no use. I don't have the voice to do it right now. My efforts to build up the ground so I can reach the ladder could take even longer than it would take Ryan to pull down another tree.

I let out a wail of frustration and throw the wine bottle I've been using as a shovel against the wall. It crashes with bravado.

The sounds above cease.

"Help!" My voice cracks. I scurry to find another bottle before whoever's up there resumes his task. I clang this bottle against the walls of the shaft. "Help!"

"Samantha?"

"Down here!" *Clang, clang, clang.*

I stare at the stream of light and pray: *open the door, see me, find me.*

"Sam?"

He sounds farther away now.

I hear voices. He's talking to someone. Maybe he never heard me at all.

No, no, no . . . Come back this way! Come back!

Clang, clang, clang go the wine bottles against the walls.

"Samantha?"

The concrete shaft practically reverberates with the sound of metal on metal. I stiffen. I'm not making that racket. What's happening?

My head pounds with every strike.

Suddenly the hatch at the ceiling opens. The incandescent barn light shines like a halo around a human figure. He's not more than a silhouette right now, but I don't care who it is, only that he heard me.

"Got her!" he yells over his shoulder.

I catch it now: the hint of Dixie in his voice.

"Ryan." I want to thank him, but all I can do is cry in relief, in gratitude.

I hear feedback from a cop's radio, someone calling for an ambulance.

Next I know, a ladder is lowered into the shaft and Ryan's climbing down. "I got you."

My arms close around him.

"I've got you." His cheek is warm against mine. "I've got you."

The beam of a cop-issue flashlight washes over us.

"Think you can climb, Sam?" Eschermann.

"I know how it happened." With Ryan behind me to stabilize me, I take the ladder rung by rung.

"Plenty of time, Sam," Eschermann says. "Let's get you to a hospital and worry about that later."

Two sets of strong arms pull me up the rest of the

way—Eschermann's and Schmidt's. "No," I tell him as Schmidt wraps a coat around me. "Now."

It's still dark outside. The sun hasn't yet risen. Maybe I wasn't in there as long as I thought.

"I was following the dog." My teeth chatter, although I'm already starting to warm up. "The passageway was open, and she went in, and—is she okay? She hasn't been out in the cold, has she?"

"The dog is fine."

"What time is it?" I'm about to ask why everyone's awake if it isn't yet sunrise, when I realize Schmidt's home. Unless he drove all through the night . . .

"It's just after seven," Ryan says.

And it's dark outside.

"In the evening," he adds. "We've been looking for you all day."

No wonder I'm so tired, so cold.

And that means Dad and Heather have been gone for over twenty-four hours. "Did you find Dad and Heather?"

Eschermann gives me a small smile. "We did. They're both all right."

"Thank God." It's so enormous but I can just barely process the news right now. They survived the crash. And Dad didn't hurt Heather.

"I called your grandmother around eleven last night to inform you. They were both admitted at Lake Forest after the accident. Which is where you should be going too. We ought to get you checked out. You've been through quite an ordeal."

"Here's your phone," Ryan adds, wiping it on his jeans to clear the mud off of its case.

"Thank you." I don't know why I try to turn it on; I know the battery is dead.

"And here's your caterpillar."

"Caterpillar?" I look up, expecting to see one of the fuzzy creatures I saw earlier. Instead, I see a pink plastic caterpillar dangling from a chain.

It's the same caterpillar that used to be attached to Mom's keys.

HHT HHT HHT HHT
HHT HHT III

"So I'm right," I say. "Mom was probably in that wine cellar. That's her pink caterpillar."

All I really want to do is shower.

But Eschermann put me, mud and all, in the back of an ambulance en route to Lake Forest Northwest Hospital. A paramedic sticks something in my ear to take my temperature.

Officer Neilla Cooper, in some ironic twist, is babysitting me again. "It could be the caterpillar was in a box and wound up in the cellar. We won't know until we look into it."

"But that caterpillar was on her keychain. You remember it, don't you?"

"I remember it was in the report Eschermann wrote after his initial interview with you."

"And my theory about Trina . . . it makes sense, right?"

"I'd say *in theory* it does, but there are a few things that won't match up. Your mother's driver's license, the records with the secretary of state, indicate that ten years ago, she was five-nine. One hundred forty pounds. Trina's five-six, one twenty. Trina likely couldn't have moved your mother's body, even from one section the passageway to the other, on her own, let alone into a vehicle. She would've needed help."

250

It takes only a second or two for me to see what she's getting at. "You think my father helped her."

"I'm not saying that. All I'm saying is that the only way your theory makes sense is if someone else helped her."

"You were around the neighborhood back then. You heard the talk. What do *you* think happened that day?"

"I think what I've always thought. That you were put somewhere out of the way while something terrible happened."

"You think my father was involved."

"The one thing missing from this whole thing, Sam, is motive. Your father is the only one having anything close to a motive."

If my mother was writing fiction based on actual events, that's not necessarily true. "If Trina was jealous of my mother . . ."

"Why wouldn't she be jealous of *Heather*?"

"Maybe she was jealous of both of them. But Mom just happened to be the one she had access to."

"Still, your mother was leaving town."

"So we're back to my father."

"Well, Heather won't budge on her alibi." Neilla shrugs a shoulder. "She insists they were together, so I don't know what to think."

"Eschermann said you found Dad and Heather last night."

Last night . . . If I'd known Heather was all right, I might not have gone into the passageway. I wonder why Gram didn't tell me. She probably thought I was asleep, but still, she should have at least looked in on me. "What happened?"

"Their two separate accounts say they were run off the road, but they're all right. Cassidy is with her mom. Heather should be released tonight or tomorrow morning."

"And Dad?"

"He's okay." She pauses. "Sami, there was open alcohol in the car. He was arrested at the hospital, once he was released."

I'm numb. I finally have a theory to clear his name, and he's locked up for something else? Worse yet, I don't know if I can bear to go through the dark days of his alcoholism again. I think of the bottle I saw tucked into the rock foundation in the passageway. "He was drunk?"

"Actually, no. But open alcohol in a vehicle is against the law. We're holding him. Given the direction the case is going, we can't let him go."

If Dad helped Trina get rid of Mom, does he deserve to pay? Absolutely. He took my mother away from me. Justice must be served.

But why do I have to pay, too?

Tell a girl her mother, whom she'd assumed had simply abandoned her, has been dead a long time.

Now tell her that her father's responsible, and she's about to lose the one parent she's relied on for most of her life.

Where's the justice in that for me?

"Knock, knock." Brooke enters my hospital room with a duffel bag. "Brought everything you asked for."

"Thanks."

She's wearing jeans and an oversized sweatshirt. Nothing out of the ordinary. But I'm struck with the realization that just a couple of hours ago, I thought I'd never see her again.

"Clean bill of health, I hear," she says. "So you managed to hide your psychosis."

I crack a smile. "Yeah, I'm getting there." I've recently taken a shower, but the sense of cold won't leave me. Beneath the heated blankets wrapped around my shoulders and tossed over my lap, I'm wearing hospital-issue scrubs, in that same bright orange you see prisoners wear, and I can't help wondering what my father is doing right now.

I don't know when, or if, he'll be able to walk through our door again. If he never again comes home, I'll never be able to ask all the questions that need answering. I've lived with my father my whole life, but over the course of the past few days, I've come to realize that I don't know him. At all.

"I was damn near ready to crack out a divining rod to track you down." Brooke begins to unpack the duffel. Leggings,

T-shirt, sweater. Thick socks, which I grab first—my feet are freezing—and a pair of hiking boots.

My gaze travels to the bag of things I arrived with. Cassidy's boots are trashed. Everything is covered in mud. And Ryan . . .

He climbed down into the shaft without hesitation.

There's so much to say to him, but no words will suffice. He was there . . . in the right place at the right time. He heard me. He helped me when every member of my family was otherwise engaged.

Eschermann told me: Gram apparently heard Kismet making a racket and went out to investigate. She closed the door to the passageway and walked the dog back inside, but she didn't bother to check on me. I wonder how she assumed the dog had escaped the house, if I wasn't out there with her, but Gram didn't question it. She didn't check my room to see that I wasn't in bed before she left for the station this morning, either. If she had, maybe people would've been looking for me.

Gram had managed to wake Cassidy late last night to tell her that Heather was at the hospital—and Cassidy subsequently booked it to Heather's side. But Gram didn't worry about telling *me* our parents had been located. She didn't worry about me, period. She told Eschermann she assumed Cassidy would have woken me, and then she assumed, when I wasn't in my room, that I'd gone with Cass.

It's also possible that Gram was blitzed out of her mind and forgot me completely.

After all, she's never been interested in protecting me. Her visits were about protecting Dad, making sure he survived. I stare at a wallpaper seam across the way, where the flowers don't quite match up.

"Hey." Brooke snaps her fingers in front of my face.

I jump.

"No one's denying you've had a shitty day, all right? But it isn't over yet. Don't check out on me."

For a few seconds, we stare eye to eye. "They all abandoned me. It was like they didn't know where I was, like my mother, but they didn't care. Like, where did they think I went? Did they assume I'd just walked out the door one day, like they thought my mom had done? Do you know how that made me feel? Growing up thinking your mom just doesn't care?"

Brooke sits on the edge of the bed. "All moms care. Some would just rather go to the Caribbean than deal."

I know she's still operating on my old theories, assuming my mother left of her own volition.

"But I know what really happened now. I know what happened, and no one cares. I could've *died* in there, and no one was looking for me."

"That's not true." Brooke drops an arm around my shoulders. "Ryan texted Cassidy and me. I texted Alex. Your sister called that cop. And check your phone. We all texted and called you."

Now that it's charged—thanks to Neilla for loaning me her charger—I can see that Cass did reply to my text. And everyone reached out to me. I just didn't know it.

"We were all looking for you," Brooke continues. "But no one thinks to look for a dungeon beneath a dungeon. If we'd known it was there, it would've been the first place—"

"Gram saw the hatch open. And the dog running out of it. You'd think it wouldn't have been too much of a stretch to search the passageway."

"She told us. We walked through it. We didn't hear you, and you obviously didn't hear us calling for you. We saw no trace that anyone had been in there. We didn't see anything that made us think that other door had been opened, and it wouldn't budge when we tried."

It must have been when I was unconscious, before I started making noise and moving dirt around.

"Sam, people love you. Maybe you felt alone—we all do sometimes—but we love you."

The words warm me up. Sometimes it doesn't feel like it, but Dad, Heather, Cassidy, and our friends . . . I know they care. Evidence: burritos. Thursday night dinners. A box full of haute couture samples I can help myself to at any time. Suddenly I have an overwhelming desire to tell them all it's mutual, that I love them too. I reach for Brooke's hand and give it a squeeze. "Brooke, thank you. For everything."

"Don't get a big head about it," she says.

"Do you think Heather would want to see me? I know Cassidy's pissed, but—"

"Cass will want to see you, and Heather too. So get dressed, and we'll head down to the first floor." Brooke moves to get off the bed, but I stop her with a grip at her elbow.

"Do you know what happened that day? The day my mother disappeared?"

"I don't think anyone really knows, Sam."

"I think I do." I tell her about my Trina Jordan theory and why the cops think it doesn't hold water. "And I get it: my whole life I've been spouting theories that clear my dad, and Eschermann always has reasons they're not valid. But this one really *is*. They're treating me like I'm just looking for other explanations, but I'm not blind. I got to the point yesterday when I faced the possibility Dad did this. I am 99 percent positive my mother is dead."

"Sam."

"No. It's true. Ryan found this little plastic ornament she used to have on her key ring. It was a pink caterpillar. And somehow, it was in the space where I got trapped, beneath the wine cellar. Whether or not she's Jane Doe Georgia, whether or not my father had anything to do with it, my mother is gone. I'm not just blindly believing—in anything—anymore."

Brooke bites her lower lip and nods. "Then we'll make that cop understand."

"You agree with me?"

"Always, Sam. No one knows better than you what happened that day. If you think this is a possibility, I'm behind you. We'll make Heather understand. And Cassidy." She moves again to leave. This time I let her go, but just as she's reaching for the door, I stop her. "Brooke?"

She turns around.

"What would've happened to me, if Ryan hadn't been there?"

"Don't think about it. Don't worry about something that didn't happen."

But if Ryan hadn't been there to visit, no one would've been in the barn stacking firewood.

With every member of my family tending to other emergencies, without Ryan to alert my friends he couldn't get a hold of me, I would've been entombed there, another piece of the puzzle, keeping track of the passing days with tally marks on the walls. And Lieutenant Eschermann probably would've found a way to blame that on my dad, too.

||||| ||||| ||||| |||||
||||| ||||| |||||

Eschermann is in Heather's room when I get there.

The door is closed, but through the window, I see my step-mother, bruised a little on the face and neck from the air bag. Her hair is pulled back into a high ponytail, and she's dressed in a uniquely-Nun ensemble: high-waisted, embellished jeans and a batwing sweater. Only Heather could be in a car that hit a utility pole and come out of it looking even more stylish than ever before.

She's sitting on the bed, feet dangling toward the floor, as if she's ready to go home.

And reading in the chair at the corner of the room is my sister.

Last week, I would've walked in without knocking, made myself at home, and made Cassidy share the only chair.

But everything is different now.

Brooke thought it best for me to come alone; she's in the waiting room with her brother. Brooke is probably right; we don't need extra people crowding this room. But I'm afraid to face Heather and Cass. They don't know what I think I know.

Depending on why Heather took a drive with Dad, instead of honoring her appointment with Eschermann,

258

Cassidy may still be calling for Dad's arrest . . .

Except that he's already been arrested.

Heather spots me peering through the window, and before I even manage to wave, she's crossing the room, opening the door, and pulling me into her arms.

"Samantha!" A heartbeat later, Cassidy's in the mix too.

"What you've been through, my sweet girl!" Heather kisses the side of my forehead.

Instantly, I let my guard down. I physically feel my shoulders relax, feel the tension release from my jaw, from my spine, from my legs.

This is what it feels like to have a mother.

I never want to lose this closeness.

But we know there's a great possibility we *will* lose it.

And I'm apologizing, and Cassidy's apologizing back.

And they're laying their hands on me, telling me they were worried, that Eschermann filled them in on my experience, telling me they love me, and I'm telling them I love them too.

"I ruined your boots," I say to Cass. "I'm sorry. I'll buy you new ones."

"I don't care about the boots, Sam."

"But I will. I shouldn't have worn them without asking, and—"

Cassidy wipes away a tear. "It's not your fault."

"None of this," Heather says, holding my face in her lovely hands, "is your fault."

I know right then and there: this couldn't possibly be the woman my mother wrote about in *Nobody's Fool*. My mother wouldn't have wanted someone else to raise me, but if she's really gone, I think she would've been grateful to Heather for loving me.

Then I catch sight of Eschermann's clipboard, or rather what's clipped onto it: the drawings I did as a child. The stick figure kid standing in the rain with a sunflower umbrella, looking from a distance at the maybe-dead larger figure with the heart on its chest.

Perhaps realizing what I'm looking at, Eschermann pulls the drawings from the clipboard and drops them atop the wheeled cart next to the bed. "I'll give you some time."

I gravitate toward the pictures.

"Sam . . . ," Heather starts. But she doesn't say anything else.

I clear my throat, which is still sore from screaming. "I'm sorry I took these from your boxes. I just saw my name, and . . . yeah."

"Eschermann told me what you thought. You thought you were drawing your mother."

I sniffle through a nod.

Heather takes a seat on the bed and pats the space next to her. "Come here."

I sit.

Cassidy sits on the other side of me.

"The year after your mother disappeared was hard on your dad. You know that."

I do.

"He'd always known how to have a good time. Usually had a bottle open, a houseful of friends to celebrate anything on any given day. But when everything happened with Delilah, things changed. He'd already lost his self-respect because . . . well, because of what *we* were doing behind Delilah's back. But when the rumors started to fly about where your mother had gone, and people started pointing fingers at your dad, he didn't have a friend left in the world."

"I'm glad you were there for him," I say. "And for me. And now . . . after everything that's happened, everything that's *still* happening . . ." I can't bear to finish the thought.

"Sami, nothing changes between us," Heather says. "We're family."

Cassidy rests her head on my shoulder.

"But your dad started hitting the bottle pretty hard after your mom left," Heather continues. "For the first time, he couldn't control it. His mother is an alcoholic. His father died an alcoholic. He knew the risk, but he couldn't stop. Even losing me wasn't enough of a reason to quit, and I think a lot of women would've simply walked away."

"But you'd loved him most of your life," I infer. "You couldn't."

"I probably could've," Heather says. "I'd left him before, you know. I loved him, sure. But I could've walked away, could've loved someone else, if I'd given myself the chance. But you know who I couldn't have left? *You.* I'd fallen in love with Christopher's smart, inquisitive, and full-of-faith six-year-old. And *Cassidy* had fallen in love with you, and you'd fallen in love with her, and there was no way we could've walked away from *you.*"

"I can't imagine life without you," I say.

"It was these drawings that turned your father around," Heather continues. "I started asking you to draw pictures of you and your daddy, and *this* is what you drew, month after month: a fall-down drunk."

"Those pictures were of *Dad*?"

"He paid attention after a while. He got his act together. And after that, there was no more alcohol."

Cassidy bursts out, "Then why are you getting divorced? After you went through all that? At first I thought he must've relapsed without Sam and me knowing. And then I thought it was—because you suspected him. Of other things."

"I did suspect him of other things," Heather says calmly. "I thought he was cheating on me."

"Was he?" Cassidy asks.

Heather holds up a hand, as if to say *one step at a time*. "Over this past year, I started noticing changes in him. I started tracking empty blocks on his calendar. He didn't want to talk about it—big surprise—so I assumed the worst. But the other day, Dad and I had a really honest chat in the station parking lot, and he told me what was really going on. Turns out, he's actually just been going to AA meetings again. He started wrestling with the urge to drink right around the time Trina Jordan's family finally reported her missing after all those years. And of course, he didn't want to talk about that with me because he couldn't admit that he may have been the last person to see Trina alive. But when you brought me that photograph, Sami, I knew it anyway."

"So maybe he's not cheating on you *now*," Cassidy says. "But he was back then? When the picture was taken?"

Heather chooses her words carefully. "When I saw that picture, the date on the back made me suspect he'd been carrying on with this other woman while he was carrying on with *me*. I knew what we'd done behind Delilah's back wasn't right, but I thought I was an exception to the rule. We'd had something special, something that we continued to revisit throughout our *entire lives*, and suddenly it was all a big lie. I figured that photograph was proof: this is how Chris Lang is wired. He's a cheater."

She takes a deep breath. "After seeing that picture, Sami, I stopped at your house and checked his email," she says. "Given

262

she's been in the news lately, I had to know if he'd been in touch with Trina. But I found no evidence of that. And when we talked in the parking lot, he came clean about a lot of things. And there were two points he was adamant on. First, that he never cheated on me with Trina. And second, that he had nothing to do with *anyone's* disappearance."

"And you believed him," Cassidy says.

"Yes. He told me Trina used to show up without warning, long after their marriage was annulled. She had trouble letting go of your father, and it put a strain on his marriage to Delilah. But he never went back to her."

If she was stalking Dad, Dad has motive. He might've decided that he couldn't let Trina sabotage his relationship with Heather the way she'd interfered with his marriage to my mom . . . But I can't think about that right now. It's Trina. It's all Trina.

"So, what does all this mean?" Cassidy asks. "If you left him because you thought he was cheating and it turned out he wasn't?"

I stare at Heather expectantly; Cassidy is looking at her in the same fashion. Could it mean that our family might stay together?

"Girls." She squeezes us in a tight hug. "This divorce is about more than infidelity. It's about trust and secrets. And Dad has issues with the former and a lot of the latter."

I think Heather has her own fair share of secrets. Case in point: the postcards that randomly show up in my mailbox. Is it mere coincidence that Eschermann's evidence techs found one at the crash site? One that hadn't been mailed but was addressed to me?

I wish I'd thought to ask Eschermann if the postcard was

one of the things we had to keep quiet in the interest of the integrity of the case. I'm biting my tongue to keep from asking her if she's responsible for Mom's correspondence. Unless . . .

I wonder if Trina Jordan would dare to come back to Echo Lake after all these years. Could she have been sending the postcards?

"Mom?" Cassidy asks. "Would you mind if Sami and I talked for a minute?"

"I think that's probably a good idea," Heather says.

The truth of the situation is that Cassidy and I don't have to be friends, let alone sisters. The events of the past few days divided us. From here forward, we can either reunite or fork further down separate paths.

I meet her gaze.

What's it going to be, Cass?

Once Heather steps out of the room, I sit on the bed and Cassidy starts pacing the floor.

"This isn't easy for me."

Her circular path—there isn't much ground to cover in this tiny space—makes me dizzy, but I keep watching her.

"This hasn't been easy for any of us," I say.

"Okay, I feel like I said some terrible things, all right? I feel like you're going through enough without me—"

"We're *all* going through it."

"Right. But I was *so sure* Dad had taken my mother somewhere. I was *awful* to you when you tried to make me realize he wouldn't have." She hiccups with the stirring of emotion, fresh tears budding in her eyes. "He's the only father I've ever known."

I nod. "I understand."

"I shouldn't have questioned his part in this."

"Actually . . ." I reach for a tissue and hand it to Cassidy. "There have been times *I've* questioned it too. Like you said before: it's not like there's a rule book for this sort of thing. How are we supposed to know how to act?"

"But I should've known."

"She's your mother," I say. "Of course you're going to jump to conclusions. Look. Over the past couple days, I've had to realize there's a possibility Dad knows what happened to *my* mom. It's been made pretty clear that I don't know him like I thought I did."

"Talk about not knowing someone. I never thought my mother would be the type of person to have an affair with a married man, and you've been trying to make me see that it happened, and I was accusing you of being blind, but *I* was the blind one. And Dad . . . what kind of a man does that sort of thing behind his wife's back? Maybe I didn't want to believe it because I didn't want to think they were capable of doing it. And there I was: letting Mom off the hook but accusing Dad."

"It's a lot to swallow."

"But, Sami . . ." She pulls a silver necklace from beneath the collar of her sweater. Dangling from the chain is a sunflower locket, identical to the one strung around my ankle. "Eschermann gave it back to Mom tonight. She brought it with her to the house the other night, when she and Dad were trying to figure out where we were and must've dropped it on the way."

Then Ryan found it and gave it to me.

Then I gave it to Eschermann.

He returned it to Heather when she told him she'd dropped it. It isn't evidence in the case, even though everything *seems* to be.

Cassidy opens the locket. "This is Dad and me. Mom said Dad bought me this locket after you and I met. I don't remember Mom having it. But this picture . . . I'm a *baby*. So obviously, Dad's known me a long time."

I've already figured that.

"But I don't get why he would have bought *me* the same locket he bought for you and your mom."

"Mom bought her locket to match mine. But I imagine Dad bought one for you because your dad was gone and he chose you for a daughter."

She meets my gaze. "Mom told me lately she'd started to think everything about our life with Dad had been a lie. She wanted to be clear she didn't want Dad to be my dad anymore—she'd been hinting at it to me for the past few months—"

It does seem as if Heather's become more vocal about my dad's flaws. That might be why Cassidy slowly stopped defending Dad, why she started believing he was capable of doing things she'd never believed possible before. I know how influential mothers can be. Mine hasn't been around for ten years, and she still affects me.

The door cracks open.

Eschermann sticks his head in. "Time to go home."

Cassidy and I look at each other. I know she's thinking what I'm thinking because it's the same look we shared when Dad and Heather told us they were splitting up. We wish we were going home to the same house. And it's not because everything's fixed—it isn't—but because you can't fix things if you don't spend time together.

I follow Heather and Cassidy to the waiting room. Eschermann brings up the rear.

Ryan's there, still wearing the same coat I muddied when I threw my arms around him in the bunker beneath the wine cellar. His jeans are stiff with dried earth, and the stuff is caked on his work boots.

He came straight from the barn.

As if there's some magnetic tractor beam connecting his soul to mine, he looks up. Smiles. Takes a step toward me.

"Thanks for coming—"

I'm silenced by the strobe of camera flashes. Stunned by the crowds of photographers standing on the other side of the windows, zooming in on Heather and Cass. On me.

"Let's get you out of here." Eschermann wraps an arm around my shoulders and steers me away from the cameras.

I look over my shoulder at Ryan. He's still smiling. He lifts a hand in a wave. "See you later, Sami."

Eschermann leads us through an employees-only exit and to a series of police cars waiting to take us home.

Heather and Cass get in one cruiser; I stay with Lieutenant Eschermann.

Home isn't going to feel like home, knowing the people who defined it for me aren't going to be with me there tonight.

Not having Mom there was something I guess I was used to.

Losing Cass and Heather was different altogether.

But no Dad?

I can't imagine it.

Maybe Heather will let me keep Kismet for a few days. Just until Dad can come home.

Something inside me aches, *hurts*, when I think of Dad alone in a cell. If he's guilty, which a part of me still refuses to believe, he must be scared to know they're honing in on him. If he's innocent, he must be even more scared. Considering the possibility he'll be incarcerated for something he didn't do. Worried he'll be separated from me forever.

"Sami," says Eschermann, "my techs unofficially verified for me: the thumbprint on the postcard we obtained at the site of the accident isn't a match to your father *or* Heather."

"Whose do you think it is?"

"If I knew that, your father might not be in a cell right now. There's obviously a third party involved. I just don't know who."

"I've been thinking the same thing," I said. "About a third party. I told Neilla—Officer Cooper. You said I should pay attention to the little details. Well, I remembered something." For the third time today, I relay my theory:

Mom released the sitter and was home with me.

Dad was out with Heather.

Trina dropped by, although I didn't know her as Trina at the time.

There was an altercation in the passageway.

I followed Mom into the tunnel.

I ran into Trina on her way out . . . by which time, my mother was dead.

And at some point, Trina moved my mother's body from where she lay in the wine cellar and drove my mom's car, with all of her belongings, away.

"It would make sense, then, that I was crying when Ryan found me. I'd lost my mother, couldn't find her. And he played with me until Schmidt found us. In the meantime, Dad and Heather came home and assumed Mom had taken me. All her stuff was gone, and I appeared to be gone too until Schmidt found Ryan and me, and then . . . you know the rest."

"Are you sure it was Trina you ran into?"

"No. I mean, maybe I'm seeing Trina's face in my mind because she really was there that day. Or maybe I'm imagining it due to power of suggestion. But *someone* was there."

"Do you think you could sit with a sketch artist? Describe what you saw?"

"Curly hair. Tall. But I was six at the time. *Anyone* would've been tall. I don't think I'd give the artist much to go on."

I pause.

"I'm also thinking . . . C. J. Lang. The person who rented the mailbox."

"Yes."

"Could it be that Trina is short for *Ca*trina?"

"Could be. It's published everywhere as Trina, but perhaps." I can tell by the way he's squinting that he's probably considering ways to disprove my theory.

"Because if she's Catrina Jordan-Lang, she's C. J. Lang."

"And you shared this theory with Neilla?"

"On the way to the hospital."

"Hmm." A long pause. His eyes get even squintier.

Finally: "Wonder why she didn't share it with me."

"What?" I'm so confused. Neilla now? Is there something *else* I don't know about people I've trusted?

Neilla was my favorite babysitter. She had access to our house. She could've known about the passageway. Maybe she *was* actually my babysitter that day. Would she have lied about it to help cover up something bad that happened on her watch?

And she's had access to this case.

"What was her reaction to all this?" Eschermann is asking.

"She said it would've made sense, except that—except that Trina would've needed help moving the body."

Eschermann nods slowly. "Why wouldn't Neilla have told me about this?" he murmurs.

My head's spinning. Was Neilla involved? Did Neilla help move my mother's body?

Neilla was eighteen back then, a criminology student at NU.

Could she have learned about covering up crime scenes while in college?

She said my mother's case was the reason she became a cop. Do people become cops to help manipulate the investigation? Maybe to steer the investigation away from themselves?

Have I been missing clues that are right under my nose?

Or was Cassidy right? Am I grasping at straws, any straw, to clear my father? Maybe I am, if I'm considering Neilla a suspect. After all, why would she want to help Trina? It makes no sense.

"It's been a hectic night," I say. "Maybe she just hasn't gotten around to it."

Eschermann's radio alerts. "Ken?" It's Neilla's voice. "Over."

"Eschermann. Over."

"I've got something you're going to want to see. Over."

"Hit me. Over."

"There's an alert on Delilah Lang's passport. We have a boarding attempt in Saint Paul, Minnesota."

My heart swells with an old sense of hope, but quickly, a tidal wave of grief washes over me.

A month ago, I would've assumed news of an alert on Mom's passport would've meant they'd found her.

Now, I know it means I'm only one step closer to knowing for certain that she's dead. But also to knowing who's responsible.

This is it. The point of reckoning.

‖‖ ‖‖ ‖‖ ‖‖
‖‖ ‖‖ ‖‖ |||

I'm sitting in a conference room at the Echo Lake police station, staring at a projector screen showing images of the woman who attempted to use a passport in my mother's name.

"Is this your mother?"

I shake my head, tears in my eyes. The hair is different, but that's not what's convincing. It's the eyes.

Sure, my mother would look a decade older today than she did the last time I saw her, but the eyes in the picture are more black than blue. Which could be attributed to the monitor and projector. But I'm not looking into my own eyes when I look at this picture, and if it were Mom, I would be.

"Is this the woman you saw in the passageway?" Eschermann asks.

"I can't be sure. It's been so long."

"How about this?"

With the click of a mouse, a younger version of the woman fills the screen. She's wearing the pale yellow jacket I found at Heather's.

I'm still not sure. "It was dark," I say. "And I caught only a glimpse of her."

"Okay. But you're sure this isn't your mother."

"I don't think it is."

"Do you want to know what your father says?"

I stiffen. It would probably be in his best interest to say it's Mom. It would get the cops off his back.

"He is almost 100 percent positive that this is Trina Jordan."

A light bulb goes on in my head. Could Trina have been in Echo Lake yesterday, even for a few days? Perhaps searching for things that would make her posing as Delilah Lang more convincing? Could she have peeked into the window at the Funky Nun? Could she have inched Dad and Heather off the road? Maybe to divert the police?

Maybe she meant to mail a postcard during her stay.

She could've driven overnight to Saint Paul.

It's possible.

The lieutenant takes a seat at the table with me. "Sami."

He's going to tell me something I don't want to hear.

"There *was* a locket found not far from Jane Doe Georgia's body."

An icy lightning bolt hits me square in the heart.

"No picture left to speak of inside, but . . ." He opens a file, selects an eight-by-ten from the stack of photographs, and slides it across the table.

It's a locket much like the one strung about my ankle. Rusted. Weathered. But I can still make out the embossed sunflower.

"It was a mass-marketed item in the late nineties, early two thousands," he says. "A picture inside would've helped, or an engraving, but . . ."

He doesn't have to finish his sentence. I know what it likely means.

My eyes have been fixated so long on the locket that it's starting to blur. I blink away the fuzz. "Eschermann?"

"Yeah, Sam."

I nod toward the picture on the screen. "Does this woman, the one pretending to be my mother . . . does her thumbprint match the one on the postcard from Gatlinburg?"

"We'll know soon."

My DNA is all over the country, it seems.

Microscopic parts of me are hard at work in Georgia, in Minnesota, at the lab in Chicago where the pale yellow jacket with the stain on the cuff has been sent. Proving or disproving, as the case may be.

I'm starting to think closure is overrated.

If Jane Doe Georgia's DNA matches mine, Jane Doe is Mom—lose.

If it doesn't, which means I still don't know where Mom is—lose.

If Saint Paul Delilah is my mother and was planning to escape the country—lose.

If Saint Paul Delilah is actually Catrina Jordan-Lang, and all the evidence that my mother might've been alive traces back to this woman instead—lose.

It's not that I've given up hope. Just that I *know* now. *My mother would never leave me.* I knew it that day, when I went into the passageway to look for her, and I knew it every time I thought to sneak back over to Schmidt's place, convinced she'd be there, waiting for me. There was a reason for that. It was the last place I'd seen her go. I'd just forgotten it along the way.

But something still doesn't add up.

Who helped Trina move my mother's body?

Who else was there that day?

Was it Dad?

Neilla?

Schmidt?

There's still no way to know.

A knock on my door jolts me back into the here and now.

It's probably Gram. And I do have a million questions for her—starting with why she didn't wake me when Dad and Heather were found—but I'm still tempted to pretend to be asleep so I don't have to deal with her. I mean, I'm glad she's always been here for my father, but that doesn't mean I have to enjoy her company.

Another knock. "Sami?"

"Dad!" A sense of relief gushes through me.

I spring off my window seat just as he opens the door, and an instant later I land in his arms.

He palms the back of my head, like he must have done when I was a baby, and his embrace is warm and tight. "God, if anything had happened to you," he whispers.

"If anything happened to *you*," I return.

I think of all the scenarios in which he may have been taken from me, or instances in which I wouldn't have even been born—a suicide mission after Mom's disappearance, a conviction for the vehicular manslaughter of Lizzie Dawson, a fatal car accident, jail time for DUI, a prison sentence for murder—and I know that no matter what, he's my father and I want him here where he belongs. Home.

"They let you go?" I say when we pull apart a little.

"My blood alcohol test proved I hadn't been drinking.

They couldn't charge me with anything."

For the moment, anyway.

"Eschermann filled me in on the developments in the case." This time he doesn't say *developments* as if the word is garbage.

We sit down on my bed.

We have so much to talk about, but I'm not sure where to start. I find myself blurting out, "So Trina Jordan . . ."

"Right." He sighs. "First of all, I didn't cheat on your step-mother with Trina."

"But you didn't tell Heather you married her, and you didn't tell her when Trina came back."

"Because I didn't want to worry her. Trina was unstable, unsafe. She turned up time and again, asking for another chance, asking for money, asking for explanations—if Delilah and I were through, why Heather and not her . . . I was as clear as I could be, but even when she wasn't getting the message, even when she became incredibly invasive, it was hard not to feel sorry for her. Things weren't good between her and her family, and I know she was looking for a home."

He looks down at his hands, maybe trying to find the words to finish the story. "The day that picture was taken was the day she finally seemed to give up on us. She said she'd come for closure, and I assumed she'd gotten it. We said good-bye, and that was the last I saw of her."

For a good minute, we sit in silence, but everything left unsaid ping-pongs in my brain.

"Dad? Do you think Mom took that picture because— because she felt unsafe with Trina around? Or do you think she just thought something was going on between the two of you?"

He lets out an exhausted sigh. "I don't know. I wish I'd known about the manuscript Delilah had written. It might've helped steer the investigation. But if Trina was here that day—the day your mom disappeared—I never saw her. I really thought, after I told her I was going to marry Heather, that she was ready to move on. If I'd suspected that Trina had any intention of harming your mother or Heather, I would've called the police, gotten a restraining order . . . I wouldn't have stood back and let anyone get hurt."

"Okay." I believe him, even if I still have questions:

How could he not remember who the babysitter was?

How could he not tell Heather about Trina?

How could he have such insanely bad luck with women?

Is he drinking again?

But as I look at him and as he draws me in for a hug, I feel the entwining of our lives. We're like that pretzel: two halves of the same heart shape, connected with a twisty, complicated path in the middle. I know without a doubt he never meant to hurt me. He loves me, and even though he's made mistakes, he's trying to make it all right.

For the first time since the delayed reporting of Trina Jordan's disappearance, I feel safe, as if I'm not alone anymore.

I'm aware this security might be temporary. Dad still isn't in the clear.

But for now, I can't ponder the inexcusable. I can only love him.

Because he's here now, and maybe if my grandmother hadn't been there that night, he wouldn't have been.

"I know I've said this before," Dad says. "Or maybe I actually haven't. Maybe I just always assumed you knew it was true. But Sam: I couldn't hurt your mother."

I lean my head against his shoulder.

"You believe that, don't you?"

"I want to believe it." It's the best I can do.

"Remember this moment. Remember this, whenever you start to doubt me."

I will.

But then it hits me, what he said:

Whenever.

Not if.

When Dad was released, he was ordered not to leave the county. That's okay; none of us feels much like leaving the house. Gram's still here, working a crossword puzzle in a chair across the room, and Cassidy and I didn't even go to school today.

We're all gathered at my house—Dad, Heather, Cassidy, and me—for the first time in months. I'm not sure what's going to happen with the divorce, but I assume they're still going through with it. True to form, Dad and Heather don't want to talk about it in front of Cass and me.

Nothing's what it used to be, but we're all here. Doing our best to pretend everything's okay—or at least that it will be.

Reporters crowd the lawn, still gaming for a scoop, yet there's a sense of calm about the place. Maybe it's because for the first time since the search for my mother began, the police have acknowledged a person of interest in the case other than my father: Trina Jordan.

The local evening news is on, and of course our family is the headliner. Cass hunts for the remote control so we can change the channel. By the time she finds it, the screen shows a reporter standing outside the hospital. The clip was obviously filmed last night. "En route to the police station on Saturday, Lang and his estranged wife were involved in an accident—"

"Turn it off," Gram says.

Cassidy pushes the button, and the screen goes black. "What happened anyway? With the accident?" Cassidy asks.

"Oh, they don't want to talk about that," Gram says briskly. She takes a sip of her soda, which sits on the table next to her. "They're okay. That's all that matters."

"We were rounding a curve," Dad says. "The next I knew, there was a big white vehicle in our lane, and I swerved to get out of the way, and we were down the embankment."

I wonder if the experience reminds my father of the night Lizzie Dawson died. There was nothing he could've done to stop it, but unlike the night Lizzie died, he was in the driver's seat, and thus, responsible for his and Heather's accident.

"But you were . . ." I'm embarrassed to ask this question in front of everyone, but I have to know. "Sober?"

"Samantha!" Gram scolds me.

"It's okay, Mercy." Dad frowns at me. "I've been sober for the better part of nine years now. I've slipped up before, but not in years."

"What about the bottle cap? The open alcohol?"

"I don't know," Dad says. "I have no idea how it got there."

"It wasn't mine," Heather says, when Cass and I look to her. "And I never would have gotten in the car, if I thought he'd been drinking."

"But it *was* there," I insist. "In the picture I saw a bottle cap, like the top of . . ." My gaze trails to my grandmother. Like the top of the vodka Dad had spilled into the sink. Like the bottle of vodka I saw in the passageway when I followed Kismet down into it.

A chill races up my spine, and I look again at my grandmother.

There's no alcohol in this house, yet Gram has still managed to drink and get drunk. I assumed she was keeping the sauce in her RV, after Dad spilled a bottle down the drain, but what if she had stashed some in the passageway? Why else would the door in the floor have been open?

The only person in this household who's been drinking is Gram.

"It was you."

"I beg your pardon?" Gram says.

Dad sits up straight, swallowing hard. Pieces of this puzzle are shifting in his head too.

A large vehicle in his lane.

The bottle cap on the floor of his car.

Gram had been inexplicably gone for a large chunk of time the day Eschermann brought Dad in for questioning, the day my entire world burst into a million little pieces. My grandmother had said she was going to the station to be with Dad, but maybe she lied.

"Where did you go after they brought Dad in?" I ask Gram.

"I was running errands," she says.

The air is still.

"Dad?"

He looks up at me with an expression of puzzlement on his face.

"Was it Gram who ran you off the road?"

No answer. He probably doesn't know. If it happened quickly, maybe he didn't get a good look at the vehicle.

"You weren't worried about them," I say to Gram. "Cass and I were scared, but you were sure they'd be okay. You knew the air bags deployed. Eschermann didn't say anything about that, but you knew."

"This is ridiculous," says Gram. But I can tell by the sharpness of her voice that I'm right.

She did it.

She ran them off the road.

And maybe Gram looked in on them in the car to make sure they were alive, and maybe she dropped the vodka, or even planted it so the police would think Dad was drunk.

She called emergency with Heather's phone, then threw Heather's purse, with the phone inside, to the brush—and in the midst of it all, the postcard she meant to mail that day fell out of her bag.

Her thumb knuckle is nearly white as she grasps her glass and glugs down some of her drink.

A scene from days ago flashes in my mind: Gram raving about a burger recipe. *A recipe I picked up in Nashville.*

She's been in Tennessee. Recently. I'll bet, if we look back over the map she's traveled, we'll see she's been in Dover, Delaware; Biloxi, Mississippi; anywhere else in my stack of postcards. And where did the first postcard come from? Atlanta. And where was Jane Doe Georgia located? Just outside of Atlanta.

"*You* were sending me the postcards," I say.

I take the glass from her hand and catch a whiff of alcohol. "If Lieutenant Eschermann tests the print on this glass against the one he found on the postcard from Gatlinburg . . ."

"I didn't want you to lose hope." Gram's voice takes on an imploring tone that I don't trust. "Do you know how important hope is? For a girl growing up without her mother?"

Coming from someone else, in other circumstances, that

might be a convincing sentiment. But this is Gram. Maybe she's been there for my dad. Maybe she's been overprotective to a fault. But she's never sympathized with me, never tried to comfort me, barely even acknowledged the hole that Mom's absence left in my life. And now, of course, there's the possibility she ran my father and Heather off the road.

"Why would you have to concoct something like that," I say, "unless you knew for certain Mom wouldn't contact me on her own?"

"That's not all you did, is it?" I ask Gram quietly. "Was it you who hid my mother's letters of recommendation behind the lathe in Schmidt's barn?"

Dad stands up now, his expression heating to a combination of anger and disbelief. "Mercy?"

She gives an almost imperceptible shake of her head, but it's less a denial than a *let's not do this now.*

"Why?" Dad's boom practically shakes the house.

Behind me, Cassidy gasps.

"The law was all over you," my grandmother says, almost hissing. "The force down in Georgia already assumed you'd gotten away with murder, and I didn't need them poking around, trying to tie more evidence to you. If they found things belonging to Delilah in your possession—"

He turns from white to bright red in a split second. "I *was not* responsible for Elizabeth's death!"

"Your car was seen following her. What were they supposed to think?"

"One witness said a woman was driving the car behind her," I say to my grandmother. "Was it you? Were *you* following Lizzie that day?"

Dad's gaze snaps to mine in shock.

"Gram's been driving a large vehicle through bad weather since before I was born," I point out. "If she was driving it while you were engaged to Lizzie, which I assume she was, driving an SUV in an ice storm wouldn't have been a problem for her."

"She was *leaving* you," Gram says.

"Maybe she should have," Dad says. "I was engaged to be married to her, and with one visit from a childhood friend . . ."

Heather.

". . . I was questioning the commitment I'd made. The moment I saw Heather again, I knew I couldn't marry Lizzie. Lizzie knew it too."

"It wasn't my fault," Gram insisted. "That girl had no business driving in that storm. It was horrific to watch."

"*Watch?*"

Gram's throat bobs with a heavy swallow.

"Is Samantha right? You witnessed Lizzie's accident?"

Gram doesn't deny it.

"You ran her off the road, didn't you?" Dad asks. "Just like you ran Heather and me off the road yesterday. Were you afraid we might compare notes with the police? Were you afraid, now that the police uncovered a body, that the case might actually be solved?"

"It was an accident. I had a drink with lunch. I just wanted to be sure you had your bases covered, wanted to make sure—"

"You ran us off the road!" Dad yells. "Do you have any idea what might've happened to us? What damage you could've done?"

"It was an accident," Gram says again, sounding desperate now. "You were getting ahead of me, and I swerved around another car, and . . . I didn't mean to do it."

She's been meddling with the investigation since day one. It's why she'd turn up unannounced. Maybe she was concerned with Dad's well-being. But isn't it more likely that the grandmother I know would have been more concerned for herself?

It adds up. Just when the investigation would kick up again, she'd be here. Every time.

"You're going to have to tell the police." Dad's fighting to stay controlled, to hold in the building rage. "About everything. About running us off the road, about following Lizzie that day—"

"The police? Why? Everything's okay now."

"*Okay?* Ask Lizzie Dawson's parents if their lives have been *okay*!"

"I did it to protect you!" Gram shouts. "Everything I've done was to protect you!"

Everything she's done.

"You were here, weren't you?" I say quietly. "The day my mom died."

"What? No—you're remembering wrong, Samantha. I came later, after Delilah was reported missing, to help take care of you—"

"No. You were here that day. You were supposed to babysit me."

"Chris?" Heather interjects.

Slowly, Dad nods. "She was supposed to be here with Sam, but she didn't show up."

"You lied to the police," Heather says.

"Because she was drunk, not because I thought . . ." He's pacing now, shaking with the realization that he'd lied to protect his mother from embarrassment, but what he'd ultimately done was remove her from the scene altogether.

I stare at Gram. "You helped Trina move my mother's body." My fingertips are numb. "Trina killed my mother, and you helped her get away with it."

"Trina didn't mean anything by it. She wasn't trying to kill anyone. Delilah started it, if you must know. She was accusing Trina of interfering with her marriage, and—"

"Trina *did* interfere with my marriage!" my dad shouts.

"—and Delilah wouldn't let it go, and Trina followed her into the passageway."

"My mother didn't come out." It feels as if the earth is rumbling beneath my feet.

"Trina didn't mean to do it! Who dies from a little bump on her head? Trina panicked. She was in the root cellar, but when Delilah didn't come to—"

"You knew about this," Dad says. "All this time, you knew. Not only that—you helped cover it up. You *moved her body*. Jesus Christ, Mercy."

"Everything's okay," Gram says. "Everything's going to be okay."

"Nothing will be okay! Do you understand the pain you've caused this family?"

Gram glares at Dad. "I was doing what I thought—"

"Apologize to my daughter!" Dad points at me. "Apologize to Samantha for the fact that she's spent half her life thinking her mother had abandoned her, and the other half thinking I might've had something to do with it! Apologize to Cassidy, who's had to grow up dealing with the accusations! To Heather! Apologize to our neighbor for the two weeks the cops had *his* place turned upside down looking for any sign of Delilah!"

Gram's head is in her hands now, and she's shaking with sobs.

My eyes are glazed over. Dad keeps at her, but his words turn to static in my ears.

All this time, my mother has been dead.

My grandmother let me believe she'd come back.

But she's dead.

Delilah Jennifer Lang never made it to eleven-seven.

She's dead.

She's really dead.

She's not coming back.

"You loaded her into your RV," I finally say, my words coming out like chips of ice. "And dumped my mother's body on the side of the road in Georgia."

"No, no. I didn't leave her. Samantha, please." Gram's rocking back and forth, reaching for me, but she'll never touch me again. "We buried her just outside of Atlanta. It's where she wanted to be. Christopher! I had to protect you! Catrina couldn't move the body alone, and I couldn't either, but if they'd found her in that passageway . . . there's no telling what might have happened to you! After Lizzie, you know—you barely recovered after Lizzie . . ."

Dad turns away and covers his face with his hands.

Slowly, I lower myself to the first chair I sense beneath me.

I pull out my phone and dial.

My grandmother knew there had been an accident. Instead of calling the police, she let my mom—my mom!—decompose for hours in a damp, dirty cell before loading her up and driving her away and leaving me all alone. She'd sent postcards to deceive me. Even wrote eleven-seven on them because that's what my mom and I kept saying to each other that day:

Eleven-seven, Samantha-girl!

Eleven-seven, Mommy.

"Lieutenant Eschermann, please."

"No!" Gram whispers. Her eyes are wide, and her face may as well be whitewashed. She's shaking her head in a tiny motion, more like a vibration. "I did it for you, Chris. So you could finally start over. Please." She's backing her way toward the door.

But there's nowhere she can possibly go, and I think she knows it.

"Eschermann." For once I'm not crying. I'm strong. I know the truth. "Can you come? I know what happened to my mother."

CHAPTER 1

This is where my life begins:

With Kismet curled on my lap as I read *The Great Gatsby*.

With my father at regular AA meetings—a preventive measure because he thinks it keeps him honest, accountable.

With Dad and Heather in a therapist's office, and their divorce proceedings on hold.

With Heather churning out new fashions at the Funky Nun while she and Cass still live above it.

With an old locket bearing a picture of Cassidy and my father strung around my sister's neck.

She's not my biological sister, but the bond between us is still vital. Blood may be an irrefutable connection, but choice is what makes us love each other, choice is what makes us family.

My mother loved me, and she never chose to leave. I know that now, and I suspect I've known it all along. But now I have irrefutable proof: Catrina Lang, carrying a passport bearing my mother's name, attempted to board a plane to Canada in Saint Paul, Minnesota. She is awaiting trial, and there's little doubt she'll be convicted. My mother's blood was on her jacket. Trina knew where to find my mother's body; she and Gram confirmed they'd buried her in the exact location the authorities recovered Jane Doe Georgia, and my DNA is consistent with Jane's.

As for my grandmother, she's going to jail too: for concealing my mother's murder, for obstruction of justice, for interfering with an investigation.

My mother is dead. She never left me.

Heather's never tried to be my mother, but she's loved me like a daughter since the day we met. I'm lucky to have her, and I have her for the long run, whether or not she and Dad can hold it together.

I'm on the porch now, with my book tented on the arm of the porch swing. The fallen leaves of Schmidt's many hickories blanket our lawn and his, and the breeze is a touch colder than it was yesterday. Second chance summer is definitely over. I pull my jacket a little tighter around my body and tuck my legs in a little closer.

"Look." I lean in close to Kismet and massage her ears. "The fairies are sweeping the clouds from the sky. Some fairies work faster than others, and that's when we get the clearer skies and harsher winds."

"Hey."

I look up to see Ryan standing in the lawn before me in running gear, with a sweatshirt draped over his left arm.

"Ready?" he asks.

"Yeah. I just have to . . ." I dog-ear my page in *Gatsby* and close the book. "Let's get you inside, Kissy."

"Brought something for you." He pulls aside his sweatshirt, and he presents me with a mason jar. Inside is a brown cocoon. "Found this little guy on a hickory twig."

I melt a little inside.

"Thank you."

"Figured we could name him. Raise him as a pet until he hatches and flies away."

"You know cocoons don't eat anything, right? They require virtually no raising."

"Well, then, this should be a fairly easy task."

"I have to agree." I set the jar on the porch railing. "Let's name him . . . Sunflower."

Once Kismet's inside, we walk past the flower bed where the sunflowers used to grow, past the row of hickories—with an extra space between the two closest to the property line, where a now-absent tree once stood.

I take his hand. "I'm going to miss you when you go back to Kentucky."

"You're coming to visit, remember?"

"Ah, yes. I'm going to learn to ride *a motorcycle*."

"That's right. A motorcycle." He gives me a playful pinch in the ribs. "I'm thinking Daisy might be a good fit for you."

"Is she a moped?"

He chuckles. "A smaller model, yes. Tame."

"Perfect."

"And I'll be here permanently next fall." He grins. "My mom called. I got the acceptance letter this morning. I'm going to Northwestern."

I'm so happy for him that I jump up and down and throw my arms around him.

He stares down at me.

I stare up at him.

"We're supposed to meet everyone at the Madelaine in an hour," he says.

Brooke, Alex, Zack, and Cassidy are probably already there, saving seats for us.

"Think we can make the loop around the lake in time?" Ryan asks.

I give him a wink. "Twenty minutes, tops."

My feet hit the pavement in even cadence with Ryan's. I count eleven steps, then seven. Eleven, then seven.

The early autumn wind rustles through the gold and burgundy leaves, reaching from both sides of the road and creating the illusion of an arbor of leaves above me.

The melody of an old song emerges from my memory. One of Mom's songs.

"Photograph" by Def Leppard.

I see her in the archives of my mind, crouching before me, the very last time I saw her. *See you Wednesday, Samantha-girl.*

She's gone, but she's all around me.

With every stride, I feel her in the wind at my back.

I smell her in the faint aromas of autumn flora.

She's a caterpillar, waiting to emerge from a cocoon.

She's a fairy, sweeping clouds from the sky.

In the spring, I'm going to plant sunflowers.

ACKNOWLEDGMENTS

Something pretty spectacular happened over the course of writing, revising, and editing this book. I acquired a new friend by the name of Alix Reid. She never gave me a business card, but I'm sure her job title is something akin to Story Charmer/Magician. Alix, we might need to consult a geneticist; there's a distinct possibility we're twins. I look forward to our next lunch, and to many more books with Lerner/Carolrhoda LAB!

Thanks, also, to the inspiring Amy Fitzgerald, whose commentary makes me laugh mid-revision. We're quite a team!

To the incomparable Andrea Somberg of the amazing Harvey Klinger, Inc.: you're a cheerleader, a careful reader, and you make my job an absolute pleasure.

The folks at Anderson's Bookshop and the Illinois Reading Council do much to promote books of all types. Thanks for many opportunities to meet readers and other writers!

To my writer friends, who understand—Patrick W. Picciarelli, Jessica Warman, Lainey Ervin—I appreciate you (and read you)!

My nephews—Alex, Zack, Jordan, Chris, and Ryan—I thank you for lending your names to this tale. My nieces—Andrea, Emily, Avery, and Julia—I assure you, your turn is coming!

My brother, Ken: yeah, I named a character after you, too. Don't get a big head about it, or anything.

Mary, Margaret, Caroline, Angela, Chelsey, and Missy: you survived Swatch Talk 2K15. I love survivors. And I know you wouldn't hesitate to work my shift at the Funky Nun . . . you rock!

Big hugs to my daughters, Sami and Madelaine, and to their friends (among them Brooke, Cassidy, Lizzie, and Neilla). You help paint a picture of teen life every time you gather for some 80s flicks. Your antics and giggles turn these pages . . . and you know how to order burritos. Next, I'm folding an origami moon. Kari and Ella should be ready; they just might share the sky with you!

Joshua, words cannot justify the measure of support, love, and loyalty you offer. I could not do any of this without you. Thanks for being a truly awesome father and an adoring husband. Thanks for your countless trips to the dance studio, to the pet supply store, and for the gargantuan stroll down the aisle. The yellow lab in this story is named after our path: Kismet. You're stuck with me!

ABOUT THE AUTHOR

Sasha Dawn teaches writing at community colleges and offers pro bono writing workshops to local schools. She lives in her native northern Illinois, where she collects tap shoes, fabric swatches, and tales of survival. She harbors a crush on Thomas Jefferson.